The Serenity Gang

Steve Parks

ISBN: 979-8-9991531-0-4

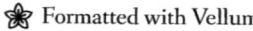 Formatted with Vellum

To my beloved mother, Marian. I couldn't have done this without you.

Chapter One

2 °19

I sat in the passenger seat of my daughter's fancy car, watching her lock the front door of my house. *Why the hell did I let her talk me into leaving?* When she got in the car, I asked for the house key. She hesitated, gave me an irritated expression, and handed it over. She started the car, backed down the driveway, and pulled out onto the street.

I'd been living alone for about four years, since my wife, Sharon, died. I didn't have much of a social life; most of our friends were connected to Sharon and stopped calling a few months after her funeral. My two college buddies who lived in the area were no longer around. One died two days after his seventieth birthday. The other had Alzheimer's and was in a memory care unit in Ann Arbor. But I kept busy reading, working in my woodshop, and watching TV. Juan, my lawn and garden guy, and his wife, Marguerite, who picked up the house, visited me regularly.

Juan and Marguerite found me after my fall down the basement stairs in early January. I couldn't get up; my hip and right arm were fractured, and I had no way of calling for help. I was on the basement floor for almost thirteen hours until they arrived and called an ambulance. While I was in the hospital, I heard the doctor mention something about a nursing home, and that motivated me to push myself in physical therapy so I could return home. I made it back home. But my daughter, April, never seemed thrilled about my achievement and had been relentless in pushing me into senior housing.

April drove slowly past the house, giving me one more chance to look at it until it vanished behind the tall hedge marking the property line. I always thought the place was too big and ostentatious, and I wasn't fond of our snobbish and snoopy neighbors. Sharon, on the other hand, loved everything about the house and neighborhood. She viewed herself as one of Detroit's elites, and the house showed the world she was loaded and successful. She paid for everything and reminded me of that when I expressed my reservations about it all.

We drove for a few miles, and April kept giving me expectant glances, as if she wanted me to say something. She always acted uncomfortable when I was quiet, so it was no surprise when she rambled on and on about my "new home" in Farmington Hills.

"I'm so excited for you, Dad. You're gonna love assisted living! Think about it. You won't have to cook, clean, or anything, and I'm sure you'll meet a lot of nice people. It'll be great!"

"I wonder if that's what criminal defense attorneys tell their clients when they've been sentenced to prison."

April shot me a puzzled look. "I'm not following. Tell them what?"

"That they won't have to cook or clean and they'll meet a lot of nice people."

April appeared to tighten her grip on the steering wheel as she took a deep breath. "Come on, Dad. You told me you'd give it a try. It's not a damn prison! It's the best assisted living facility in Southeast Michigan, and you're fortunate to be going there."

"As I told you before, April, I don't need assistance with living."

"You can't back out now, Dad. I'm sorry, but it's all arranged. Your apartment is set up with furniture from Mom's beach house, and we have an appointment with one of the owners when we arrive."

April turned off the highway onto a long blacktop driveway leading to a sprawling one-story brick building that looked like a ski lodge. The landscaped grounds were impressive, with old-growth oaks and white pine dotting the property, along with flower beds bursting with colors. I kept my mouth shut because I didn't want April to think my resistance to the move was starting to wane.

I noticed a brightly colored van, a Mercedes convertible, and a few nondescript vehicles as we drove by the parking lot adjacent to the building. I turned to her. "When are you going to bring me my car?"

"No reason to have a car here, Dad. They have everything you need."

I slapped my hand on the dashboard, startling her. "Wait a minute! You never mentioned I wouldn't have my car."

"Oh, I'm sure I did. Maybe you just don't remember."

"Don't remember? Are you kidding me? I never would have agreed to stay here without a car."

"Dad, I'm sure we talked about the car. And frankly, I

don't think it's safe for you to be driving. Remember your accident last month?"

"Sure, I remember! The son of a bitch jammed on his brakes, and I rear-ended him. It was just a fender bender."

"But you got a ticket."

"Big deal. How many tickets and fender benders have you had, April?"

"Dad, this isn't about me."

I felt my face reddening. "And the house?"

April looked in the rearview mirror, casually fluffed her bleached blond hair, checked her lipstick, and adjusted her sunglasses. "We'll put it up for sale when the time is right."

"It's not yours to sell, April! I'll decide when to—"

April stopped the car in the circular drive near the entrance, opened her door, and got out. A short, trim man with curly dark hair came flying out the door toward her. He was wearing boating shoes, khaki pants, and an unbuttoned navy blazer over a pink golf shirt. I stayed put as a final protest.

"April, so nice to see you again!" the man said. He and April hugged.

They let go of each other. Then April walked over to my side of the car and opened the door. "Dad, I want to introduce you to Brett Beaudry. Brett and his partners own this beautiful place and two others."

I reluctantly got out of the car and shook Brett's hand. What else could I do?

"Great to meet you, Mr. Livingston. May I call you Bud? April told me all about you. I'm thrilled you and your family chose Serenity Assisted Living as your home away from home. You'll be happy and safe here, my friend." Brett droned on and on while April smiled and nodded, as if she was endorsing his sales pitch.

I felt as if I needed an alcohol wipe to rub Brett's slickness off my hand before it soaked into my skin. He was definitely impressed with himself and apparently spent a lot of time in a tanning booth, darkening his skin to complement his bleached white teeth and the gold around his fingers and neck. His fake charm and smooth-talking manner really turned me off. When you're over seventy, I figure you have enough life experience to evaluate a flashy guy who hugs your daughter.

April had a history of not making good choices involving men, so it was no surprise she seemed enamored with Brett and bragged that he'd obtained his bachelor's from Cornell and his MBA from President Trump's alma mater, the Wharton School of Business at the University of Pennsylvania. It was as if April expected me to sing his praises, but I said nothing.

Puzzled by their connection, I asked, "How do you two know each other?"

"I met April through your son John," said Brett. "John and I were in the same high school class at Cranbrook. We graduated together."

Cranbrook. That word stirred memories of my many disagreements with Sharon about the elitist attitudes our kids had developed at that private and expensive prep school she insisted they attend.

"I see," I said.

"I'll have one of the aides get your suitcases out of the car and take them to your room. Just like a five-star hotel, but you don't have to tip," said Brett, winking at me. "Let's go to my office."

Chapter Two

There was a commotion on the other side of the spacious lobby, where three men were watching the Tigers baseball game on a wall-mounted TV. The inning had apparently just ended, and the distinctive introductory drumbeats of the sixties rock classic "Up Yours" were blasting. The men were laughing and high-fiving each other. I remembered "Up Yours" as a powerful rallying tune during my protest days as a student in Ann Arbor, but its message of resistance to authority and opposition to the Vietnam War was lost long ago.

April looked at the men and then back at Brett. "What the hell are they so excited about?"

"The tall one there with the ponytail gets a royalty check every month because that asinine tune is played in stadiums," he replied. "It's pathetic."

"Wait," I said. "That guy wrote 'Up Yours'? Wow."

Brett sneered. "Right. He and his friends get all excited when it's played. You'd think they'd have something better to do." Apparently sensing my interest, Brett added, "Stay away from him. He's a liar and a troublemaker."

Brett motioned for April and me to follow him into his office. I noticed on the wall a large framed photograph of Brett, President Donald J. Trump, and a buxom woman in a tight-fitting, low-cut shirt and golf skirt standing next to a golf green. Brett was smiling so broadly I was surprised the glint of his artificially whitened teeth didn't ruin the photo. The president seemed to be casting a side-glance at the woman's large endowments.

Brett launched into his spiel when we were seated.

"Well, super! We're so happy to have you here at Serenity, Bud. You're going to love it! There are some amazing people who live here, and I'm certain you'll make new friends. We take care of everything—meals, laundry, medication. We even provide entertainment! Birthdays are a big deal. You get the meal of your choice, and we make the day very special. We have bingo, exercise classes, card games, occasional music nights, and church services. Sometimes, the residents get together and work on elaborate puzzles."

Brett's well-memorized speech about all the benefits of living at Serenity stopped for a moment as he looked past April and me to the front of his office and into the lobby. I turned to see what had caught his attention. A short, heavyset woman with an unruly mop of brownish-gray hair and a shirt with cat faces was peering into the office as she slowly pushed her wheeled walker.

Brett continued. "Okay, where were we? Anyway, as I was saying, we serve you just about anything you want for breakfast between 6:30 and 8:30 a.m. Lunch is served at noon, and dinner is at 5:30. Our meals are outstanding, so be prepared to gain weight, Bud. The evenings are yours . . . Excuse me a moment." He sprang from his chair, bolted past April and me, and quickly opened the door. This time, we both turned to see what was happening. The woman with the cat shirt had returned and was again peering into the office.

"Is there anything I can do for you, Mrs. Miron?" Brett asked.

"No. Just getting a little exercise."

The woman began moving along, so Brett closed the door, sat back in his chair, and asked if we had any questions. When we didn't, he extracted the housing contract from a manila folder on his desk and gave it to me. "I put a red X by all the places you need to sign."

I picked up a pen, wondering if my signature would lock me into an expensive long-term contract that would leave me marooned with no means of escape. I asked, "Can the contract be canceled?"

"Yes, with thirty days' notice. But our residents rarely cancel." Brett smiled, flashing his pearly whites.

The residents don't cancel because they die here, was my first thought, but I decided to keep that comment to myself. I signed the contract with the intent of canceling in a few days. That would get April's attention.

Chapter Three

After giving April and me a tour of the apartment, Brett said he had to head off to the golf course for an early-evening tee time. He gave April another hug, and we shook hands. As he was leaving, he mentioned that Nurse Jackie would be stopping by to collect my medications and explain the policy for storing them.

The apartment was nicely furnished with the items April had delivered. My suitcases were eventually brought to the apartment, and my daughter quickly unpacked them, stashing clothes in the bedroom closet and dresser drawers. After we finished making my bed, she put my toiletries next to the sink in the bathroom, along with a towel and washcloth.

April's phone chimed. She glanced at a text message and said abruptly, "Dad, I've got to get going. I know you're going to like it here. Just give it a chance. Oh, one more thing." She pointed at a small unopened box on the bedroom floor. "There's a couple framed pictures of you and Mom in there." She gave me a kiss on the cheek and said curtly, "Love you," and left.

I picked up the box and put it in the closet.

Nurse Jackie arrived a few minutes later. She was clearly younger than April and appeared confident and organized.

She told me that all prescription medication was kept in a locked cabinet at the nurses' station and dispensed to residents by staff nurses. She asked me what prescription medications I was taking, and I told her I took Zestril for blood pressure and Lipitor for cholesterol. She was surprised to learn I didn't take pain medication. I told her my doctor had prescribed thirty pills when I was discharged from the rehab facility but that I'd only taken two because they made me feel loopy.

Nurse Jackie looked concerned. "Mr. Livingston, with the injuries you had, you may develop arthritis in those areas and experience toothache-like pain. It's very important to address that pain as soon as it flares up, so don't hesitate to let us know if you feel uncomfortable. With today's medicines, no one should experience chronic pain."

I thanked Jackie for her advice and gave her a large Ziploc bag containing the pill bottles I'd brought from home.

After she left, I sat on the edge of my bed, thinking about April and our discussions over the last few months. I remembered her complaining about the twenty-five-mile drive from her apartment in downtown Detroit to my place and how she seemed put out and preoccupied every time she stopped by. She'd always been self-centered and not particularly compassionate, but I took her concerns about me seriously. Then it hit me: She'd manipulated me out of my house.

I stood and cursed at myself for being so trusting and naïve. I imagined April calling her friends and gloating that she'd off-loaded her caretaking responsibilities and wouldn't have to check up on me.

I looked at my watch and realized dinner would be served soon. The last thing I wanted to do was go into a dining room full of strangers and pretend I was happy to be with them. I thought about skipping dinner, but I was hungry. And I'd be in the same spot in the morning when breakfast was served. I had to pull myself together.

I went into the bathroom, closed the door, and took off my shirt. Then I turned on the hot water at the sink and picked up the washcloth April had laid out. I held it under the water until it was saturated, then squeezed out the excess water and placed the warm washcloth over my face. I concentrated on my breathing and tried to relax by thinking about floating on a calm lake on a warm, sunny day.

After a few moments, I pulled the washcloth off my face, intending to hold it in the hot water again and start the process over. I looked at the steamed mirror in front of me and saw a dark figure. I nearly fell over as I spun around and faced Gene Simmons of the rock band Kiss.

His life-size poster was taped to the back of the bath-room door.

Simmons was decked out for a concert, with his black-and-white painted face, a one-piece leather outfit gener-ously adorned with steel studs and chains, matching black boots with eight-inch heels, a black bass guitar in his hands, and, of course, that extraordinarily large lizard-like tongue hanging out of his mouth.

I shook my head in disgust as I wiped the water off my face and chest with a towel.

The previous resident must have been a Kiss fan or had some weird obsession with Gene Simmons.

Chapter Four

S hould *I stay put or go to dinner?* I mulled over this question for several minutes and eventually decided to go to the dining room and eat, then return to my room and write a thirty-day lease cancellation notice, which I'd give to Brett first thing in the morning.

I entered the dining room and spotted Mr. Up Yours sitting at a table with his two companions. When they looked at me, their conversation seemed to become more animated. *Were they talking about me?* Remembering Brett's warning, I veered away from them and walked toward an empty table on the opposite side of the room.

Someone yelled, "Dude!"

I kept walking.

"Hey, new guy!"

I looked and saw Mr. Up Yours waving me over to their table. I froze, unsure what to do. *If I don't go to their table, they'll think I'm a jerk. If I go to their table and Brett sees me with them, he'll think I'm a jerk for ignoring his advice. I'm screwed no matter what. This is the kind of crap you don't have to deal with when you live alone.*

I sighed and approached the three men. Mr. Up Yours stood and introduced himself.

"Hi, I'm Clayton Davis. And you are?"

"Bud Livingston."

We shook hands.

"Have a seat, Bud. We're always interested in getting to know the new inmate."

I sat in the only available chair.

Clayton leaned forward in his chair and seemed to be sizing me up while stroking his mousy-brown Fu Manchu mustache. His long brownish-gray hair was tied in a pony-tail and hung down to the center of his back. He'd apparently taken a page from Ringo Starr's or Liberace's playbook and wore rings on most of his fingers. And his Sex Pistols T-shirt was a bold statement of his musical taste that undoubtedly drew the ire of some of the residents. His high cheekbones, inquisitive blue eyes, and disarming smile gave me the impression he'd probably been a lady's man in his younger days.

"So, Bud . . ." Clayton glanced at his pals. "Oh shit! Excuse me! Ever hear of the "Sylvester Stallone in a wheelchair" look-alike competition for seniors?"

"Can't say as I have."

"Well, if they had one, my good friend here, Jim Rogers, would win hands down."

Jim shifted in his wheelchair and looked at me. I could definitely see his resemblance to Sylvester Stallone. His wavy dark hair, streaked with gray, hung well past his ears and down the back of his neck. There was hardness in his craggy face, and he had round, dark, penetrating eyes. I could tell he wasn't very tall—definitely less than six feet. He had a broad chest and short, muscular arms. I noticed a tattoo of an eagle head on his right forearm. But when Jim smiled, his face lit up, and his intimidating appearance vanished.

"Welcome aboard, Bud!" Jim said.

I noticed a nasty white scar on his wrist as he reached out to shake my hand. A quick glance confirmed a matching scar on his other wrist.

"And this fashionable young man with the slightly receding hairline is my buddy, Charlie Johanson," Clayton said.

Charlie shrugged, and I smiled. He was bald as an egg! His soft, round face, ruddy cheeks, bright-blue eyes, and friendly smile reminded me of a beardless Santa Claus.

"Nice to meet you, Bud," Charlie said. "Where ya from?"

"I grew up in a small town in the Upper Peninsula, but I've been living in the Detroit area since the early seventies."

"A Yooper! I used to have a hunting camp near Newberry. My boys and I shot a lot of bucks there over the years.

"Love the Upper Peninsula!" said Jim. "I went up there in the late sixties when I was on leave to check out Northern Michigan University in Marquette. I was thinking about going to college up there after I got out, but . . . Well, things didn't work out."

"Jim was in the 101st Airborne," Clayton said.

Jim frowned, then smiled and said, "What a beautiful place! I remember looking out over Lake Superior and thinking I really was in God's country. I can't believe you'd leave that for metro Detroit! What the hell is wrong with you?"

I laughed. "My wife and I met in Ann Arbor when we

were students in the late sixties. We fell in love, and the rest is history."

"Love can make a man do some crazy shit," said Clayton. "I bet you wanted to go back, but she didn't want to live in the boonies. Am I right?"

"Well, it was a little more complicated than that. I wanted to go back, but my wife got a job outside Detroit when she was done with her schooling, so we moved to this area. Been here ever since."

"What kind of job?" asked Clayton.

"She was a doctor."

"No shit! What kind of doctor?"

"A thoracic surgeon."

"Wow! Wait. What kind of surgeon is that?" he asked.

"Her surgery focused on the chest organs, like the heart and lungs."

"That's big-time surgery."

"Definitely," I said, nodding.

"So . . . is your wife . . ."

"Yeah, she died four years ago. Breast cancer."

"Sorry, man," Clayton said.

After an uncomfortable, quiet moment, Jim said, "Bud, I'm not done talking about the Upper Peninsula. Ever fly-fish?"

"Sure. The Escanaba River has some really big brown trout."

Jim's eyes widened. "Bow hunt?" he shot back.

"Yeah."

"Backcountry camp?" he asked.

"All the time. Spent a lot of time in the Huron Mountains and on Isle Royale."

"Oh my God, Bud! You were a regular Tom Sawyer!" Jim exclaimed. "You had the life I wanted! You and Clayton have so much in common. He loves the wilderness. Right, Clayton?"

"My ass!" Clayton jumped in. "Don't listen to that BS, Bud. I'm a concrete-and-steel kind of guy. The one time I went camping, I damn near needed a transfusion, I lost so much blood. The mosquitoes were after us from the moment we arrived, a leech attached himself to me while I was swimming, and I found a wood tick burrowed into my leg after I got home. Literally, everything I encountered that weekend sucked. In fact, the whole damn weekend sucked."

"I used to have a hunting camp near Newberry," Charlie said again.

I made a point of looking surprised. "I bet you shot a lot of big bucks. I've heard there's some monsters in that area."

Clayton smiled and gave me a sly wink. "We did. I had some great times with my boys."

"Charlie can be a little forgetful at times," said Jim. "But we're all forgetful at times, right, fellas? That's part of getting old."

We nodded in agreement.

Chapter Five

Dinner was served, and we began to eat. "How long have you been here, Clayton?" I asked.

"Hmm. Let me think. It's been over three years since my accident."

"Accident?"

"Yeah. I rode my Harley up from Florida to visit my mom, who lived just outside Detroit. I was minding my own business, riding down the road, when a banker who'd had a few too many martinis blew a stoplight and hit me. I lost my leg below my knee." He reached down and knocked on his prosthetic leg. "When the ambulance came, the attendant took one look at my leg, opened the ambulance door, and told me to hop in."

I smiled at Clayton's offbeat humor. He grinned, looked at his friends, then turned back to me. "Okay, where were we? Oh yeah. After I got out of the hospital, I stayed at my mom's house. But I had all sorts of complications, and she couldn't take care of me. So, to answer your question, I came here temporarily almost two years ago. When the lawsuit settled, I had enough money to stay put until I came up with a new plan."

"You must like it here."

"It's okay. The place is clean, the food is good, staff is great, and I have my pals." He flashed Jim and Charlie a quick smile. "The only negative is the manager, Brett. He's a douche."

"Tell Bud about your court thing," said Charlie.

"Okay, I'll give you the short version. I have occasional pain in my stump, but I don't like pills. I prefer natural medicine. So I got a medical marijuana card with the help of my doctor. Everything was totally legit. One evening, Brett pulled up to the building and saw me outside smoking a joint. He flipped out and tried to evict me. We went to court, and the good guy won. He's hated me ever since."

"Tell him what the judge said at the end," said Jim.

"It was great, Bud. He called Brett a dickhead. Said he'd kick his ass if there was any hint of retaliation."

"You're kidding," I said.

"Yeah, I'm kidding. I don't remember exactly what he said, but he definitely implied that Brett would be in a world of shit if he tried to mess with me."

I put my fork down and was reaching for my glass of water when there was a sharp and loud *rrruupp*.

Clayton, Jim, and Charlie stared at me with disgusted looks.

"Did you fart?" Clayton asked.

"Of course not." I could feel my face getting flushed.

Clayton looked at Jim and Charlie, sniffed a couple times, then appeared to rule them out as suspects. He turned back to me. "Do you have wheels?" he asked.

"Not here. My daughter thinks I shouldn't drive."

"Then you're branded and stranded. It happens all the time, Bud."

"What do you mean?"

"You've been branded too old, too senile, or just too fucked-up to drive. You're dumped here without wheels, so you're stranded in this place. You're branded and stranded. It's a clever way for your family to stop taking care of you and know where you are at all times. Unless . . ."

"Unless what?" I asked.

"Unless you know someone who has wheels." Clayton leaned back in his chair and smiled. "Have no fear, Bud. The Mothership is on the launching pad."

"What?"

"Clayton has a custom van in the parking lot, Bud," explained Jim.

While I was trying to process *branded and stranded*, there was another abrupt and violent *rrruupp*, followed by a gentle, fading *pa pa pa poop*.

"If you're going to fart, I wish you would do it away from the dinner table," Clayton said in a serious tone.

Jim chimed in, "Where I come from, it's not good manners to fart at the table."

"I didn't do it!" I almost shouted.

Clayton, Charlie, and Jim looked at me skeptically.

Embarrassed and humiliated, I wiped my mouth with a napkin, tossed it on my plate, and slid my chair away from the table.

A tall, attractive woman with stylishly cut salt-and-pepper hair was approaching. We made eye contact, and she smiled. I stayed put, feeling my face go flushed. She had to be just shy of six feet tall, with a slender and athletic build. She was a sharp dresser, wearing white pants and a light-blue blouse. I wondered if she was the social director or something like that.

When she reached our table, she stood next to Clayton. Then she looked at me and smiled again. Her right arm hung loosely by her side as if it was dead weight. Then she looked at Clayton, who avoided her gaze. She put her left hand on her hip and seemed to be studying Jim's and Charlie's faces.

"How's my favorite cribbage player?" Charlie asked her.

"I'm doing well, Charlie. Thanks. What's going on over here, boys?"

"Nothin'," said Clayton. "Just getting to know our newest Serenity resident, Bud Livingston."

"Yeah, I bet you are. Hi, Bud. I'm Kathleen Adams. I'm just down the hall from you."

I stood and shook her left hand. Her warm smile and genuineness somehow made me feel awkward and unsure of myself.

"Nice to meet you, Kathleen," I said. It was all I could muster.

She motioned to me to sit. Then she fixed her dark eyes on Clayton. "Now, we don't want to scare Bud away on his first day, do we?"

"What do you mean?" he asked.

"You know what I mean." She opened her hand. "Fork it over, mister."

"Fork what over?"

"The remote."

"What remote?"

"The remote sitting on your lap."

Clayton picked up the remote off his lap and looked as if he was surprised to find it there. "This?"

"That's the one."

Clayton reluctantly gave it to Kathleen. She pushed the button, and a fart noise came from underneath my chair. Everyone laughed. This time, I did too.

The woman wearing the cat shirt apparently heard the laughter and saw Kathleen talking to us. She left her table, pushed her walker over, and stood next to Kathleen, who was about a foot taller and much thinner. Her face was wrinkled, with deep worry lines around her eyes. Her bright-red lipstick, liberally applied, reminded me of the candy lips I used to buy as a kid.

"What's the ruckus over here?" she asked in a deep, raspy smoker's voice. She looked up at Kathleen and grinned.

"The boys were up to their customary welcome prank again," replied Kathleen.

Looking at me, the woman asked, "Did it work?"

"They got me good."

Clayton, Charlie, and Jim smiled. Her eyes brightened, and she giggled for a moment. "Nice going, guys!"

"Bud Livingston, this is Abbie Miron," said Kathleen.

I rose again, and we shook hands. The cat heads on her shirt were of every breed, shape, and size, so I asked the obvious question: "You a cat lover?"

"Hell no. I bought it for a buck at Kmart years ago, before they went out of business. They had a super blue light special that day. Remember those?"

I nodded.

She looked me up and down as if she were assessing a giant. "You're one tall drink of water. How tall are you?"

"Six four and shrinking."

"I know how that goes," said Abbie. "My problem is I get wider with every inch I shrink. Shit, I used to be your

21

height." Everyone laughed. "Hey, Charlie. Can you believe it? Bud actually has more hair than you."

I still have hair. But, unlike Jim and Clayton, I keep mine trimmed over my ears and off my neck.

Charlie laughed. "Ya think?"

"Was that you walking by Brett's office when I was getting checked in?" I asked Abbie.

"Sure was! Please sit down, Bud. A man of your advanced age shouldn't be standing for long periods of time."

I sat. She crossed her arms and looked at Clayton and the others. They smiled, seeming to know what was coming.

"Let me tell you what these SOBs did to me," she finally said. "For days, they told me about seeing a big rat digging a hole near my window. I had rats on the mind after that. I even dreamed about them. That damn Jim even told me an aide found rat droppings in the hallway."

"It was a perfect setup," said Clayton, smiling at Jim and Charlie.

Abbie continued. "Anyway, one morning, I'm heading down to breakfast, and I see a great big rat with a long, disgusting tail zigzagging down the hallway toward me. I was petrified. It's not like I can turn and run. The damn thing saw me and came straight at me. I thought I was going to have a heart attack. It went under my walker, between my legs, and down the hall. Then I heard these three morons laughing. It was a remote-controlled rat. I could have killed them at the time, but now I think it's pretty funny."

"Do you still have that rat, Clayton?" asked Kathleen.

"Damn right! Robo Rat is hibernating. He only comes out on special occasions."

Chapter Six

I didn't write a thirty-day notice after I woke up. I actually smiled when I thought about the fart prank and the laughter that ensued. After almost four years of being alone, it was nice to feel I was among friends, even if I was the butt of the prank. I couldn't remember the last time I'd laughed and enjoyed myself like that.

The first breakfast reminded me of breakfast in a college dorm. Kitchen workers were bustling about as residents trickled into the dining room. Some of the residents were nicely groomed and in street clothes, and others were disheveled and still in pajamas and bathrobes. There were coffee klatches here and there, and a few residents were sitting alone at the tables.

I saw Abbie sitting by herself, working on a crossword puzzle. She looked up, saw me, and motioned for me to join her. She yelled, "Come sit, Bud. No fart machine here!"

I laughed and joined her.

"You got quite a reception at dinner last night," said Abbie, "but I think you passed the test. I'm just glad Kathleen intervened. Who knows what those knuckleheads would have done next."

"Where is she from?" I asked. Concerned she'd tell Kathleen I'd asked about her, I added, "I swear I've seen her before."

"I can't remember where she lived before she came here, but I know her two daughters live in Farmington. She's my best friend in this place. She got married in her late teens and was a stay-at-home mom. Her husband was in the insurance business. She was kinda sheltered and is a bit naïve, but you couldn't find a better person. I love her. She's super down-to-earth and is always positive."

Abbie asked me if my check-in with Brett went well and confirmed that the woman who accompanied me was my daughter. She mentioned she'd seen April in Brett's office on another occasion.

"Brett sure seems to have a lot of visitors," she said.

"I'm sure he does. Managing a place like this is a big undertaking."

"I don't know, Bud. It's weird. People drop by, have a quick conversation, then they're out the door. That just seems strange to me."

"He's definitely a smooth operator. I'll give you that."

"I feel like he's up to something."

"Like what?"

Abbie looked around the room, as if checking to be sure no Serenity employees were within earshot. "Like, maybe he's in the Mafia."

Jim rolled up to the table in his wheelchair just as I was about to explore Abbie's theory.

"We were just talking about Brett," said Abbie.

"Oh boy," said Jim, grinning. "The Mafia thing?"

She nodded.

"Abbie is our resident detective, Bud. Big fan of *Law and Order*."

Jim looked suspiciously around the room and then said quietly to Abbie, "I've been thinking about our conversation last week. Remember you told me about all sorts of people coming and going? Well, I think you may be onto something."

"Really?" said Abbie, seeming happy to finally have some support.

"Yeah. The other day, I saw Brett make a call from his office. I thought it was odd he'd be making a call at the dinner hour. A while later, a car pulled up in front of the building, and a man in dark clothing got out. He pulled a square box from the back seat, came into the building, and went directly to Brett's office."

Abbie's eyes widened. "No kidding?"

"Yeah, Brett took the box and gave the guy cash. Then the guy beat a path out the front door, got in his car, and split. I'm sure it was a Mafia transaction."

"What makes you so sure?" she asked.

"When the car drove away, I noticed it said *Godfather's* on the side."

"You're an ass, Jim."

He grinned. "I know."

Abbie stood to leave. "Someday, you're going to admit I was right all along."

Jim and I watched Abbie steer her walker around people and tables until she vanished down the hall.

So, Jim," I said. "Last night, Clayton said you were in the 101st Airborne. Did you serve overseas?"

"Two tours in Vietnam."

"That must have been rough."

There was a flash of pain across Jim's face. "It was." Just

as quickly, he appeared to shake off whatever dark memories my question had triggered, then smiled. "I keep thinking about you growing up in God's country. When I was up there checking out NMU, I actually thought about going AWOL. I felt at peace at a time when I was questioning a lot of things."

"It's a special place. After I cross the Mackinac Bridge and pay the toll, I feel like I'm home, even though I'm over one hundred and twenty-five miles from my hometown. I haven't been back in years. My wife and kids weren't fans."

"Maybe we should talk Clayton into taking us up there," said Jim.

"You think a self-described 'concrete-and-steel guy' would want to leave the city and travel north for six hours?"

"I kinda doubt it. We'll have to work on that. Have you seen the Mothership?"

"I glanced at a bright-red van in the parking lot when we were pulling up yesterday. Is that it?"

"Yup. You'll be blown away when you see it, Bud. It's cherry deluxe—leather seats, carpeted walls, a kick-ass sound system, and even a wheelchair lift."

"Really? A wheelchair lift?"

"Yeah, he had it installed before his mom went into the nursing home. He's very close to her. Visits her all the time. Be sure to check out his license plate the next time you're outside."

"Why?"

"I'm not going to be the spoiler. Just check it out."

"All right. I will."

"What are your first impressions of this place?" Jim asked.

"I like the people I've met so far, and my apartment is comfortable. I wish I had wheels, but that's another issue."

"There's some really great people here, Bud. Charlie is a gem of a guy, and Kathleen is a sweetheart. They came here around the same time and are close friends. You'll see them playing cribbage from time to time. Charlie occasionally has difficulty counting his cards, but Kathleen is amazingly patient and understanding. Did you notice her right arm?"

"I did."

"She had a major stroke a few years ago—after her husband died. She was in rehab for months but never regained the use of her arm. Her daughters and grandchildren are regular visitors. Abbie's a bit rough around the edges, but she's a good egg. And Clayton is impulsive, unpredictable, and has a reputation for bullshitting and name-dropping. But he's a blast to be around. I love the guy. He's a great friend and an amazing musician. I've never seen anyone play the piano like him. No kidding, Bud. It's magical. Come to think of it, I haven't seen him play since Sister Mary Katherine died."

"A nun?"

"Right. She used to live in your apartment. Everybody loved her."

Jim must have noticed me flinch. "What's wrong?"

I smiled. "Nothing."

Chapter Seven

Another benefit to living alone was that I wasn't on a schedule. I could come and go as I pleased and eat when I felt like it. That wasn't the case anymore. Meals were served at specific times, and my day revolved around those times. I looked forward to the meals because they gave me opportunities to get more acquainted with my new friends, but the dead time between the meals was driving me nuts. I wasn't into bingo, blanket making, yoga, watercolor painting, and some of the other organized activities. I felt cooped up and bored. So I decided to take long walks in the morning and afternoon.

One afternoon, I returned from a walk and found Charlie and Kathleen playing cribbage. Kathleen was counting Charlie's hand.

"Fifteen-two, fifteen-four, fifteen-six, and a pair is eight," she said. "Looks like you beat me again, Charlie! Good game."

Charlie smiled and moved his peg to the end of the board.

Kathleen and Charlie greeted me, and Kathleen asked me if I knew how to play cribbage. I said I did but admitted I hadn't played in a long time. Kathleen suggested I play Charlie, but Charlie declined, saying he wanted to keep his winning streak intact. Kathleen challenged me to a game, and I accepted.

I shuffled and dealt the cards. She said that when she and her husband were first married, they were so broke that they spent many Friday nights playing cribbage. I told her I tried to get my wife interested in the game but that she would have none of it.

As the game progressed, we chatted about our lives. Charlie and Kathleen spoke glowingly of their children and grandchildren. As we talked, I felt a touch of envy mixed with sadness. When Kathleen eventually asked me about my children, I put on a fake smile and told her that April lived in a condo in downtown Detroit and my son, John, was an investment banker in California.

Kathleen said Clayton told her my wife had been a surgeon, so I knew it was only a matter of time before she or Charlie asked me about my occupation. The expected question still made me feel uneasy. Not everyone respected a man who stayed home with his children while his spouse worked. When the kids were in high school, they told me some of the parents said I didn't work, and that bothered me.

"Were you also in the medical field?" Charlie asked me.

I shifted in my chair. "No, Charlie. I was a high school teacher."

"Really? That's great," said Kathleen. "How long have you been retired?"

"Well, I *was* a high school teacher, which I thoroughly

29

enjoyed. I loved the kids, and I felt as if I was contributing to their social and intellectual growth. For years, several of them kept in touch with me. But circumstances took me in a different direction. When Sharon finished her residency, she took a job with a high-powered medical clinic. She was pregnant with April, who was born a few months later. Sharon's career was just taking off, and we didn't want to put April in day care. So I took a leave of absence to care for her. Then John came along, and that delayed, and eventually ended, my return to teaching."

I didn't want Kathleen and Charlie to think I begrudgingly gave up my career to care for John and April, so I said, "Don't get me wrong. I enjoyed being with my kids every day. Sometimes it was hectic, especially when they were teenagers, but we had a lot of fun. And I learned how to cook." Kathleen smiled. I sighed. "That's the way things went, but I admit it was disappointing not being able to return to the classroom."

"I'm sure you were a great teacher," said Kathleen, "but you should feel good about the sacrifices you made for your family. As far as I'm concerned, you had the toughest job in the house."

The conversation was making me feel vulnerable, so I collected and shuffled the cards, then steered the conversation in a different direction. "Brett told me Clayton wrote, 'Up Yours.' Does Clayton ever talk about it?"

"Not much," said Kathleen. "I talked to him about it once, and he went on and on about the encouragement he got from Graham Nash in writing the song. But I checked Wikipedia, and there's nothing about that."

"He knows Graham Nash of Crosby, Stills, Nash and Young?" I asked her.

"That's what he says."

"Clayton is a great guy, but he is full of it sometimes," said Charlie.

The game ended when Kathleen pegged out. I congratulated her, and we agreed to play again soon.

Chapter Eight

Abbie looked out the window of her apartment and watched a large black car with tinted windows pull into the parking lot. A tall, thin man with slicked-back black hair and dark sunglasses got out of the driver's side. He stood behind the open door and appeared to survey the parking lot and grounds. After a few moments, he bent down and said something to the passenger.

The passenger-side door opened. A rotund blond man holding a briefcase emerged. The two men began walking toward the building.

Abbie quickly picked up her iPad and placed it in a bag attached to her walker. She hurriedly left her apartment and went to the lobby, where the two men would make their entrance. As she went by the office, she noticed the closed door and Brett sitting at his desk, talking to Nurse Jackie, who sat in a chair across from him.

Abbie positioned herself in a chair facing the entrance, took out the iPad, turned it on, and aimed the built-in camera toward the entrance doors. A few moments later, the men entered the building, and Abbie let loose with the camera shutter button.

Abbie watched as the two men joined Brett and Jackie in the office and began talking. The conversation appeared heated. No one laughed or smiled. At one point, Brett raised his voice and slammed his hand on the desk. Jackie nodded and seemed to agree with whatever Brett said.

The short man in the tan suit eventually handed Brett the briefcase. Before opening it, he looked out the office window and saw Abbie looking at him. He said something to Jackie, and she turned in her seat and looked toward Abbie. Abbie pretended to be reading her iPad. Brett turned his attention back to the briefcase, opened it, and peeked inside. He said something to the man, who nodded. Brett closed the briefcase and gave it back to him.

"What's happening, Abbie?" said Clayton, who was standing next to her.

"Damn it, Clayton! Don't do that ninja sneaking-up shit on me."

"I didn't sneak up on you! You were so engrossed in your iPad that you didn't hear me."

"I'm sorry." She whispered, "I'm doing some surveillance on those clowns in Brett's office. There's something going on in there."

"Still think it's a Mafia operation?" Clayton said with a smile. "That blond dude definitely looks Sicilian."

"Piss off. Every mob operation has an accountant. You know, someone who cooks the books. I figure the blond guy is the accountant, and the other guy is his bodyguard."

"I'm on my way to the van to get something. I'll check 'em out." As Clayton turned to leave, he saw a photograph of Graham Nash on the front page of the entertainment section of an abandoned *Detroit Free Press* on a chair adjacent to Abbie. He picked up the paper, studied the photograph, and read the accompanying article.

"Holy shit! That's incredible!" said Clayton as he tossed the paper back on the chair.

"What?" asked Abbie.

"Graham Nash is playing in Royal Oak in August."

"That's nice," said Abbie dismissively. Concentrating on the two strangers in Brett's office, she added, "They were in that big, dark car in the parking lot. Check that out too."

"Will do." Clayton winked at Abbie, walked over to Brett's closed office door, and knocked. He glanced back at Abbie, who stared in disbelief.

"What?" yelled Brett rudely.

Clayton slowly opened the door a few inches until he could see Nurse Jackie. "Excuse me. Nurse Jackie, I think I've got . . ." Clayton looked down and pretended to be embarrassed. "I think I've got a hemorrhoid. A lot of itching and burning in the Batcave, if you know what I mean."

"Clayton, I think this can wait until later," said Jackie sternly. "We're in the middle of a meeting."

"Oh, sorry, man. I'll talk to you later." Clayton quickly walked away from the partially open office door and smiled at Abbie as he headed out of the building.

"Who the hell was that?" asked the short man as Brett stood to close the door.

Keeping her eyes on her iPad, Abbie listened intently.

"The medical marijuana asshole I took to court last year," said Brett. "I've had it with him. His time is coming."

A few minutes later, Clayton came in carrying some sheet music and a paper grocery bag. Still stunned that he had interrupted the meeting, Abbie whispered forcefully, "What in God's name did you say to them?"

"Brett and the boys?"

"Right."

"Oh, that." Clayton looked at the goings-on in the office, smiled, and said, "I told them I was sorry to be such a pain in the ass, but I was itching and burning to know what they were talking about."

"You're kidding."

"Yeah."

"Quit jerkin' me around, Clayton. What the hell was that about?"

"Just wanted to see what was going on. It all came together when I checked out their car."

"Really?" Abbie glanced suspiciously at Brett's office. "What did you see?"

"There were flyers for the Serenity facilities in Grand Rapids and Traverse City. I figure one of those dudes is from Traverse City and the other one is from Grand Rapids, and they're here to plan . . ." Clayton took a deep breath and ran his hand across his forehead.

"What?" said Abbie impatiently. "What do you think they're planning?"

"I'm afraid you and the others may not be able to deal with what I am about to say."

"Just tell me, Clayton!"

"Okay, I think they may be meeting to plan a rent increase." Grinning, Clayton added, "I'm really scared, Miss Abbie."

"You ass! Laugh all you want. Something is going on here. Why does Jackie need to be in there the entire meeting? What does she have to do with Traverse City and Grand Rapids? And what's up with the briefcase? Brett opened it, looked in, and closed it like there were a bunch of snakes inside. There must be something incriminating in there."

"I already told you why Jackie is in there. She's servicing her boss, and he has to be nice to her or she'll blab to his old lady."

"And the briefcase?"

"Investment documents. Bank records. Pictures of Brett's love child. Snakes. Who knows?"

"Okay. You're right, Clayton. I'm an idiot." She jammed her iPad into her bag, hung the bag on her walker, then abruptly got up and headed toward her room.

Chapter Nine

Abbie passed me in the hall without saying a word. I spotted Clayton and asked, "What's up with her?"

"Oh, she's pissed. I gave her a hard time. She has this wild theory about Brett and the Mafia, and I'm not buying it. Wanna get out of here?"

Thrilled with the invitation, I said, "Sure. When you leavin'?"

"As soon as I drop this stuff off in my apartment."

I glanced at the items in Clayton's hands and noticed he was carrying sheet music. "What's up with the sheet music?"

"Jim has a birthday coming up. I want to do something fun."

"I see. Well, I'll wait for you here."

While I was waiting, I watched Brett and the other people in his office. The men seemed agitated, and it appeared they were arguing.

"Ready?" said Clayton.

"Well, that was quick." I nodded in the direction of Brett's office. "Boy, those guys are really going at it in there."

Clayton looked. "I guess so."

As we walked the short distance to the parking lot, he said, "You know what I just read in today's *Free Press*?"

"What?"

"Graham Nash is playing at the Royal Oak Music Theatre in late August."

"It's amazing he's still touring. It'd be fun to go."

Clayton sighed. "I guess."

"You don't sound enthused."

"I'm thinking logistics. Getting Abbie and Jim to a concert venue would be a real challenge. Plus, he probably wouldn't remember me. It's been over forty years."

I knew from my conversation with Kathleen that Clayton claimed to know Nash, but I decided to keep that to myself. "Are you serious? You really know Graham Nash?"

"Yeah. Spent a lot of time with him in the late sixties and early seventies."

"How so?"

"In recording studios and partying. Neil Young, Joni Mitchell, Frank Zappa, and all sorts of people had places in Laurel Canyon, just outside LA. We hung out there. It was crazy. So many talented people in one place. But that was a long time ago."

"I see. Well, okay. I just thought it would be a good time."

Chapter Ten

I took a walk around Clayton's van before climbing in. On each side was an intricate painting of a flying saucer sailing through space with the word *Mothership* cleverly superimposed over the images. I laughed when I saw the Up Yrs license plate.

"Love the license plate."

"I get a lot of comments about it. I figure most people think I'm a grumpy old man with ED. Point of clarification. I'm not grumpy."

"So, where we goin'?"

"A flower shop and then a short jaunt to the nursing home where my mom is an inmate serving a life sentence. You'll love her! She's ninety-two and a bit frail but still very sharp. You'll see. I surprise her every week with a little razzle-dazzle. Today, it's flowers. Last week, it was a beautiful DeWalt circular saw."

"You're kidding."

Clayton laughed. "You think?"

"I can't tell when you're serious or when you're kidding."

"You'll get used to it. Go to bullshit.com and get an app for your phone. It might help."

I laughed. "I'll look into that."

I'd never met anyone in the music business and was tempted to pepper Clayton with questions about "Up Yours," the people he knew, and the places he'd seen. But I read somewhere that's a turnoff to famous people.

I was thinking about a topic unrelated to music, touring, or performing when Clayton stopped for a traffic light. "You know," he said as we began moving again. "Growing up in Hamtramck, we didn't have much. My dad was an iron-worker, and my mom had a part-time gig at a bakery, but there was always music and love in our house."

"Were your folks musical?"

"Not at all. They just enjoyed listening and were big-time dancers. We had an old upright piano, and I spent a lot of time messing around with that. It was a magical time. Detroit was exploding with music back then, and they took us to all sorts of concerts."

"Really? What concerts?" I asked.

"Every genre—blues, rock 'n' roll, Motown, and jazz. It must have cost them a small fortune. If their plan was to inspire me . . . well, their plan worked. By the time I turned sixteen, I knew I wanted to be part of the music scene."

"I'm really jealous. What was your favorite concert?"

"I don't know. Probably Bavarian Frank and the Polkateers."

I laughed.

"I loved them all, Bud. I was blown away by Aretha Franklin's pipes, and I was fascinated with the complexity of Dave Brubeck's arrangements. But good old rock 'n' roll really stuck with me. I was a big fan of the Stones and The Who."

40

We stopped at the flower shop, Clayton picked up a bouquet of flowers, and we were soon back on the road.

"Ever get married, Clayton?"

"Naw, the rock 'n' roll lifestyle, the temptations, and being on the road—not a good mix for marital bliss. I had a special lady for a while, but that didn't work out. I haven't heard from her in years. I don't even know if she's still alive. You've got two kids, right?"

"Right. April, the oldest, lives in the Detroit area, and John lives in California."

"Cool. What made you decide to come to Serenity?" he asked.

"I fell and fractured my hip and arm after the first of the year. I thought I was doing fine, but a month or two ago, April made me think I was losing it. She'd say things like I was becoming forgetful, that I shouldn't be driving, and it was unsafe for me to live alone. My dad died of Alzheimer's, so her comments really struck a nerve."

"So, you think you're running on all cylinders and April fed you a line of shit?"

"My dad drifted away from reality and didn't recognize he couldn't take care of himself. For a while, I wondered if that's what was happening to me. I kept telling myself I was fine, but she planted some seeds of doubt. One day, I caved and said I'd give it a try. That was all she needed to hear. Within days, she was arranging for me to move. So, in answer to your question, I think all eight cylinders on this old jalopy are still running. She fed me a line of shit to get me out of her hair."

"Man, that's brutal. You said all this happened in the last couple of months. How long was it between you caving in and arriving here?"

"I don't know. Around two weeks."

"Really? Two weeks? That's weird."

"What's weird about that?" I asked.

"There's a long waiting list for people to get into Serenity. I didn't get the green light for at least three months after I submitted the paperwork."

I thought about the date of my fall and when I agreed to move to Serenity. "April probably applied when I was in the hospital in January because she didn't want to look out for me after I got home."

"Sorry, man."

"The truth hurts, Clayton, but that's April. She's always looked out for number one."

"Your son John?"

That question was like another punch in the gut. "He lives in California. I haven't seen him for a couple years. We talked briefly at Christmas."

Clayton winced. "I see."

Embarrassed for myself and Clayton, I said, "I bet you feel like you walked into a family minefield."

"Not a minefield. I'd say *quicksand* is a better term."

"I suppose it is." I didn't want to talk anymore about April and John, and I was sure Clayton sensed that. I stared out the window, thinking about my conflicts with Sharon and the discord between my children and me. I turned to Clayton. "I'm sure there are things I could have done better as a parent, and I don't wanna sound like everything is my wife's fault. But she kinda lost sight of the things that matter in a marriage and family. The status, prestige, and money changed her, and all that rubbed off on the kids. I'm sorry to say they've grown into spoiled, selfish, self-centered adults."

"You guys stay married?"

"Yeah, we did. I guess I was hoping we'd get it together after she retired, but the cancer was found, and—well, you know the rest. I guess the one thing I'm grateful for is that she did very well, so I don't have to worry about paying the bills."

Clayton didn't respond. He turned on the blinker and waited for traffic to clear before turning into the nursing home parking lot.

His silence made me feel uncomfortable. "Sorry to lay all that on you, Clayton. I got a little carried away."

"No problem. We've all got stuff, Bud. Sometimes, it's good to get it out in the open."

Chapter Eleven

W e walked down a long hall past the nurses' station. A smiling nurse in scrubs looked at Clayton and the flowers in his hand, then said, "Are those for me, Clayton?"

"You bet, Corrine. I just wanna show 'em to my mom first to see if she approves."

Corrine laughed. A beeping sound drew her attention to a control panel. "Gotta go. I'm wanted in 127. Have a great day."

We walked a short distance down the hall from the nurses' station until we reached Room 115. Clayton knocked softly on the door and proceeded in. I followed.

Clayton's mother was in a wheelchair at the foot of the bed, facing the entrance door. She was a small woman who couldn't have weighed more than ninety pounds. Her head was dropped forward with her chin resting on her chest. Her facial features were obscured because of the position of her head and her disheveled silver-gray hair hanging over her eyes.

Clayton handed the flowers to me and quickly pushed

aside the tray table next to the wheelchair. He bent over, gently put his hand on her shoulder, and said, "Mom." No response. He straightened up and glanced at the cord for summoning the nurse. Again, he bent over, put his hand on her shoulder, and said, "Mom, it's Clayton."

She didn't stir. Just as he was straightening up, she yelled, "*Boo!*"

Clayton and I jumped.

"Damn it, Mom! You scared the crap out of me."

Clayton's mother burst into laughter. Looking quite pleased with herself, she said, "You thought the old goose was cooked, didn't you?"

Clayton looked at me and shook his head.

She continued laughing. "I heard you talking to Corrine and couldn't resist. Her eyes went to the flowers in my arms. "Are those for me? They're beautiful. I love the lavender. The answer is yes."

"Yes what?" I asked.

"My husband always brought me flowers when he wanted to get lucky."

I felt a flash of warmth in my face. "They're from Clayton."

"Oh, bummer." She smiled at Clayton. "Thank you, sweetie. Come here and kiss your mama." Clayton bent over, and she kissed him on the cheek. She looked at the flowers admiringly and said, "You are so thoughtful. There's a vase under the bathroom sink. Honey, would you put the flowers in the vase with a little water?"

Clayton found the vase, arranged the flowers a bit, and placed them on the windowsill.

Eyeballing me, she said, "Who's this hunka burnin' love, Clayton?"

"This is Dr. Mel Practice. He just got his license back

after a few botched procedures, so he's performing free colonoscopies for nursing home residents. I figure you deserve one after the stunt you pulled."

She laughed. "Oh, Clayton. Can't a girl have a little fun?"

"I guess. Just don't do that again, or you'll be grounded. Mom, this hunka burnin' love is my new friend, Bud Livingston. He lives down the hall from me at Serenity."

"Nice to meet you, Mrs. Davis." I reached out to shake her hand.

She took my hand and winked. "I prefer Marian, Bud. That's what all my boyfriends call me."

I laughed. "Okay, Marian. Nice job playing possum."

"You liked it? You know, an opossum will pretend like it's dead when it feels threatened. We had one of those things in our garage once, and when my husband went to smack it with a shovel, it rolled over on its back, closed its eyes, and didn't move. I thought it had a heart attack and died from stress. I wouldn't let my husband hit it. It was dead, right? Anyway, my husband scooped up the damn thing with a shovel and was carrying it out into the backyard to bury it when it popped up, jumped off the shovel, and ran right at me. I tripped on the hose and fell on my ass. It went right by me under the fence and was gone, just like that. Clever lil sons of bitches."

"I guess so. That's quite a story," I said.

Marian looked at Clayton and frowned. "When the hell are you going to shave off that mustache and get a haircut? You know it's 2019, right?"

"Come on, Ma. I promise I will one of these days. Maybe when you stop asking me about it." Clayton turned to me. "She asks me every time I'm here."

"Damn right!" Marian said. "It makes you look like an

old hippie clinging to the past. Look at all your heroes—Clapton, Page, Townshend. They all have short hair. I bet you'd look a lot younger with short hair. And that mustache . . . no girl wants to kiss a walrus. Clean yourself up, and you might find a girlfriend."

"Okay, okay, stop, Mom. I said I'll do it one of these days."

"You promise?"

"If you stop bugging me about it."

"Bud, have you ever heard Clayton play the piano?"

"No."

"Oh my God, Bud, you have to. He can play anything, and he can sing too. Elton John and Billy Joel are lightweights compared to Clayton."

"Oh, come on, Mom. Stop."

"I'm not kidding you, Bud. He's a musical genius. When he was a baby, he'd sit in his high chair and beat his silverware in perfect time to the music on the radio. Then, when we got a piano, he was maybe five or six. He'd spend hours plunking away on the keys, making up songs and playing ones that were popular at the time. My friends used to come over just to watch him. It was amazing. I have no clue where he got all his talent." She rubbed her forehead, eyebrows pinched. "Well, maybe I do." She gave me a devilish grin. "Our milkman was a helluva musician."

"Real funny, Mom."

"Then we got Clayton an electric guitar and amp when he turned sixteen." She turned to her son and asked, "What was the name of that guitar?"

"A Fender Stratocaster," he answered.

"Right, a Fender. He just had to have this guitar, and my husband and I saved for over a year to buy it for him. It was 1964, and those were the days of the British Invasion.

47

He was all over that stuff. He just picked up that guitar and seemed to know what to do. He's really gifted." She smiled at Clayton. "Did you tell Bud about your band?"

"No, Mom. That was a long time ago."

"After the Beatles became popular, Clayton had a band called the Bugspots. He got the name from the marks bugs leave on the windshield when they get smacked. Anyway, they had Beatles haircuts, and the band was really popular in Hamtramck. They had gigs all the time. A couple of times, record company guys came to see them play." Marian winked at me. "Clayton was really popular with the girls."

Clayton frowned. "Was not."

"We took him to all sorts of concerts starting in the late fifties. Jerry Lee Lewis, B.B. King, Ray Charles . . . I can't think of them all. We figured exposing him to different musicians and styles would help him if he had a career in music. It was really fun before he was a teenager. After that, he totally hated it."

Clayton responded emphatically, "I did not!"

"Oh yes, you did, honey. You didn't like being seen with us. It's okay. We understood. When I was sixteen, my mom used to take me shopping for clothes, and my friends would see me and laugh. I wanted to crawl under a rock and die. But sometimes, I just beat the crap out of them." She looked at me. "Just kidding on the last part, Bud." Marian shifted in her wheelchair. "Bud, tell me about yourself."

Clayton answered. I figured he wanted to head off the questions that would likely come. "Bud's wife died four years ago. He's a former teacher, and he has two great kids. One lives around here, and the other one is in California. He moved into Serenity a couple of weeks ago, and we've been having a blast. We had a big food fight yesterday in the cafeteria, and Bud got sent to his room for misbehaving. Right, Bud?"

I didn't respond.

"Really?" asked Marian.

Clayton shook his head. "Of course not."

"Oh, Clayton, you're such a bullshitter. But I still love you."

I laughed. It was entertaining, seeing a rock star getting needled by his mother.

"I think we should get going, Bud. We don't want to miss bingo." Clayton rolled his eyes. He bent over and kissed Marian on the cheek. "See you in a couple of days. Love you, Mom."

"Love you too, sweets. Thanks so much for coming by, and thanks for the beautiful flowers."

"Nice to meet you, Marian." I extended my hand.

Marian slapped it away and said, "Get in here and give me a hug." I bent over and hugged her. She kissed me on the cheek. "I really enjoyed meeting you. Ditch Clayton and come on by sometime." She giggled as I felt my face getting warm again.

Clayton laughed, and we headed out of the room.

Walking down the hall, I said, "Thanks for covering for me. I really didn't want to talk about my wife and kids again."

"I understand. Glad I could help. She's something else, isn't she?"

"She's great. I can see the apple didn't fall too far from the tree."

Chapter Twelve

As we passed the nurses' station and headed toward the exit door, I heard a man's loud voice coming from one of the rooms ahead. He seemed to want assistance, but his words were unintelligible. I glanced in the room as we passed and saw an old man with unkempt white hair and sunken cheeks. He was wearing a food-stained white hospital gown and sitting in a chair with what appeared to be a catheter bag hanging from its arm. I looked at Clayton, and he shook his head.

When we reached the Mothership, I said, "I don't know how people can work in a place like this, but God bless those who do."

"I sure as hell couldn't do it," said Clayton as he started the van. "People like Corrine are the closest thing to angels."

Seeing that man was a reminder of what could happen to me or my new friends. As Clayton was backing out of the parking space, I said, "Sure hope a nursing home isn't in the cards for me."

"I'm with you, brother. A massive heart attack in my sleep would be terrific. Just go to sleep and drift away to never-never land."

We proceeded down the road with little discussion as the radio softly played tunes from a classic rock station. When we reached an intersection and stopped for a red light, a car pulled up next to us. Rhythmic thumping coming from its stereo drowned out the tune we were listening to. The thumping seemed to vibrate right through the van.

Oblivious to my gaze, the three occupants, who appeared to be high school age, were moving in time to the beat and mimicking the male voice blasting from the speakers.

Clayton frowned. "It's rap. I hate that shit. I respect people who can actually play an instrument or sing, but sitting in a studio with a bunch of electronics and talking smack does nothin' for me. It ain't music. You know, Bud, rap is like scissors. It loses to rock. Get it?"

I laughed as the light turned green and the Mothership proceeded into the intersection. Meanwhile, the car with the young rap lovers turned the corner, tires squealing, and sped away. "Yeah, I get it. I'm not a fan either. But I suppose people in our parents' generation didn't like the music we listened to."

Grinning, Clayton said, "Oh man, don't go layin' logic and wisdom on me. I hate that."

I laughed and apologized for being too intellectual.

After a couple of minutes, Clayton reached down and turned off the stereo. "Bud, I've been thinking. Some of the things you said about your family kinda hit home."

"How so?"

"Well, back in the late sixties and early seventies, I was living with that special lady friend I mentioned earlier. Her name was Candace. We'd been together for about three years. She was fucking beautiful, Bud, and had the heart of a saint."

"What happened?"

"Back then, I was just like your kids—selfish and self-centered. It was all about me and chasing my crazy dream of fame and fortune. In the process, I lost sight of the things that were important in a relationship—kinda like your wife. I took her for granted and wasn't the friend and partner I should have been. One day, she told me she needed to move on. I begged her to stay and promised to change, but the damage was done. It was the saddest day of my life."

"That must have been rough."

"It was. I was lost without her. I tried to numb my pain with alcohol and marijuana, but I couldn't get her out of my mind. I was a bloody mess for a long time." Clayton jammed on the brakes to avoid colliding with a car that had shot out from a parking lot, crossed in front of us, and headed in the opposite direction. "You're an asshole!" Clayton yelled as he honked and flipped off the driver. He looked at me and shrugged. "Sorry about that. I flunked anger management."

"No problem. A little road rage from time to time never hurt anyone." I leaned back in my seat. "So, did you ever see her again?"

Clayton didn't respond for a moment and seemed to be deep in thought. He swallowed and said, "One time. She told a mutual friend she wanted to get together with me and talk, so he passed along her phone number. I called her, and we arranged to meet at a quiet little bar down by the ocean. I was hoping she wanted to get back together."

"And did she?"

Clayton shook his head. "Far from it! She told me she was pregnant and planning to get married to some wealthy businessman. I think his last name was Whittaker, Whitcomb, or something like that. Anyway, she claimed she had found stability and happiness with him. I tried to seem happy for her, but I was heartbroken."

I could see the pain on Clayton's face. "I'm sorry."

I was about to change the subject to something less personal when Clayton said, "It gets worse, Bud. She told me the child was mine. She found out she was pregnant after she left me, and when she met her new man, she decided not to tell him."

"Oh my God. What did you say?"

"Not much. I was blown away. She said her man would be a good provider and father, and I knew deep down I couldn't give Candace and the child the stable and predictable life they deserved. She begged me never to tell anyone or ever try and contact our child."

"Did you agree to that?"

Clayton nodded. "I did. There've been many times I regretted that decision, but I did what she asked because I loved her. Does that make any sense?"

"It does. It absolutely does."

"Eventually, I received a postcard with no return address. It said, 'Marie, eight pounds, two ounces.' My daughter, Marie, would be in her mid-forties. I don't even know her birthday."

"Do you ever wonder if she knows about you?"

"Yeah, sometimes."

"Maybe she'll reach out to you. With the internet and things like Ancestry and 23andMe, it's much easier for children to track down their birth parents. I know a guy who did it."

Clayton looked at me and smiled ruefully. "Well, she better hurry up. I'm not getting any younger."

"Have you thought about trying to track her down?"

"I wouldn't know where to begin. Plus, I promised Candace I wouldn't try."

"I understand."

The next morning, I woke up thinking about Clayton, his stories about his time in LA, and his penchant for bull-shitting. I sent a text message to April, requesting that she drop off my laptop and printer, which had been left behind in the move.

* * *

Abbie was in her apartment, examining the Serenity website, which contained information about the facilities in Farmington Hills, Grand Rapids, and Traverse City. She clicked on the Staff tab and found photographs of the employees of each facility. She closely examined the pictures of the general managers of the Grand Rapids and Traverse City facilities and compared them to the iPad pictures she took of the two men who visited Brett.

Abbie admitted to herself that Clayton was right. The tall, dark man, Lou Ricci, managed the Grand Rapids facility, and the short, chubby blond man with the briefcase, William Pennington, managed the Traverse City facility. The only common thread between them appeared in the website description about the founding of Serenity. Brett and the others were all 1993 graduates of Cranbrook, a private college prep school in Bloomfield Hills, Michigan.

Abbie was unable to forget the sequence of events in the

office that led to Pennington passing the briefcase to Brett. Brett's furtive behavior before he opened the briefcase confirmed something was going on. But what?

Sometime later, Abbie found a note slid under her door. It was an invitation from Kathleen to attend a birthday celebration and happy hour for Jim.

Chapter Thirteen

Charlie and I sat together during breakfast. He had a pained look on his face, and eventually confessed to not remembering my name.

"It's Bud," I said. He let out a sigh and shook his head.

"Don't worry about it, Charlie. I have the same problem."

"Thanks for that, Bud, but I'm sure you've noticed that my memory problems are a little more significant. The doc says I have mild cognitive impairment.

"When did you first notice it?"

"A year or so after my wife died, I got lost a couple of times going home from work, and that scared me. My two boys started getting on me about forgetting and misplacing things, and that's when they took me to the doctor. I didn't want everybody worrying about me, so I turned over the business to my sons, sold the family home, and moved here."

"What kind of business were you in?" I asked.

Charlie's eyes brightened. "Bus repair. My grandfather started the business in the thirties."

"That's a real niche business. How'd he get into that?"

"He was a first-generation Swede who worked as a mechanic for the Detroit school system. All he did was repair and maintain school buses. He was a mechanical genius, no doubt about it. Anyway, he thought he could make more money with his own bus repair business, so he bought some property out in the country with an industrial-size garage and began soliciting every school district within fifty miles. He showed them it was cheaper to hire him for repair work rather than employ a bunch of full-time mechanics."

"Sounds like the American dream. He must have bought a big chunk of land to accommodate a bunch of school buses needing repairs."

"He did. Fifteen acres, just north of Warren. It was farm country when he bought it, but now warehouses and some light manufacturing surround it. My grandpa did a great job getting the business off the ground, and I did a pretty good job keeping it going. But my boys have taken the business to the next level. They have state-of-the-art technology and the best diagnostic equipment on the market. They've branched into repairing heavy equipment."

I asked him, "Do you miss it?"

"I do. I loved working, being with my boys, and talking to the customers. I'd do just about anything to spend a couple days a week there. I see my boys and their families almost every weekend, and I'm grateful for that, but during the week . . . I don't know, I'm kinda drifting." There was sadness in Charlie's bright-blue eyes and Santa Claus face.

"How do you mean, Charlie?"

"Well, work and running the business was such an important part of my life. I'm kind of empty without it." He looked around the dining room for a moment, then added, "I don't know what I would do if I didn't have friends here."

It's weird. Some people retire and are busier than they were when they were working. Other people, like Charlie, are lost. I suppose a family business is in your blood and part of your identity. When it's gone, you've lost your identity and sense of purpose. I was glad Charlie had friends because, without them, I thought he'd give up.

"From what I see, Charlie," you've got some very good friends. You're a lucky man."

"I know." He smiled and seemed to shake off his sadness. "Yeah, Bud. We're all stuck here on Gilligan's Island, and we have to make the best of it. Speaking of making the best of it, I assume you got an invitation to the party Kathleen is throwing for Jim."

"I did. It's nice of her to do that."

"Yeah, it is." Charlie smiled. "It may also be a convenient way for her to get to know you better."

"What? Why would you say that?"

"I don't know. I've known Kathleen for two years. We've spent a lot of time together. She seems different when you're around."

"Different?"

"Yeah. Her eyes twinkle, and she smiles more. Who knows? Maybe she likes you."

Chapter Fourteen

pril surprised me by actually making time to retrieve and drop off my laptop. She didn't stop by and see me but left the laptop and a note with Brett:

Hi Dad,

Sorry I didn't have time to stop by. Your next-door neighbor saw me at the house yesterday and asked if it was going to be for sale. He said he has a friend who is a big shot at GM and is very interested. You should think about it.

I'll be gone for ten days. I'm going to LA to meet John and his new girlfriend. We're going to wine country.

Love you, April

Notice that April didn't ask how I was doing or if I'd met anyone? I'd be lying if I said her behavior didn't bother me.

She had been very close to Sharon, and I'd thought Sharon's death would bring us closer. But it seemed to do the opposite. April had put up a wall that I hadn't been able to penetrate. I'd told her many times that I loved her and wanted to talk to her about our relationship, but she insisted that everything was fine. Her relationship with me was purely superficial and transactional. It's sad. I digress.

I began my research soon after I received the laptop, and I was eager to get back to it. I finished my breakfast and headed to my apartment. I was thinking about Charlie's comment that Kathleen seemed different around me when I looked through the library door's window and saw her sitting at a table, reading. I gently knocked on the door. She looked up, put the book on her lap, and waved me in.

I thanked Kathleen for the invitation to the party, and she excitedly told me about her plans for decorating her apartment and ordering the birthday cake. As I was about to leave, I decided to ask her about my apartment's former resident.

"You mind if I ask you something way off topic?" I asked.

"Not at all. What is it?"

"Jim mentioned Sister Mary Katherine. What was she like?"

"Oh, Bud. I wish you could have known her. She was a fascinating person. She'd been all over the world and had a lot of great stories. She was a bundle of energy and was very generous with her time. She helped me through some rough stuff."

I wondered what Kathleen was alluding to, but I didn't feel comfortable diving into that. Then I heard a moaning sound and turned to see Clayton pressing his face against the library door's window with sufficient pressure to flatten and distort his nose and lips. It was something a ten-year-old might have done, but it was still damn funny. Kathleen and I laughed and waved him in.

"Top of the morning, fellow senior citizens!" Clayton said. "Sorry for interrupting. Did I interrupt?"

"No. You're fine. Come on in," said Kathleen. "What's up?"

"I saw you guys in here and thought about giving you a pressed ham or pickle on a platter, but I decided to keep it PG and went with the ran-into-the-window thing."

Kathleen gave me a blank look, then turned to Clayton. "I don't get it. Pressed ham? Pickle? What am I missing?

Clayton laughed, giving me a friendly, high-schoolish, the-joke's-on-her shoulder push. "Go ahead. Tell her, Bud." I hesitated, and he egged me on. "C'mon, spill the beans, son."

"Ah . . . a pressed ham is a butt pressed against glass, and I assume a pickle on a platter is—"

Kathleen cut me off. "Okay, okay. I get it! That's gross, Clayton! How you come up with this stuff blows my mind."

He shrugged. "I guess I'm just a word wizard. Kinda like Bob Dylan, but I don't dabble in silly stuff like love and peace."

As usual, Clayton was wearing a shirt related to music of the sixties. This time, he was wearing a Grateful Dead shirt tie-dyed in bright orange and blue.

"Love the shirt," I said. "I was kind of a Deadhead back in the day."

"You were? Cool!" He looked down, appearing to proudly admire his colorful shirt. "I love this shirt, man. I've had it for . . . gosh, close to twenty-five years. Jerry Garcia, one of the best guitarists ever, gave it to me about a year before he died. You know who he was, right? The Dead's lead guitarist."

I glanced at Kathleen, and she shot me a skeptical look.

"Oh yeah," I replied. "I saw him play with the Dead at the Grande Ballroom in Detroit in 1968. He was unbelievable.

"The man could play, that's for sure. Interesting guy." Clayton seemed lost in thought for a moment, then he turned to Kathleen. "Awesome idea about the happy hour. Thanks for the invitation. Now, I'm supposed to pick up that cake tomorrow, right?"

"That's right. No later than three. And be sure to stop by and get my grocery list before you leave, or we'll be drinking tap water for happy hour."

"Okay. Gotcha. I need to stop somewhere and have some copies made. I'll do that first, then I'll pick up the stuff at the grocery store. I'm on it."

"Clayton," she said. "I was just talking to Bud about Sister Mary Katherine. You talked to her as much as I did. She was a really special person, wasn't she?"

"The best!" He slapped me on the back. "I'm not kiddin' you, dude. She was the most compassionate person I've ever met. She loved music and was a pretty good piano player."

At first, I smiled and nodded.

"She turned me on to some amazing bluesy gospel tunes," he continued. "But inevitably, she'd want to listen to Kiss. She loved their *Destroyer* album."

Stunned, I looked at Kathleen.

"Come on, Clayton! Kiss? This is another one of your stories, isn't it?" she said.

"No, man! She was a big-time Kiss fan—had all their albums. She even had a life-size poster of Gene Simmons."

"Gimme a break," Kathleen said.

"I'm serious. She had a Gene Simmons poster on the back of her bathroom door. I saw it with my own eyes! Maybe they took it down when they cleaned out the apartment. Who knows?" He looked at me. "Bud, did you see the Kiss poster?"

"Yeah. It's still there."

"See! I'm surprised you never saw it, Kathleen. You spent a lot of time in there." Clayton grinned. "I'm very hurt you would accuse me of making up a story about our dear friend Sister Mary Katherine."

"Yeah, you really look hurt, Clayton," she said.

"Well, sometimes, people conceal their hurt with a smile."

Kathleen laughed. "Oh, that's what you're doing. I got it. I just wonder if Sister Mary Katherine put up the poster by herself or if someone helped her."

"Hmm, I don't know." Clayton scratched his head. "That's a puzzler. Let me think on that while I'm running errands. I'm outta here." He smiled and headed out the door.

Kathleen smiled and turned to me. "So, you've got a Gene Simmons poster on your bathroom door? Now that's funny! I'd love to see it. Is he in full costume?"

"Definitely. Painted face, leather, studs, chains, elevated shoes, the works! The darn thing scared the bejesus out of me my first night here."

"You're kidding!" She giggled. "How so?"

"I went into the bathroom and closed the door." Kathleen covered her mouth to stifle her laughter. "I was trying to relax before the first dinner. I ran hot water, saturated a washcloth, and held it over my face. When I pulled it off, I looked in the mirror and saw someone standing behind me." I paused for a moment and added, "I nearly wet myself."

Kathleen erupted in laughter. I smiled as I watched her. She was lovely.

Then she looked up at me. "Sorry, Bud. The image of that is really funny."

"Yeah, I think it's funny now too. I'm beginning to realize Clayton is quite the prankster."

"Oh, it's not just Clayton. I'm sure Jim was in on it too."

"Really? Jim?"

"Absolutely! Every comedy team needs a straight man, and that's Jim. The poster may have been his idea, and Clayton helped him implement it. You never know. The two of them feed off each other." Kathleen gazed up, rubbed her chin, and smiled.

"What? Is there more?" I asked.

"No. Just thinking that Sister Mary Katherine would be laughing her . . . habit off if she knew those two went in her apartment after she passed and hung a Gene Simmons poster on her bathroom door."

Chapter Fifteen

We gathered in Kathleen's apartment for Jim's birthday celebration. Jim was nicely dressed in khaki pants, a white golf shirt, and penny loafers. Beer in his hand, he sat in his wheelchair, smiling at Clayton, who was standing by the window and razzing him about his "yuppie outfit."

Charlie and I were on the couch, sipping our beer and talking about the predicted storm. Meanwhile, Abbie and Kathleen were in the kitchen, yakking, while Kathleen poured wine into two glasses.

When the women finished their business in the kitchen, I got up from the couch, and they sat on either side of Charlie, each holding a wineglass. I stood next to Clayton with an eye on the darkening sky.

Kathleen said we needed to toast Jim on his birthday, so we raised our glasses and wished him a happy birthday and a healthy year. Jim returned the toast, thanking us for our friendship.

"You're the man, Jim!" said Clayton. He took a drink of beer, wiped his lips with his hand, and froze for a moment as he looked at Abbie, who was wearing what appeared to be a polka-dotted sweatsuit. She looked at him quizzically.

"Oh my God, Abbie! Are those dots little cakes with lighted candles?" Clayton asked.

"They are. I bought it special for Jim's birthday."

"It's cute," said Kathleen.

"And festive," said Clayton. "Do they come in men's sizes?"

"Stick it, Clayton." Abbie poured a second glass of wine.

"Okay, before I got distracted by our fashion plate," said Clayton, "I was going to ask Charlie if he remembered his birthday entertainment."

"Why do I suddenly feel nauseous?" said Charlie, making everyone laugh. "What the hell was his name?"

"King Karaoke," said Kathleen.

"Right!" said Charlie. "Bud, you should have seen him. He had a terrible hairpiece, and he looked like he slept in his suit. He even tried to get Abbie to dance. It was hilarious!"

"The guy gave me the creeps. Thank God Clayton came to my rescue," said Abbie.

"What did you do, Clayton?" I asked.

"I gave him $150 to leave. Best damn money I ever spent."

Everyone roared.

I heard a faint rumbling and looked out the window. The sky was dark, and thunderclouds were rolling in. Charlie said he'd heard on the news that the area was under a severe thunderstorm watch.

"Forget about the thunderstorm," Kathleen said to him. She turned back to the group. "Who'd like another beverage?"

Kathleen and I distributed another round of beer to the men, and the talk continued about some of the past birthday entertainment.

"I sure hope whatever entertainment torture is in store for us doesn't involve an accordion," said Clayton.

"You don't like accordions?" I asked.

"Bud, do you know what baseballs and accordions have in common?" he replied.

"No. What?" I said, smiling as I waited for the punchline.

"People cheer when you hit them with a bat." The room erupted in laughter. "Does that answer your question?"

"Okay, enough of accordions and King Karaoke," said Kathleen. "Does anyone have plans for the Fourth of July?"

"I plan to get naked and run all over the Serenity grounds with a sparkler," said Abbie, making her friends laugh again.

"Count me in," said Charlie.

Kathleen sighed. "My kids always ask me to join them on the Fourth. But it's such a bother for them to pick me up when they should be enjoying the time with their kids and their friends and not worrying about me. I loved the Fourth of July growing up. The parades, the good food, and the fireworks. It was the best. My mom used to dress my sisters and me in red, white, and blue outfits. We'd get together at my uncle's farm and play baseball. We had so much fun. What about you, Bud?"

"When I was a kid, you couldn't buy fireworks. But I had a friend whose parents were divorced. So, every couple of weeks, he went to the Soo to visit his dad, who took him across the river into Canada to buy the good stuff. We stockpiled firecrackers, M-8os, and bottle rockets until the Fourth. Then we blew them off all over town. We never stayed at one location because we knew someone might call the cops. So we moved around on our bikes."

"You were the first mobile missile launchers," said Jim.

"And a smuggler and confessed criminal. I knew you had issues," said Clayton. "What about you, Abbie?"

"My husband and I were heavily involved in the UAW, so we always walked in the parade with the float and then got together with UAW families in the park. My two boys loved it. There were games and races for the kids, and the food was out of this world. The union went all out." Tears came to her eyes, and she quickly picked up her wineglass and took a large gulp. "Those were good days." She reached into her pocket, pulled out some tissue, and wiped her eyes. "Okay, Mr. Birthday Boy. What was your most memorable Fourth of July?"

Jim shifted in his wheelchair and seemed to be searching for words. He graciously smiled and said, "Gosh, I don't know, Abbie. We always went to the parade and then to the park for our annual picnic with my family. It was a long day, and half the time, I fell asleep during the fireworks."

"Let's get some fireworks," said Clayton.

"Not a bad idea. But where would we shoot 'em off?" I asked him.

"Right here."

"I don't think that would be a good idea," cautioned Kathleen.

"Motor City Bus Repair," said Charlie.

"What are you talking about?" asked Clayton.

"My business, where my boys work. We've got fifteen acres, and it's only thirty minutes from here. Just outside Warren," said Charlie.

"Really? You really think we could do that?" Clayton asked excitedly.

"Sure. If we get enough fireworks, my boys and their families may want to join us," said Charlie.

Clayton stood and yelled, "Let's do it! The Fourth of July at Motor City Bus Repair!"

Chapter Sixteen

When we were seated at our dining room table, I remembered that Brett told me that residents celebrating birthdays got the meal of their choice.

"Whatcha order for dinner, Jim?" I asked.

He grinned. "You'll see."

"Wait," said Clayton. "You made something up to mess with them?"

"Sort of. I'd call it East Asian culinary horseplay."

"Ladies and gentlemen," said the head chef in a loud voice. "May I have your attention, please."

The dining room quieted. The residents were looking toward the kitchen entrance, where the chef was standing next to Nurse Jackie, who was holding a food tray covered with a white cloth. "I am pleased to announce that tonight, we are celebrating the birthday of Jim Rogers, the only Serenity resident who proudly served our country in Vietnam."

Many of the residents clapped. Jim looked down at the table and appeared to sink into his wheelchair.

"Two weeks ago," the head chef continued, "we provided Jim with our Birthday Dinner Request Form. He returned that form with an interesting story and an unusual request. Tia Ni Po Ni. Right, Jim?"

Jim gave him a thumbs-up, seemingly relieved that the chef had no idea he had been pranked.

Kathleen looked at Jim and mouthed the words *Tiny pony?*

He grinned. She giggled and whispered it to me. I winked at Jim. Clayton looked at us and barked, "Quit horsing around."

"Unfortunately," the chef said, "we were unable to provide the meal Jim requested, so we decided to go all out and celebrate his birthday and thank him for serving our country." He turned to one of the kitchen workers and nodded. The refrain from "God Bless the USA" began playing over the ceiling speakers.

That was Nurse Jackie's cue to walk toward Jim's table with the mystery food tray. As she arrived at the table, she stood erect, appearing to wait for her next command. When the song finished, she carefully placed the tray on the table and dramatically pulled off the white cloth, revealing salad, a fruit dish, a vegetable dish, and a plate with a stainless-steel cover.

"Ladies and gentlemen," said the head chef, "in honor of Jim's birthday and his service to our great country, we have prepared an all-American meal that would make George Washington's head spin. From the great state of Wisconsin is an all-American salad with Parmesan pepper-corn dressing. We have beautiful, fresh Michigan green beans sprinkled with pomegranate arils and mint, and a fresh fruit salad made with honey-vanilla Minnesota yogurt, Michigan strawberries, Georgia blueberries, and Washington raspberries. Now, the main course. Go ahead, Jackie."

She removed the plate cover to reveal a huge cut of meat with an American flag stuck in the middle and a side of potatoes.

"A USDA prime-cut T-bone steak and some good, old American fries!" the chef announced. "How about that, people?"

The residents clapped, and the chef turned toward Jim, solemnly saluted, and went back into the kitchen.

Jim looked at us and said, "I need a drink."

"Excuse me, may I have your attention!" Nurse Jackie blurted as the residents were being served. "I just want to remind everyone to save room for cake and to stick around for some fantastic entertainment!"

Chapter Seventeen

Most of us had finished eating and were waiting for the entertainment. The occasional rumbling of the approaching thunderstorm was quickly drowned out by drumbeats coming from the ceiling speakers.

"Ladies and gentlemen!" yelled Nurse Jackie. "From the beautiful city of Dearborn, Michigan . . . the one and only . . . *Gordy Accordee!*"

The door to the kitchen flew open, and out popped a man in his fifties playing the "Beer Barrel Polka" on an accordion. He was dressed in brown lederhosen with red suspenders over a white shirt, white knee-high socks, hiking boots, and an Alpine hat with a feather. He smiled broadly as he pranced to the music, dipping and spinning toward the spot that had been cleared for him. His hat fell off, but a resident picked it up and handed it to him. He high-fived the resident, put the hat back on, and resumed playing. Some of the residents were clapping in time to the music.

Clayton stood and put his hands over his ears, saying, "This is my nightmare."

"Where are you going?" I asked.

"I need an accordion sickness bag." He walked out of the dining room.

Gordy began singing as he pranced and danced his way toward Jim.

"Roll out the barrel, we'll have a barrel of fun. Roll out the barrel, we've got the blues on the run. Zing boom tararrel, ring out a song of good cheer. Now's the time to roll the barrel, 'cause Birthday Jim is *here*."

On *here*, Gordy extended his arms and pointed his index fingers at Jim, who was probably wishing he'd left with Clayton.

"Good evening, ladies and gentlemen," our entertainer said. "I am Gordy Accordee, and I'm delighted to be here with you to celebrate Jim's birthday and his service in Vietnam. How old are you, Jim?"

"Seventy-three."

"Wow! Jim is seventy-three. He doesn't look a day over seventy! Did you enjoy your all-American dinner?"

"Yup."

"Jim's a man of few words. They say a quiet man is a thinking man. A quiet woman is just plain mad, right?"

"That's right!" yelled a resident, who was rumored to have been married four times.

Gordy put his hand on Jim's shoulder. "Seriously, Jim, a couple of months ago, I didn't think I would make this gig. I was really struggling. It was hard, but I had to finally accept I had a serious addiction." Gordy hung his head. After a moment, he looked up and yelled, "I was addicted to the Hokey Pokey, but I turned myself around! Let's get it on, Serenity!"

Gordy began playing "The Hokey Pokey" as he spun

and dipped his way back to the front of the dining room. Along the way, he encouraged four female residents to follow. They left their tables, went to the front of the dining room, and began dancing.

From the back corner of the dining room, someone played a few notes on the piano, but Gordy played on. A few more notes came from the piano.

"It's Clayton," said Charlie.

Clayton was flexing his fingers as if he was trying to loosen up. After a few moments, he put his hands on the keys and began to play a beautiful up-tempo melody that filled the dining room with a sweet sound.

Jim signaled that he was joining Clayton. Abbie gave him a thumbs-up and followed. I looked at Kathleen and Charlie, then shrugged. We agreed to join our friends. Soon, we were joined by almost all the other residents and some of the nursing staff and kitchen workers. Appearing irritated, Gordy was the last to join us, but his mood quickly dissipated as we watched Clayton's agile fingers move up and down the keyboard.

When Clayton ended the piece, he said, "Gordy, come on over here." The audience became quiet as Gordy made his way through the crowd with his accordion slung over his shoulder. When he reached the piano, Clayton said, "Hey, everybody. How about a big hand for our friend here, Gordy Accordee!" Clayton began clapping, and we quickly joined in. "Gordy, you were absolutely outstanding, and I'm very sorry I interrupted your performance. But I want you to know that it was *your music* that inspired me to go to the piano after a long time away. Thank you for that!" Clayton extended his hand, and Gordy shook it.

One of the residents yelled, "He wrote 'Up Yours.'"

"You wrote 'Up Yours'?" asked Gordy.

"I did," said Clayton, "but I've always wanted to play the accordion. Have you ever heard of Eric Clapton or B.B. King?"

"Of course I have," said Gordy.

"Their first love in music was the accordion. I was on the road with them in 1970, and they got together at the end of a concert and played their accordions until the break of dawn. It was the most amazing thing I've ever seen."

Clayton grinned and winked at Kathleen and me when Gordy's attention was momentarily drawn to his accordion, but his serious look returned when Gordy looked back at him. Then the bullshit continued to flow.

"Wow! I never knew that," Gordy said to Clayton.

"You didn't? Many of the most important and innovative musicians over the last fifty years have been accordion players. Thank you for sharing your gift with all of us."

"Yes, thank you," said Jim, who appeared to be biting his lip so he wouldn't laugh.

Gordy smiled and proudly replied, "You're welcome."

"Gordy, do you mind if I play a couple of tunes to celebrate Jim's birthday?" asked Clayton.

"Not at all."

Clayton reached under the piano bench and retrieved a brown bag. He tossed the bag to Jim and said, "Put that on."

"What is it?" Jim asked.

"You told me you were in glee club in high school, so I know you can sing. Don't ask questions. Just put it on."

Jim reached in the bag and pulled out a black wig of long, straight hair. "Cher hair? You want me to put this on?"

"Yes. Come on, brother. Get with the program. Put it on."

There were giggles as Jim rolled his eyes and put the

wig on. Then there was more laughter as he tossed his head back, ran a hand through the long hair, puckered his lips, and blew me a kiss.

While Jim was putting on his show, Clayton stood, grabbed a stack of sheet music from the piano, and handed it to me. "You'll find fifteen packets," he said. "Each packet contains the music and lyrics for the five songs we're going to sing. Mind passing them around? People will have to share."

I gave half the stack to Kathleen, and we distributed them.

Still standing, Clayton said, "Okay, everyone. Remember "I Got You Babe" by Sonny and Cher? You'll note that I slightly modified the lyrics. All you have to do is follow along and sing, 'Brett, I got you, Brett,' every time that phrase comes up. Jim and I will handle the rest. Any questions?" No one responded. "Jim, I highlighted your lines."

Jim seemed to have fully embraced playing the role of Cher. "I understand, Sonny, my love," he said in a falsetto voice as he ran his hand through his long, black wig and winked at Clayton.

"Smokin' hot, isn't she?" said Clayton. Everyone laughed, and Clayton sat. Jim wheeled himself up close, and Clayton asked, "Can you join me on the piano bench, Cher?"

"Yes, sweetheart." Jim pushed the wheelchair footplates to the side and stood with someone's assistance. He walked a couple steps, then slid next to Clayton on the piano bench.

"Are you ready, Cher?" Clayton asked.

"I'm ready, you big hunka man."

With that, Clayton began playing the melody to "I've

Got You Babe," and Jim launched into the opening lines. "They say we're old and past our prime. We're stuck in this place, just biding time," he sang.

Rocking back and forth on the piano bench, Clayton responded, "Well, that's true, but don't you fret, 'cause I've got you, and baby, we've got Brett."

All around the piano, groups of three and four people were huddled together around their sheet music, smiling and following the lyrics. Then came the refrain, and everyone joined in.

"Brett, I got you, Brett, I got you, Brett."

Clayton and Jim continued hamming it up and belting out the song, and their antics and enthusiasm seemed to energize the audience. Several nurses in the back had their arms over each other's shoulders and were swaying in time to the music. Gordy put down his accordion, climbed up on a chair, and waved his hands wildly in time to the music as if he were conducting a chorus. Every refrain was sung louder and with more gusto.

"*What the hell is going on here?*" screamed Brett. Clayton stopped playing. Brett barked at his employees, "Get to work. *Now!*"

A nurse tried to explain. "We were just—"

"I said get to work!" Brett said.

Gordy was frozen like a statue on the chair.

"Get down from there and get in my office now!" commanded Brett. He glared at Clayton as Gordy stepped off. Then he looked at Gordy in disgust and turned back to Clayton. "I hired that idiot, not you."

Red-faced with anger, Brett stormed out of the dining room with Gordy dejectedly following several paces behind. Everyone seemed rattled by Brett's outburst, and they began to scatter. I stayed with Clayton, Jim, and the others at the piano.

"Can you believe that asshole?" said Clayton.

"That was the most fun I've had since I got here, and that son of a bitch spoiled it," said Jim.

I was a little surprised by Kathleen's reaction. She'd always seemed so easygoing and unflappable. But now, she looked downright pissed off. Her jaw was extended, and there was no longer any friendliness or warmth in her dark eyes. "He's a . . . a . . ." She looked around, and I assumed she was about to call Brett a son of a bitch or worse. "He's a . . . jerk, and that was incredibly rude and disrespectful to our birthday boy."

"Whose birthday?" asked Charlie.

"Jim's birthday. Remember?" said Kathleen sweetly.

"Oh, that's right. Sorry."

Gordy walked back into the dining room, seeming utterly defeated. He looked at Clayton and Jim, who were still sitting on the piano bench, and said, "He fired me." He picked up his accordion, then headed to the front of the dining room to collect the rest of his belongings.

"Wait!" said Clayton. Gordy stopped and looked back. Beckoning with his forefinger, Clayton said, "Come here a second." Gordy walked back to the piano. "How much was he going to pay you?"

"One hundred fifty dollars."

Clayton feigned shock. "That cheapskate. With your talent? That's offensive!" He pulled out his wallet and dug out three crisp hundred-dollar bills. "Here you go." Gordy accepted the money and thanked Clayton. "Listen, Gordy, from one musician to another, I want to thank you again for lifting my spirits and motivating me to play again."

"You're welcome. Say, do you think I could have your autograph?"

"I was just about to ask you the same thing," said Clayton.

The two exchanged autographs and shook hands. "I expect big things from you," said Clayton.

As Gordy turned to leave, I told him he was awesome and gave him a fifty-dollar bill.

Chapter Eighteen

W e were still wound up after Gordy left. Clayton said Brett's behavior was in retaliation for his court victory. Jim complained that Brett ruined the evening. As Abbie commented on what had happened, her anger clearly began to build, and she erupted with a stream of colorful epithets.

Seeming to recognize that the continuing hostility was not productive, Kathleen looked at me as if she was asking for support, then announced, "Everyone to my apartment for Jim's surprise."

At her apartment, we sang "Happy Birthday," and Kathleen cut and distributed cake. "This is from all of us," she said.

"Fantastic cake!" said Jim as he savored his first bite from the large slice in front of him. "Thank you all. This means more to me than you could imagine."

"Glad to do it, buddy," said Clayton.

We all agreed.

I noticed that Clayton and Abbie still seemed preoccupied about the Brett incident and whispered that to Kathleen.

She glanced at them and agreed. "After-dinner drink, anyone?"

Abbie eagerly requested a glass of wine, and Clayton and Jim accepted Kathleen's offer of another beer.

I looked out the window toward the parking lot. "The storm is definitely getting closer," I said. "Hey, guys. Check it out. The top is down on Brett's ride."

As we gathered at the window, Clayton said, "Hmm. Maybe the rain gods will be delivering some payback."

"Payback," Abbie muttered under her breath as Kathleen handed her a glass of wine. She took two long gulps, put down her empty glass, and said, "Clayton, I need to talk to you." She began pushing her walker toward the entrance door.

Looking puzzled, Clayton replied, "Now?"

"Yes, right now!"

He put his beer down and followed.

"Where are you guys going?" asked Kathleen as they neared the door.

"I just need to talk to Clayton real quick, and then we'll be right back," Abbie said.

As Clayton and Abbie left Kathleen's apartment, I asked, "What's that all about?"

"I have no idea," said Jim.

After a few minutes, the rumbling was louder and the sky was darker.

"We're gonna get hammered," said Charlie.

I glanced out the window and saw Abbie pushing her walker down the sidewalk toward the parking lot. The wind was howling, and the carry bag on the walker was swinging back and forth.

"What the hell is she doing out there?" I asked.

"Who?" asked Kathleen.

"Abbie!"

Charlie, Kathleen, and Jim joined me at the window.

"She's gonna get drenched," said Charlie.

"Or struck by lightning," said Kathleen.

When Abbie was about halfway between the entrance and the parking lot, she looked around furtively and pushed her walker off the sidewalk to a large oak tree a short distance away.

"What is she doing?" said Kathleen. "Maybe we should go get her. She really sucked down that last glass of wine."

We watched as Abbie vanished behind the oak tree for a few moments, then popped out on the other side. She pushed her walker back on the sidewalk and began heading toward the entrance. A hard rain was imminent, and Abbie was going to get wet.

"Why is she smiling, and where's Clayton?" asked Kathleen.

Before anyone could respond, Brett came flying out of the building and ran past Abbie toward his car. Abbie stopped and turned to watch him while looking anxiously at the building.

As Brett passed near the oak tree, Abbie screamed loudly, causing Brett to stop and look back. She screamed again while pointing at the tree. At that moment, a large rat came scooting around the oak tree, heading directly at Brett. He screamed and raced down the sidewalk with the rat on his heels. He threw open the door and jumped in his car as the rain came pouring down. The rat turned and scooted back into some bushes alongside the building. Brett backed up his car and slumped over the steering wheel in the pouring rain as he waited for the convertible top to finish closing.

For a moment, we looked at each other in disbelief, which quickly erupted into hysterical laughter. Abbie, who was soaking wet, and Clayton, who was still holding the remote control for the rat, soon joined us in the apartment.

Clayton grinned. "I could see that dipshit perfectly from Abbie's room. With the rain and all, I was concerned Robo Rat wouldn't pick up the signal, but he definitely did. You're a friggin' genius, Abbie."

Jim laughed so hard he had tears streaming down his face. "This definitely was the best birthday I've ever had."

Chapter Nineteen

After the party, Jim joined me in my apartment for a nightcap.

He took a long drink of his beer and looked around the room. "I spent a lot of time in here talking to Sister Mary Katherine. She really helped me work through a bunch of stuff, but I could never get my head around her obsession with Gene Simmons." Jim grinned, and there was mischief in his dark eyes reminiscent of his look during my fart machine initiation night. "Are you familiar with Gene Simmons?"

"Very funny, Jim. I know you were in on it too."

"Me? In on what?" he protested with a smile.

"The Gene Simmons poster on the bathroom door."

He laughed. "I guess you got me. Clayton and I saw the poster at a record store, and all I did was mention that it would be a nice welcome gift for the new tenant. The housekeepers left the door open after the apartment was cleaned out, and we couldn't resist. What'd you do with it?"

"Oh, it's still there. Gene and I have the best conversations when I'm in the shower."

"I'm so glad you two hit it off," Jim said with a chuckle.

"Tell me about Sister Mary Katherine. Kathleen and Clayton speak highly of her."

"You would have liked her, Bud. But I gotta admit she was a pain in the neck when I first arrived here. She had one helluva motor and was always moving and doing. I intended to stick to myself, go to meals, and return to my room for an exciting day alone. She would have none of it. She'd stop by to visit, bring me goodies, and get me watching the Red Wings and Tigers. She even convinced me to start playing chess again. I think I was her pet project. She was bound and determined to get me out of my funk. She drove me nuts at times, but it's hard to be rude to a nun with a big heart."

"Who's a Kiss fan," I said.

Jim laughed. "Exactly! Sister Mary Katherine gradually introduced me to the others, and I began to feel a sense of belonging that I hadn't experienced since being with my pals in Vietnam. Our conversations became deeper, and I understood her intentions were pure. She cared about me and wanted me to be happy. Honestly, I might not be here if it wasn't for her. She opened my eyes, Bud. She made me realize that by hanging onto the past, I was blind to the goodness that surrounds me, starting with my friends here. She always encouraged me to 'go out strong,' which means I should zealously embrace all that life has to offer until the Big Guy upstairs decides to punch my ticket."

"Have you been able to do that?"

"For the most part, but there are times when the past creeps up and bites me in the ass. Like tonight." Jim took a drink from his beer and put his empty can on the coffee table.

"Another one?"

"Sure. One for the ditch." I gave him another beer. He opened it and took a drink. "Remember when Abbie asked me about my most memorable Fourth of July?"

"I do."

"Aside from a couple counselors, I've never told anyone about this, even Clayton." Jim took another drink of beer. "It's a memory I've tried to shake for almost fifty years. It was 1970, and we were at a godforsaken place called Firebase Ripcord. Nixon had thrown in the towel, and the war was winding down. But some idiot decided the 101st Airborne should go on the offensive, and Ripcord was our staging area. The bad guys knew this, and starting July 1, they pounded us with mortars and all sorts of other fireworks. It was terrifying." Jim took a long drink from his beer and added sadly, "My best friend was killed by a mortar round three days later, on July 4. I can still see him lying there, all blown to shit. I still have dreams about it."

"I'm so sorry." I could feel my long-suppressed guilt welling up.

"Thanks. Anyway, the next few weeks are kind of a blur. The history books say it was a twenty-three-day siege, but to me, it was twenty-three days of living hell. The fuckin' politicians took a beating after the debacle at Hamburger Hill a year earlier, so the media was kept away, and we were denied reinforcements. We were on our own, fighting for our lives. Over seventy of my brothers died for nothing. Many times, I've wondered why I wasn't among them."

"How'd it end?"

"You're gonna love this. After all that bloodshed, the higher-ups decided Ripcord was not defensible, so we were withdrawn. The place was carpet-bombed by B-52s. Such a waste."

"Oh my God."

Jim sighed. "So, there you go, Bud. Every Fourth of July, I'm reminded of shit I saw and the tears I shed."

I felt ashamed. While I was in Ann Arbor, protesting the war and the military-industrial complex, Jim was trying to stay alive and enduring unimaginable horrors thousands of miles away.

He took another drink of beer and stared at me, seemingly waiting for a response. I didn't know what to say. He continued. "It was a lot to deal with—the senseless loss of friends and being abandoned and sacrificed by politicians and generals. I thought coming home would help with the healing, but it only made things worse. People from my generation treated me like the enemy. They thought going to Canada was nobler than answering this country's call. I felt unwelcome and unappreciated. I was pretty bitter about it all."

It was as if Jim was talking about me, and my guilt was nearly unbearable. I was one of those people who didn't think about the hardships, sacrifices, and patriotism of the soldiers. I remembered shunning returning soldiers because I viewed them as willing participants in the war. God, I regretted that. People like me hurt and alienated good people like Jim. What the hell were we thinking? I knew I should apologize but couldn't bring myself to do it then.

"So that's my story," said Jim. "With Sister Mary Katherine's help, I was able to let go of most it. What about you? When you first got here, I had the impression you weren't happy about it."

"You're right. I wasn't happy. I didn't want to be here and felt my daughter forced me into it. Maybe Sister Mary Katherine's spirit continues to be at work. I've been trying to let go of some of the disappointments in my life. I want to go out strong too."

"Like what disappointments?"

"Nothing like what you went through, Jim—an unhappy marriage, two disappointing children, and an unfulfilled career."

"Geez, Bud, that's plenty." He raised his beer can. "To Sister Mary Katherine."

I agreed. "Yes. To Sister Mary Katherine."

We clinked our cans and finished our beers. I wondered what Jim would think of me if he knew I'd been one of those people who hurt him so badly.

Chapter Twenty

We arrived on the Motor City Bus Repair property the evening of the Fourth of July and Charlie's sons, Dean and Tony, greeted us. After a few minutes, Dean's wife, Karen, and Tony's wife, Rose, joined us. Kathleen and Abbie hit it off immediately with Karen and Rose, and they were soon sitting and visiting at prearranged picnic tables while Dean and Tony helped Clayton and me unload the fireworks from the van. Jim was interested in watching Charlie's teenage grandsons and their friends play wiffle ball and convinced Charlie to push him toward their makeshift playing field.

"I can't believe how much you look like your old man," said Clayton to Dean. Dean had Charlie's height and stocky build, as well as his blue eyes and friendly smile.

"I'm just hoping I can keep my hair." Dean handed a box of fireworks to Tony, who put it in the bed of the company pickup truck. "Yup, there's no doubt who my father is. Can't say the same for my big brother."

Tony, who had dark features and was taller and thinner than his brother, laughed. "I don't care who my father is as long as that guy who pretends to be my father wills the business to me as he promised."

"Settle down, boys," said Clayton facetiously. "I don't want to have to break up a fight."

"I've had some nice visits with your dad," I said as I picked up another box. "He's very proud of you two. He said you're expanding the business and have around fifty employees."

Tony put down the fireworks box he had just picked up and put his hands on his waist. "Dad said that?" He gave Dean an astonished look.

"He sure did."

"That makes me happy. He didn't like the idea of expanding the business when we first brought it up a few years ago," said Dean.

"Yeah, he definitely was not enthusiastic about it," added Tony.

"Well, maybe he was unsure at first, but you proved to him that you made the right move."

Dean and Tony smiled.

"That makes my day," said Tony. "Thank you."

"We were afraid he thought we maneuvered him into Serenity so we could run the business the way we wanted," said Dean. "That wasn't the case at all."

"There's no way he thinks that," I said.

"Fellas, tell me something," said Tony. "We see Dad on the weekends, so it's hard to tell how he's really doing, you know, day by day. What do you think?"

Clayton looked at Tony seriously and responded, "I'd be a little concerned about his violent tendencies, and I don't think it's appropriate for him to be dating a twenty-year-old. Right, Bud?"

The brothers looked at me incredulously. "Ah . . ." I

smiled, gathered my wits, and responded, "I thought she was twenty-three."

Tony and Dean laughed.

"Good one," said Dean.

"Okay, okay, okay," said Clayton as the laughter subsided. "This is serious, boys." Dean and Tony stopped smiling. "I don't know if you noticed, but your dad suffers from . . ." Clayton turned toward me and winked. "Damn, I forgot what it's called. What's it called, Bud?"

Embracing my new role as the straight man for Clayton's ongoing shenanigans, I responded, "Oh boy, I think it has something to do with . . . Gosh, I don't remember."

"His memory?" asked Dean.

"That's it!" said Clayton. "Sometimes he's forgetful. What was your name again?"

Dean looked at Tony, unsure if Clayton was kidding.

I blurted, "That's Tony!"

"No, I'm Dean!"

Dean's emphatic reply was the last straw. Clayton and I laughed hysterically while Tony and Dean stood grinning, watching us carry on.

Their laughter was interrupted by Rose calling to Tony. "Hey, honey, we could use a hand over here." She was struggling to extract the cork from a bottle of wine while the other women at the picnic tables held their glasses in anticipation of a pour.

"I'll be right there!" said Tony. "Sorry about that. Clayton, I think you were going to tell us about Dad."

"Right. He's definitely with the program. He knows he's forgetting things, and we see that. But it's not a big deal. Shit, half the time, I don't know what day it is myself."

Chapter Twenty-One

The teenagers took a break from their wiffle ball game and stopped by the picnic tables to grab some snacks and soft drinks. Rose introduced them, and within minutes, they dispersed to resume the game. While Jim and I were talking, I heard Karen ask Kathleen and Abbie if they had children. Kathleen proudly told her about her two daughters, Martha and Elizabeth, and her four grandchildren. Abbie suddenly seemed distant and told Karen she had two sons and two grandchildren.

"Abbie's oldest son is a doctor in Ohio," said Kathleen enthusiastically.

"Wow! That's impressive," said Karen. "And the other boy?"

The pain on Abbie's face was undeniable. "Things aren't quite right with that one."

Apparently trying to change the subject, Kathleen nudged me and pointed to an old school bus, which was painted with psychedelic colors and parked at the back of the property. "Hey, Charlie, what's the story on that bus?" she asked.

"The hippie bus?" Charlie thought for a moment. "Hmm, I used to know . . . Hey, Dean, where'd the hippie bus come from?"

"It's an old school bus. Some college kids from Warren bought it for some sort of Woodstock celebration in August. They spent days painting the damn thing, but no one bothered to check the oil in the crankcase. The engine blew on their way to Detroit to show it off."

"Not the sharpest tools in the shed," added Tony.

"I bet those kids were planning to go to a big concert in upstate New York to celebrate the fiftieth anniversary of Woodstock," said Jim. "I think it's the weekend of August 16. I just read about it."

"Woodstock. Wow, does that bring back memories," said Kathleen.

"Did you go?" asked Jim.

"Good grief, no. I was a stay-at-home mom with two little girls. But I remember being so envious of people who dropped everything and headed to upstate New York. It seemed so exciting and adventurous, and I was blown away by the number of people who attended and the bands that played."

I looked to my left, where Clayton had been. "Where'd Clayton go? I wonder if he went to Woodstock."

"He's helping the guys get the fireworks ready," said Rose. "They said they're launching soon."

"We should do something to celebrate Woodstock," said Jim.

"Like what?" asked Kathleen.

Abbie took a gulp of wine and said, "Like, have a big old party with music and dancing and love beads and flowers and shit."

Jim laughed. "I'm with you all the way, Abbie! I just don't see us throwing a shindig like that at Serenity."

"We'll do it at my house," I said.

Abbie, Kathleen, and Jim looked at me in surprise.

"Are you shittin' me? You still have a house?" asked Abbie.

"Well, I do unless my daughter figured out a way to sell it without me knowing."

"Where's it at?" Abbie asked.

"Bloomfield Hills." I braced for a smart-ass comment from her.

"Ooh! You're Richie Rich," she said.

The grin on her face vanished when I replied, "Abbie, it was my wife's house, if you know what I mean. I just lived and worked there."

"Sorry, Bud. Me and my big mouth."

"That's okay. It's my house now, and that's where we're going to have Woodstock!" When I looked at Karen and Rose, I noticed puzzled expressions on their faces. "Do you know about Woodstock?"

"Sort of," said Rose.

"Google it, and you'll understand why we're excited about celebrating it. The party will be August 16, and I want you and your hubbies to come. The only condition is that you must wear sixties attire. It'll be a blast."

As soon as I said "blast," the first firework was launched and a loud *kaboom* followed. Jim flinched and looked at me while the others admired the sparkling colors illuminating the sky, followed by a loud "Right on" from Clayton and hoots and hollers from the teenagers.

Remembering what Jim told me about his struggles on the Fourth of July, I leaned in and quietly asked him if he was okay.

"Thanks for asking, Bud. I'm fine. Really"

A second launch produced another deafening boom, but I heard Jim shout, "It's been a great day!" Our eyes met, he smiled, and we fist-bumped.

When the fireworks ended and goodbyes and thank-yous were said, the brothers helped everyone into the van. Just as Clayton started the engine, I asked him to give me a minute. I stepped out and called to Dean and Tony. They followed me around the corner of the garage, out of sight from the van, and I told them about the conversation I had with their dad.

Chapter Twenty-Two

During breakfast the next morning, I told Charlie how impressed I was with the building and repair bays. Kathleen joined us and complimented Charlie on his nice family.

Charlie was beaming. "My grandfather started the business . . ." I smiled and nodded. "Did I already tell you the story?" he asked.

"You did," I replied. "Your grandfather had a lot of guts and business savvy to leave a comfortable job and start his own business. He must have been quite a guy."

"Good morning, everyone," said Abbie as she pulled up a chair to the table. Her hair was a mess, and she was wearing the same white sweatsuit with tiny American flags that she wore the night before. "Charlie, thanks so much for hosting last night. It was nice to get the hell out of here and spend time with your family."

"You're welcome. I think everybody had a good time." Charlie looked toward the dining room entrance and said, "What the hell?"

Dean and Tony walked in and were looking around.

Charlie waved, and they came over to the table. "Is every-thing okay?" asked Charlie.

"Everything is fine, Dad, except . . ." said Tony.

"Except what?" asked Charlie.

"Well, Dad," said Dean, "a lot of our old customers have been asking about you. We think they like you better than us. We wondered if you'd be willing to spend a few days a week at the shop."

"Yeah, we think it would be good for the business," said Tony.

Charlie seemed stunned. "You want me at the shop? When?"

"How about today? We already have a couple of employees making an office space for you," said Dean.

"I'd be honored." Charlie stood and hugged his boys. "I have to get a couple of things out of my apartment."

"No problem," said Tony.

Grinning, Charlie turned to us. "I'll see you guys tonight. I have to go to work!"

We wished him a great day as he and his sons departed.

"That was so nice of the boys to do that," said Kathleen. "Did you see the smile on his face? He just lit up."

Abbie looked at me suspiciously and said, "That was you, wasn't it?"

I didn't respond.

"*It was you!* I wondered why you got out of the van just before we left. I figured you were up to something."

"What are you talking about?" I asked.

"Don't gimme that crap, Bud," Abbie said. "The evidence shows we were all in the van and ready to leave when you jumped out without explanation. You called to Dean and Tony, and you and the boys entered the garage so no one could see you. A short time later, you returned to the

98

van without explaining what you had been up to. I thought that was weird. Less than twelve hours later, Dean and Tony are here telling their father they want him to return to work. I'd say that's very strong circumstantial evidence that you told the boys something about their dad, which prompted them to come and pick him up."

Appearing pleased with her intuition and deductive reasoning, she smiled, crossed her arms, and leaned back in her chair. "How do you like them apples?"

"Okay! You got me, Sherlock. I plead guilty!"

Abbie laughed. "Take him away, Officer!"

Kathleen touched my arm. "That was very thoughtful, Bud."

"The boys asked how Charlie was doing, and I wanted them to know what he told me about feeling lost since he left the business."

"He pretty much told me the same thing during one of our cribbage games. I suggested he tell his sons how he felt, but for whatever reason—pride maybe—he said he couldn't do it. Maybe he'd been waiting all along for them to reach out to him."

"I agree. You done good," said Abbie. "It bothered me to see him sitting alone in here in the mornings. One day, I sat and talked to him, and he told me he felt useless and wished he hadn't retired. I tried to cheer him up but didn't get anywhere."

I was smiling when I got back to my room. I felt a sense of purpose and accomplishment that I hadn't experienced since I left teaching.

Chapter Twenty-Three

C harlie was a new man after he began working. He was happier and more engaged, and he seemed less forgetful. One of his sons picked him up in the morning three days a week and returned him in time for dinner.

Conversely, Abbie had become quiet and withdrawn. Clearly, something was troubling her, but Kathleen's attempts to encourage Abbie to confide in her were politely rebuffed. Kathleen approached me one morning while I was sitting at a dining room table, working on my laptop.

"Hi," she said. "Mind if I sit for a moment?"

She looked great as usual, wearing a floral-print peasant dress and sandals, but her somber look concerned me.

"I don't mind. What's up?"

Kathleen pulled out a chair and sat across from me. "I don't know what to do, Bud. Abbie seems depressed, but she won't talk about whatever it is that's bothering her."

"Do you think she's overly concerned about that business with Brett and those other men? The Mafia thing?"

"I don't know. I keep wondering if she has some health

problem she's keeping to herself, or maybe she's got financial problems. I know that her son Brian, the doctor, helps her financially."

"Wait! What about her son? Not the doctor, but the other one. Remember how, on the Fourth of July, she said something about things not being right with him?"

"I do. That was a shocker. She never mentioned there were issues with him."

"Maybe there's something going on with him."

The next morning, I saw Kathleen and Abbie sitting at a table after breakfast hours. They appeared deep in conversation, oblivious of the kitchen crew cleaning the dining room. As I approached, I noticed that they both appeared red-eyed.

"Sorry," I said, "Didn't mean to interrupt."

When I turned to walk away, Abbie said, "Don't go, Bud. Come and sit."

I pulled out a chair, then sat next to Kathleen and across from Abbie.

"Sorry, Bud. I'm not doing very well. I was telling Kathleen about my boy."

"Your doctor son?"

"No. My younger son, Mark."

Abbie took a deep breath and wiped her eyes with her hands. "I don't know where to begin." Kathleen handed her a napkin, and Abbie blotted the tears running down her cheeks. "My son Mark has been a drug addict for over twenty years. The last time anyone saw him was four years ago in Ohio, when he tried to convince his brother to write him a prescription. A few days ago, Brian told me Mark got busted again for heroin almost two years ago in Warren."

"I'm so sorry, Abbie," I said.

"I go from telling myself I don't care, to feeling like a

failure as a mom, to wondering if I could have helped him if I hadn't been working all the time. Oh God, it's so painful."

"I'm sure it is."

"We tried so hard to help him, Bud. Three times, we took early draws from our pensions to put him into treatment. Every time he got out, he'd tell us what we wanted to hear and then go right back to using. He stole thousands of dollars from us. I think he even stole my wedding and engagement rings, but he always denied it. He tore our family apart, and I'm sure the strain of it all killed my husband.

"By all rights, I should hate him, but I can't. He's my son. He was so smart and had so much potential. It breaks my heart that he's thrown away most of his life. He's been living on the street for years. I don't know how he ended up in Warren."

Abbie was no longer the confident and boisterous woman I was used to seeing. She was broken and vulnerable.

"You said Mark was arrested almost two years ago. Where's he now?" I asked.

"I don't know. I called the court clerk and confirmed that he pled guilty, but she wouldn't elaborate on his sentence. I checked the Department of Corrections website, but he's not in prison. I even called the Macomb County Jail, and he's not there either. So I don't know what's going on. I'm praying he's not dead." She straightened in her chair and blew her nose into the napkin. "I'm sorry," she said between sniffles.

"No need to apologize, Abbie," said Kathleen.

Abbie stood. Her face showed the depth of her pain and worry. "Thanks for listening. I need to go." She turned and pushed her walker out of the dining room.

Chapter Twenty-Four

As we were finishing dinner, Clayton turned to me. "Let's go see your house. If it's going to be the venue for celebrating the fiftieth anniversary of Woodstock, then I think we should check it out. Who wants to go on a road trip?"

Before I could respond, Clayton raised his hand like a child in school, and the others did the same.

I shrugged. "Well, I guess we're going on a road trip."

Less than an hour later, we reached Bloomfield Hills, and I directed Clayton into the neighborhood.

"Wow! Check out the real estate," said Abbie.

The others quietly marveled at the size and opulence of the houses and the neatly manicured lawns.

I directed Clayton to turn onto the long driveway that led to my house. It was designed by Sharon's architect friend, who specialized in creating sprawling Tudor-style brick homes with sharply angled rooflines and beautiful windows. I surmised that April was continuing to pay Juan because the grass was freshly cut and the flower beds looked nice.

Clayton put the Mothership in park while the others stared at the house.

"Holy shit, Bud! Your friggin' garage is bigger than my old house," said Abbie.

"Yeah, it's big. That was important to Sharon. Wanna go in?"

The Mothership had already drawn the attention of my neighbor, who was gawking at the brightly colored van. I got out and yelled, "Hello, Glen!" as I opened the sliding side door and helped my friends climb out. Abbie immediately started pushing her walker toward the front door while Clayton lowered Jim with the lift.

"Is that you, Bud?" replied the neighbor.

"It is."

"What are you doing here?"

"I'm planning to sell my house to the Mothership Corporation."

"What's that?"

"It's a nonprofit that provides housing to elderly parolees. I brought a few of them with me to check it out." I turned and walked with the others toward the front door.

"You're learning, kiddo," said Clayton, smiling.

I whispered, "I never liked that guy."

I was concerned April might have changed the lock. But when I inserted the key, the front door popped open. The foyer led to a large living room, and Abbie and Kathleen gushed about the beautiful decorations, furniture, and grand piano.

We walked down the hallway, toward the back of the house, and into the kitchen and dining area. Kathleen and Abbie stood in the kitchen, admiring the large space, custom cabinets, ornate table and chairs, convenient island with four stools, and state-of-the-art appliances. Someone asked about the bedrooms, and I said there were four on the other side of the house.

"Well, Clayton. Do you think this will work for Woodstock?" I asked.

"Are you kidding me, dude? This place is fucking beaut —" Clayton looked at Kathleen, who seemed to wince. "This place is awesome! Can we crash here after Woodstock?"

"Of course."

"I am so stoked!" he said. "Got any booze around? We should have a drink!"

I pointed Clayton toward the booze cabinet, and, in short order, we all had drinks in our hands.

"To Woodstock!" said Clayton. We clinked glasses and talked excitedly about the party. "I saw the piano in the living room," he said. "Do you have a stereo?"

"It's wireless. There are speakers in the living room and above the cabinets in the kitchen."

"Great."

"What should we do for food?" asked Kathleen.

"Order pizzas," said Abbie. "Let's keep this simple."

"We should get a keg of beer," said Clayton. "Then we won't have to deal with beer bottles or cans. Also, if anyone wants to expand their sixties wardrobe, I'll be going to Goodwill. Just let me know if you want to tag along."

"Charlie, do you think your boys and their wives will come?" I asked.

"I do. They've been talking about it. The other day, I heard Rose and Karen talking about miniskirts and go-go boots," said Charlie.

"Miniskirts and go-go boots! What a wonderful combination," said Clayton. "Speaking of boots, do you guys remember the rain and mud at Woodstock? It was brutal.

There were repeated rain delays. The concert was supposed to finish on Sunday but was pushed over until Monday due to the rain."

"Wait. Come on. Were you actually at Woodstock?" asked Kathleen.

"I drove straight through from LA with some studio friends in a Volkswagen bus. It was an amazing adventure. Woodstock is where Graham and I became buds."

"Graham who?" asked Charlie.

"Graham Nash."

"You mentioned him before when I talked to you about 'Up Yours.' But was he really a friend or just an acquaintance?" Kathleen asked Clayton.

"A friend. We kinda knew each other before Woodstock, but that's where we really connected."

"Did you stay up late and play accordions with your friend, Graham Nash?" Abbie asked sarcastically, remembering what Clayton had told Gordy Accordee.

"What I told Gordy was bullshit. This is not," said Clayton defensively.

"You told me a while ago that Graham Nash is playing at the Royal Oak Music Theatre in late August," I said. "You were concerned about logistics, but we can deal with that. We should go."

"That'd be great," said Clayton. He hesitated, then added, "Graham probably wouldn't remember me. It's been such a long time."

When Clayton wasn't looking, I saw Abbie nudge Kathleen and heard her whisper, "He's so full of it!"

Chapter Twenty-Five

A few minutes later, we were in the Mothership, heading back to Serenity. Giddy with excitement, we were singing "The Letter" by the Box Tops as the tune blasted from Clayton's high-priced speakers when he yelled, "Oh crap!" We stopped singing as he frantically turned off the stereo.

"What?" asked Kathleen.

Clayton was looking in his driver's-side mirror. "Cops! We're getting pulled over."

Jim opened the curtain, looked out the rear window, and calmly said, "Indeed we are."

"I knew I shouldn't have brought all that marijuana," said Clayton with a panicked tone as he turned on his blinker and drove the Mothership off the road and onto the gravel shoulder. He glanced at Kathleen, who looked as if she was about to pass out. "Just kidding, Kathleen. Relax. Nothing to worry about."

Clayton watched out the driver's-side mirror. "He's out of his car and checking out the license plate. Looks like it's a

Bloomfield Hills cop who's eaten his share of donuts. Here he comes, people."

The officer appeared at the driver's-side window. Clayton rolled it down and said, "Greetings and salutations . . . " He leaned toward the open window and appeared to be trying to read the cop's name tag. "Officer Bacon."

Officer Bacon appeared to be in his late forties or early fifties. He was in uniform, and his large stomach protruded well over his black gun belt. He ignored the greeting and requested Clayton's license, registration, and proof of insurance. As Clayton was getting his papers out of the glove box, Officer Bacon tugged on the back of his pants and asked, "Do you know why I pulled you over?"

"Not really," said Clayton.

"You seemed to be weaving a little bit in your lane back there. Have you had anything to drink this evening?"

"I had one drink at a friend's house."

"Where are you headed?"

"We're going back to Serenity Assisted Living in Farmington Hills."

"Is that where you live?" asked Officer Bacon.

"Yes, sir. That's where we all live. You should drop by sometime."

The officer peered inside the car, and Abbie winked at him.

Clayton handed over the requested documents. Officer Bacon took them and said, "Stay put. I'll be right back." Then he walked back to his car and got in.

"What's he doing?" asked Abbie.

"Talking on the radio," said Jim, who was peeking through the back-window curtains.

After a few minutes, Officer Bacon returned Clayton's

documents. "Do you have any illegal drugs or firearms in the vehicle?"

"No."

"Do you mind stepping out, please?" Clayton looked at me, shrugged, and climbed out of the van. "I'd like to talk to you, but I'd prefer we do that at the back of the van. It's a little safer back there."

"No problem," said Clayton as he followed Officer Bacon.

Jim watched through a crack in the curtain and reported to us what he was seeing.

"Clayton has his hands in the air, and the cop is patting him down. Clayton just put his hands down. Now they're talking. The cop is looking at Clayton's eyes. The cop is talking. Now Clayton is saying something. Maybe the alphabet. More talking. Okay, the cop is using his right hand and showing Clayton some kind of fingers-to-thumb touch test. Clayton is imitating what the cop showed him. Now the cop is showing him how to stand on one foot with his arms extended. What is Clayton doing? Oh my God, he's taking off his prosthetic leg."

Kathleen gasped, and Abbie said, "No way!"

"He just gave the cop his leg to hold," said Jim. "Now he's standing on his good leg with his arms extended. The cop looks really flustered. The cop just gave back the leg. Clayton is leaning against the patrol car and putting the leg back on. They're talking, and the cop is pointing at the fake leg. Clayton is talking and making a sawing motion with his hand. Oh shit."

"What?" said Abbie.

"What's going on?" I asked.

"The cop just put his hand to his mouth and turned

toward the grass along the shoulder. He's bent over, and his hands are on his knees. Looks like he's gonna puke."

"Now what's happening?" said Kathleen.

"The cop is still bent over with his hands on his knees. Clayton just saw me peeking and smiled. Okay. The cop just stood erect. No puking today! They're talking."

"Can you tell what they're talking about?" asked Charlie.

"Not really. Oh wait! The cop just extended his hand. They shook hands. Clayton is coming in."

Clayton opened the door and climbed in as Officer Bacon drove past, politely tooted his horn, and waved.

"What the hell happened out there?" I asked.

"He told me I was the bravest person he has ever met," said Clayton.

"Why would he say that?"

"I told him how I lost my leg."

"Oh no," said Jim. "What'd you tell him?"

"I told him the truth. You know I always tell the truth." Clayton grinned.

"That's a lie right there!" yelled Abbie.

"Okay. Let's hear it," said Jim.

"I told him about the time my leg got wedged in a rock while I was exploring a cave near Carlsbad Caverns in New Mexico."

"And?" said Jim.

"Well, I was alone, and no one knew where I was, and I was stuck for three days."

"I think I know where this is going," said Jim. "And?"

"I had no choice but to cut it off with my pocketknife."

"Ewww," said Abbie and Kathleen in unison.

"There's more. I just know it," said Jim. "And?"

"I was just inducted into the Spelunkers Hall of Fame."

"And he bought that?" asked Jim.

"The truth set me free."

"Truth, my ass," snapped Abbie.

Jim and I laughed, but Kathleen wasn't amused. "I sure hope you don't run into him again. He'll be really mad if he googles what you told him and finds out you lost your leg in a motorcycle accident."

"Oh, come on, Kathleen. The chance of me running into Officer Bacon again is slim to none. Don't worry about it."

Chapter Twenty-Six

I was heading out of the building for my afternoon walk when I ran into Abbie coming down the hall. She seemed to be in a hurry and was pushing her walker faster than usual. When we met, she looked suspiciously at the wall-mounted camera and whispered that we needed to talk. I asked if she was all right, and she told me to come to her apartment. I put off my walk and went with her.

She closed and locked her door after we entered her apartment. She was her usual disheveled self, but there was something more. She was frazzled.

"What's going on? Are you okay?" I asked.

She plunked down in one of her kitchen chairs. I moved a pile of *People* magazines off the other chair, put them on the counter, and sat across from her.

"Somethin's goin' on here that ain't right, Bud."

"What are you talking about?"

"You know how when you check in here, they ask you if you are taking pain medication, and then they keep it in a locked cabinet at the nurses' station?"

"Sure. Nurse Jackie took all my medication when I arrived."

"If more pills are prescribed while you're living here, they keep those pills in the cabinet too."

"That makes sense. So what's the problem?"

"Last month, my back was so painful that my doctor gave me a prescription for thirty Vicodin to be taken as needed. I took two pills on the day he wrote the prescription. I've been pretty good since then. But yesterday morning, I woke up with back pain, so I took one at seven a.m. and another one at one."

"Okay. So, you've had four Vicodin pills in a month. Go on."

"Something told me to ask about the pills. So I played dumb and asked the head nurse how many pills I had left. She told me eleven."

"Wait. You're telling me you got thirty pills a month ago and only took four of the pills. So there should be twenty-six left?"

"That's exactly what I am telling you."

"Are you sure, Abbie? Maybe you took more pills than you remember. Vicodin can make a person forgetful."

"I'm damn sure. Someone stole my pills. What do you think I should do?"

Knowing Abbie's suspicious nature and propensity to jump to conclusions, I thought it was premature to suggest she call the police or tell Brett. I decided that maybe her son could talk her down. "Have you thought about calling your doctor son?"

"Good idea. She picked up her cell phone. While she was dialing, she said, "I don't call him very often, so he'll probably think something is wrong. I'll work that out first."

She held the phone to her ear, and when it began to ring, she put it on speaker and placed it on the table.

Brian answered. I kept quiet. They had a lengthy conversation about Brian's family and the goings-on at his clinic. As they were getting ready to end the call, Abbie said, "Oh, I almost forgot. I have a question for you."

"I'm listening."

Abbie told him everything she had told me, and Brian also seemed cautious—and possibly skeptical. "Why don't you tell the head nurse or owner?" he said.

Abbie looked at me and mouthed, *No way.*

Brian said that the theft of prescription medication was not unusual and typically involved a nurse or nurse's aide with a drug problem who had access to the locked cabinet.

Abbie backtracked when he pressed her to report the matter. "You know, Brian," she said. "I could have lost count, or the nurse may have looked at the wrong record. Maybe I'll just keep an eye on things for the next month or two."

"Okay, but let me know if you continue to think there are discrepancies. Hey, Mom. On another note, I got a call from Mark a couple of days ago."

Abbie's eyes widened, then she looked down and put her hands to her forehead.

"You still there, Mom?"

"Yeah, I'm here. Did he want you to write him a prescription?"

"No. Actually, he sounded pretty good. He's said he's in some kind of program, and he hasn't been using."

She shook her head. "Yeah, well, we've heard that before."

"I know, but let's just hope he means it this time. Actually, he called because he wanted your address. I hope you don't mind, but I gave it to him."

She put her hands on the table and sat up straight. "You what?"

"I gave him your address."

"I sure hope he doesn't show up asking for money."

"I don't think that's going to happen. He sounded like his old self. He said he's been clean for months."

Abbie looked at me and rolled her eyes. "He's a good actor."

"Yeah, I know, Mom. This seems different."

After a few more minutes of light conversation, Abbie told Brian she loved him and thanked him for helping her. She hung up the phone and said, "Let's go talk to Jim."

I'd never joined Clayton and Jim in teasing Abbie about her theory that Brett was in the Mafia, and I definitely didn't want to go down this new rabbit hole. "I should go," I said. "I want to get a long walk in before dinner."

"Come on, Bud," she pleaded. "You're neutral and sensible. I need you to be with me."

I suspected she wanted me with her so Jim would be less dismissive and would think I was on board with her suspicions. I reluctantly agreed but said I wasn't staying long.

Chapter Twenty-Seven

When the three of us were seated in Jim's apartment, Abbie began. "Jim, I need you to promise that what *we're* about to tell you stays in this room."

That one word officially sucked me in.

"I promise," he said.

"I mean it, Jim. It stays here, right?"

He tossed the book in his lap on the floor and sat up straight in the recliner. "Absolutely."

"I know Clayton thinks I'm nuts, but there's something going on here, and it involves . . ." Abbie looked around the room as if she was looking for listening devices, then whispered, "Prescription drugs."

"What?"

"*Bud and I* just had a long conversation with my son."

I rolled my eyes at Jim, hoping to signal that I hadn't participated in the conversation and had doubts about what he was about to hear.

She repeated her story for the third time. "Someone's stealing from me, Jim."

"Are you sure, Abbie? That's a serious accusation."

"Jim, I know for a fact I took a total of four."

"Why are you telling me this?"

"I figured if someone is stealing from me, they may be stealing from you, assuming you take the kind of pills they want. I hope you don't mind me asking, but I wondered if you take any pain medication. Do you?"

"I do. I have a standing order for Percocet. I take it when I have pain in my back and legs."

"When was the last time you filled that prescription?"

Jim shrugged and leaned back in the recliner. "Whew! I'm guessing maybe two months ago."

"How many were prescribed, and how many have you taken?"

"Sixty were prescribed. I'm guessing I've taken around fifteen."

"Can you do me a big favor? Tomorrow, act like your back hurts and request a Percocet. When Nurse Jackie gives it to you, ask how many are left. Would you be willing to do that?"

"Sure. I'll do it."

"In the meantime, I'll request a Vicodin here and there until it's used up, then I'll get a refill and see what happens. This is just between us, right?"

"You got it."

I was relieved Abbie didn't ask me about the pain medication I had when I checked in.

Chapter Twenty-Eight

I was sitting outside near the Serenity entrance, enjoying the warm sunshine after a long morning walk, when Clayton came hustling out the front door. "Where are you off to in such a hurry?" I asked.

Without stopping, Clayton said, "They found my mom on the bathroom floor this morning. Gotta go."

I watched as he hurried to the Mothership and quickly drove away. I said a silent prayer for his mom as I left the bench and walked inside the building. I spotted Jim coming my way. He confirmed he had heard about Clayton's mom, but he couldn't talk at the moment because he had to meet with Nurse Jackie.

I went back to my apartment, turned on my computer, and opened the electronic file labeled "Clayton." I was reviewing information stored in it and comparing it to my notes when there was a knock at the door.

I got up, opened the door, and was greeted by Abbie and Jim, who asked to come in but ignored my offer to take a seat.

"Tell him, Jim," said Abbie.

"Bud, I never thought I would say this, but I think Abbie may be right. I told Nurse Jackie that I must have slept in a cockeyed position and my back was really bothering me. After she gave me a Percocet, I asked her if we should think about ordering a refill. She told me that was a good idea because I only had fourteen pills left. I started out with sixty pills and took approximately fifteen. Now I have fourteen left. That means around thirty pills are missing. Maybe Nurse Jackie or one of the other nurses is an addict. I'm thinking we should tell Brett."

I was about to agree with Jim's suggestion, but Abbie interrupted. "Hold it right there, mister. What if Brett is involved?"

"You think he's an addict too?" said Jim.

"No. Not at all. But it might be more than that."

"What do you mean?" I said.

"Listen, you guys. Probably everyone here is prescribed something that's sold on the street. There are people here just like us who have pain, so the docs have given us generous prescriptions for Percocet, Vicodin, oxycodone, and God only knows what else. Some folks can't sleep. Or maybe they have anxiety, so their docs have given them prescriptions for pills like Xanax or Valium. All these drugs have street value and are abused. Believe me, I know."

"This blows my mind, Abbie," said Jim. "How do you know so much?"

Abbie glanced at me. "Jim, my son Mark has been a drug addict for well over twenty years. I've already talked to Bud and Kathleen about this. Anyway, because of Mark's struggles, I had to educate myself about these things. Don't you see? If everyone at Serenity is being ripped off like we are, those pills could be worth a fortune."

"Wow, I'm really sorry about your son, Abbie. How awful for you."

"Yeah, it's been a living hell. You understand now why I'm suspicious?"

"I get it."

"The thing is, there may be more."

Jim shot me a puzzled look. "More? Like what?"

Abbie whispered, "What if the same thing is being done at the places in Traverse City and Grand Rapids? Brett's prep school buddies are his partners, and they could all be in it together. There's probably at least a hundred and fifty people between all three facilities, and if every resident is being ripped off, those guys are rolling in the dough."

Jim leaned back in his wheelchair, and our eyes met. I shrugged. He said, "I don't know, Abbie. It seems pretty farfetched to me. What you're talking about would involve a bunch of people. Some of them would have to steal the drugs, and others would have to unload them. I just don't know, man. Why would Brett be involved in something like that? He'd risk losing everything and would probably end up in prison. I just think whoever is stealing the pills is an addict or someone who has a little drug-dealing side business."

"Yeah, maybe you're right," Abbie said. "I just keep going back to the day Brett's partners were here and the odd way they behaved. Nurse Jackie was definitely part of that meeting too—and why? Clayton thinks Brett and Jackie are getting it on, but my gut tells me it's something different."

"I don't want to argue, Abbie, but I'm trying to understand why you're so quick to rule out Clayton's theory."

"C'mon, Jim. Think about Brett—the expensive clothes, gold jewelry, dark tan, perfect teeth, and flashy car. And Jackie, to put it bluntly, isn't in his league."

"Okay, okay. Abbie," Jim said. "If you feel uncomfortable telling Brett, maybe we should call the police."

"I think that's a good idea," I said.

Abbie frowned. "Right! Then what? The police are going to want proof. If the records have been altered to show we received the medication, it would be our word against theirs, and we know how that would come out. I think I should use up the rest of my Vicodin, get a new prescription ordered, and see where that takes us. You should do the same with your Percocet. My son Brian is in the loop. He said he would help if there are any more discrepancies."

Glad the discussion was ending and anxious to get back to my research, I said, "Okay, that sounds like a good plan."

Jim agreed.

Abbie cautioned, "Remember! This is just between us!"

Chapter Twenty-Nine

Clayton spent his days at his mother's bedside and kept us updated about her condition. He reported that she had a vertebral compression fracture but didn't require surgery. She'd been transferred from the hospital back to the nursing home, where she was on bed rest and receiving pain management.

I sent Clayton a text asking if there was anything I could do, and he soon answered: *How about grabbing Kathleen and coming with me tomorrow? She adores Kathleen and thinks you're sizzling hot. Maybe she won't bug me about shaving and getting a haircut if you're around.*

The next morning, Clayton was subdued as we traveled to the nursing home. Kathleen and I exchanged puzzled glances.

"What's going on?" I said to him. "You're not your chipper ol' self this morning."

"Nothin'."

"Come on, Clayton," said Kathleen. "You've hardly said a word since we left. What's goin' on?"

"Sorry, man. I just keep wondering if Mom's fall is the

beginning of the end. She's not eating well, and she can't afford to lose weight. She sleeps away half the day. I just . . . I know she won't be around forever, but the thought of losing her . . . Everything I've ever accomplished is because of her. I'd be nothing without her."

"Have you told her that?" asked Kathleen.

"I don't know. I'm sure she knows."

"She probably does, but maybe you should think about telling her. Clayton, I didn't always get along with my daughters. When they were teenagers, we clashed all the time over just about everything—clothes, curfew, even some of their friends. They thought I was an old-fashioned idiot. Now that they're moms themselves, they understand. They've thanked me many times for raising them the way we did. Hearing that makes me happy. You'll make your mom happy if you tell her how you feel."

"That reminds me of a student I once had," I said. "She was a free spirit—constantly at odds with her mother. A few months into the school year, her mother was diagnosed with cancer and given six months to live. The poor woman barely made it three months. It was incredibly sad, but the girl made an about-face and cared for her mother until the end. They made things right between them. Toward the end of the year, I had the students write an essay on death or dying. The girl wrote an essay about a poem that helped her during those last three months. I'll be honest, I was moved to tears when I read her essay, and I've never forgotten the poem that meant so much to her."

"Hit me with it," said Clayton. "I love poetry."

"Yeah, let's hear it," said Kathleen.

"Okay, but I'm warning you, it's heavy duty." I cleared my throat and began. "'If you have a tender message, or a loving word to say, do not wait till you forget it, but whisper it today; the tender word unspoken, the letter never sent, the long-forgotten messages, the wealth of love unspent. For these some hearts are breaking, for these some loved ones wait; so show them that you care for them before it is too late.'"

"That was beautiful, Bud," said Kathleen, her eyes glistening from unshed tears.

"Wow. That was heavy," said Clayton as he wiped a tear from the corner of his eye. "Who wrote that poem?"

"Frank Herbert Sweet."

"That really was a sweeeet poem," Clayton said.

Kathleen looked at him as if he'd committed blasphemy. "Clayton, you are something else."

He grinned. "You know, poetry is at the heart of a lot of song lyrics. I'm thinking Kiss may be able to do something really cool with that poem. Whaddya think, Bud?"

My mouth opened, but I couldn't respond.

Chapter Thirty

As we walked by the nurses' station, I recognized the nurse from our last visit.

"How's she doing today, Corrine?" asked Clayton.

"She's been sleeping a lot. The pain medication really knocks her out."

When we got to Room 115, Clayton opened the door, and we entered. Clayton's mom was lying on her back with the covers pulled up to her neck. Her mouth was open, and her face was pale. Clayton signaled to Kathleen and me to sit in the two chairs to his mom's right while he went around the foot of the bed and sat on the edge of it on the other side.

He whispered, "Good morning, Mom. It's Clayton. Feel like waking up?"

I was hoping she would pop up and yell, "Boo," as she had done before. Instead, she moved her legs slightly and slowly opened her eyes to look at Clayton.

"Oh, hi, honey," she said softly. She raised a hand and lovingly stroked the side of his face. "Sweetheart . . ." Her voice trailed off.

"Yes, Mom."

"When are you going to shave and get a haircut?"

"Someday, I'll do it for you. I promise. You have some visitors today, Mom."

"I do? Where?" she said groggily.

"Can you look to your right?"

Clayton's mom slowly turned her head and saw Kathleen and me sitting in the chairs next to her bed.

"Well, I'll be." She took a breath. "If it isn't Snow White and Mr. Hunka Burnin' Love. Thanks for stopping by. Tell me." She swallowed. "Tell me how much Clayton had to pay you."

I winked at her. "This one was on the house, Marian. We're so sorry about your accident."

With a faint twinkle in her eye, Marian asked Kathleen, "Do Snow White and Mr. Hunka Burnin' Love have a little something going?"

Kathleen blushed. "No, Marian. We're just friends."

I felt obligated to respond too. "Just friends from Serenity."

"Don't know why. You'd make such a cute couple." She reached out and clasped Kathleen's hand. "So nice of you to drop by. It makes me happy Clayton has friends like you. I've really enjoyed getting to know you. Do you mind if I have a few minutes with Clayton?"

"Not at all." Kathleen released her hand, leaned forward, and kissed her on the forehead. "Get well, Marian. We'll be praying for you." She looked like she was on the verge of tears as she got up and hurried out of the room.

I stood, looking down at Marian. Her eyes were closed. As I began to leave, she opened them and seemed to be struggling to keep them open. She said, "Hold my hand, Bud." I glanced at Clayton, and he nodded his approval. I gently grasped her hand. She looked into my eyes and said, "She's a keeper, Bud. Don't let her slip away."

I whispered, "I know. I won't." I let go of her hand and kissed her on the forehead. "Your son is a good man, and I'm honored to know him. Getting to know you has been a double bonus."

"Thanks," said Marian faintly before she closed her eyes.

"We'll be praying for you," I said as she faded. I went out in the hall, where Kathleen was waiting. Corrine saw us and suggested we go to the dining room for a cup of coffee. We thought that was a good idea and decided to wait there for Clayton.

We sipped our coffee while we thought about the love between mother and son and the tears that were likely being shed. Kathleen used her napkin to wipe the tears from her eyes.

"Oh, Bud, I feel so sad. She told me she enjoyed getting to know me. That sounded like a goodbye."

"I know." I gently patted her hand, and she smiled meekly. We both thought Marian wasn't likely to be around much longer. I pictured Clayton and Marian holding hands. Then I imagined him thanking her for her steadfast love and support and her telling him how proud she was of him.

Kathleen and I were talking about the poem I'd recited when Clayton came into the dining room and poured a cup of coffee. He walked to our table and plunked down in one of the empty chairs. He seemed somber and reflective as he poured powdered creamer into the coffee and stirred it.

"Are you okay?" asked Kathleen.

Without answering her question, he said, "I'm sorry my mom booted you guys out of the room like that. You didn't get to spend much time with her."

"Not a problem for us," I said. "We were glad to give you some time together. Right, Kathleen?"

"Absolutely! We wanted you to have that time."

"She had something personal she wanted to discuss and didn't feel comfortable with you in the room," Clayton said.

"We understand," I said. "How'd it go?"

"It was a little awkward at first, but after a few minutes, she opened up and told me what was on her mind."

Kathleen gently touched Clayton's arm. "That's good. I'm happy she did that."

"I told her I was glad she didn't wait until it was too late."

"That's so sweet," said Kathleen. "Just like the poem."

"What poem?"

"The poem Bud recited on the way here."

Blank-faced, Clayton stroked his mustache as he stared at Kathleen. "Huh?" Then he laughed, leaned back in his chair, and slapped his knee. "Oh my God! No, man! The poem had nothin' to do with it. Mom's been constipated from the pain meds, so they gave her something to help with that. Whatever they gave her worked, like right now. I buzzed Corrine as soon as Mom told me. Corrine hurried into the room to help, and a crisis was averted, if you know what I mean."

Kathleen looked at me as if she was pleading for help.

"Okay, then," I said. "I think we should hit the road."

Chapter Thirty-One

We met in the dining room the morning of Woodstock day to discuss our final plans. There was much laughter, joking, and excitement. Clayton said the "warden," Brett, was going to "shit bricks" when he found out we'd busted out.

I noticed that Abbie seemed a little detached and quiet. I asked her if she was okay. She said she'd had a bad night and was tired.

Everyone except Charlie had assembled a Woodstock outfit, and we agreed not to divulge what we'd be wearing. The "big reveal," as Kathleen put it, would be when we met by the Serenity sign just before we left. Charlie explained that the big reveal for him would be when his daughters-in-law delivered the sixties clothes they wanted him to wear.

Charlie confirmed that his sons and their wives would be at my house late afternoon but would not be spending the night. I reminded everyone to pack overnight bags. We agreed to order pizza after a few hours of partying.

"I am so stoked!" said Clayton. "We took the keg to the house last night. You know, back in the day, we'd party till the sun came up. I suppose that's a little ambitious for this crew. Let's shoot for midnight! Who's with me?" He eagerly looked around the table. We hesitatingly agreed.

"Well, I guess that's it," I said. "Can't wait to see you all this afternoon."

Jim backed his wheelchair away from the table, and Charlie and Clayton stood. Abbie whispered to Kathleen and me, "Can I talk to you guys for a minute?"

"Here?" I asked.

"Sure," said Abbie.

We remained seated while the others headed toward their apartments.

"What's up?" asked Kathleen.

Abbie reached in the hip pocket of her sweatpants and pulled out what appeared to be an invitation. She handed it to Kathleen. "What do you make of this?"

Kathleen showed the invitation to me.

"Our greatest glory is not in never failing, but in rising up every time we fail."
— Ralph Waldo Emerson

We are proud to announce the
graduation of Mark Thomas Miron
from the 37th District Drug Court.
We invite you to share with us
this remarkable achievement
on Tuesday, the 20th day of August, 2019
at 11:00 a.m.
37th District Court Courtroom
Warren, Michigan

.   .   .

"It says my son is graduating from drug court. What the hell is that?" asked Abbie.

"I don't know a lot about drug courts, Abbie," I said, "but I think they started when people realized that throwing drug addicts in jail wasn't accomplishing anything because they'd get out of jail and continue using. You know that from your own experience. I think the focus is on treatment and rehabilitation. That's about all I know."

"Are you going to the graduation?" asked Kathleen. "It must be quite an accomplishment for the court to send out an invitation like this."

"I don't know. Every time there's been a glimmer of hope over the last twenty years, he ends up breaking my heart. I just don't think I can go through that again."

"You should go, and we'll go with you. We'd love to meet your son," I said.

"He was such a good kid until the drugs," said Abbie, tears in her eyes.

"Maybe this time will be a breakthrough," said Kathleen. "I'm sure the others would also want to be there to support you. I agree with Bud. We all should go."

Abbie put her face in her hands and began to weep. I slid my chair over and put my arm around her as Kathleen held her hand.

"This will be great," I said. "You'll see."

Chapter Thirty-Two

I returned to my apartment and tried to take a nap, but I was Christmas Eve excited and couldn't sleep. I got up, took a shower, laid out my outfit, and tried working on my research project, but I had difficulty concentrating. I looked at my watch. We wouldn't be leaving for three more hours. I grabbed two cans of beer out of my refrigerator and went to Jim's apartment.

When I knocked at his door, his and a female's voice yelled almost in unison for me to come in.

Jim was out of his wheelchair and sitting shirtless on a kitchen chair, wearing only cut-off army field pants. Brenda, his favorite aide—dressed in light-blue scrubs—stood next to him, holding a white T-shirt. A short, stocky redhead in her early twenties, Brenda was taking courses at a community college to become a licensed practical nurse. She once told me that her brother—a marine who'd fought on the streets of Fallujah, Iraq, during the second Gulf War—had struggled mentally and emotionally when he returned home. I wondered if that was why she seemed to have a tender spot for Jim. Her smile was a mixture of curiosity and amusement.

Smiling, Jim said, "What the hell are you doing here, Bud? I thought we were going to dress up in secret."

"I had no idea you'd be primping three hours ahead of the party! I've known teenage girls to do that, but not a grown man. I'll leave and put this ice-cold beer I brought with me back in my refrigerator."

"Now, Bud. Don't be too hasty!"

I laughed, opened both cans, and handed one to Jim. I raised my beer, and he did the same. "Happy Woodstock," we said as we clinked cans and each took a drink.

"Brenda, I'm feeling a little guilty that Jim and I are having our pre-Woodstock party and you can't partake. Would you like a soda? I have Diet Coke back in my apartment.

"I'm good, Mr. Livingston. Thanks." She looked at me and back at Jim. "Can I ask you guys something? What the heck is Woodstock, anyway?"

Jim looked at me and grinned. "Go ahead, Bud. You're the history teacher. Tell her about Woodstock."

"Woodstock was a huge outdoor concert held in 1969 on a guy's farm in Woodstock, New York, where some of the best musicians in the world played. The concert lasted three days. Over four hundred thousand people attended."

"No way! That's crazy! I've never heard of a concert even close to that size. So, tell me about the bands. Did the Jackson Five play? My mom had all their records. She's always been a Michael Jackson fan."

The image of little Michael Jackson and his brothers dancing around the Woodstock stage while legends like Joe Cocker, Janis Joplin, Carlos Santana, and Jimi Hendrix watched made Jim and me smile.

"No Jackson Five," said Jim. "I think they were a few years later, and their music appealed to a different crowd."

Brenda seemed unfamiliar with the names of the bands I ticked off. She looked at the white T-shirt she'd been holding and read out loud the words printed across the chest. "'Make love, not war.' Now, that's an interesting slogan. What's up with that?"

I deferred to Jim. "Your turn, buddy."

"Thanks a lot, Bud," he said with a tone of playful sarcasm. "Brenda, there was the sexual revolution, and we were at war. Young people preferred lovemaking over war-making."

"Sexual revolution? Oh my." She paused and put a hand on her hip. "Now explain that one."

Jim hesitated, took another sip of beer, then punted. "You'd probably do better to look it up. It was a kind of social movement that changed the way people thought about sex and sexuality."

As Brenda assisted Jim in putting on his T-shirt, he told me he wanted to be the first one to the Serenity sign so he could film everyone as they came out the door. That's why he was getting dressed early. After his T-shirt was on, he leaned over and picked up off the floor a vintage olive-drab army shirt with the sleeves cut off. He put it on with a little help from Brenda, leaving it open so the message on his T-shirt could be seen.

Brenda held in each hand a white tube sock with a red band at the top. "Interesting socks, Jim." She helped him put on the knee-high socks and sandals, and he completed the outfit by putting on a green Vietnam War boonie hat. She stepped back and appeared to be sizing him up.

"What do you think of the outfit?" said Jim.

"I'm not hot on the socks," said Brenda.

Jim looked at me. "Don't tell anyone, but I went for the disgruntled Vietnam veteran look."

"You nailed it."

"Did Woodstock happen around the same time there were riots in Detroit and a bomb went off in Ann Arbor?" asked Brenda. "I've heard my uncle talk about those things. I think he was going to U of M around that time."

"They were the same time frame," I said. "I think the Detroit riots were in 1967, and your uncle was probably referring to the bombing of the CIA office in Ann Arbor in 1968. Woodstock was a year later. There was a lot of social unrest, and there were ongoing student protests in Ann Arbor about the war, women's rights, and social injustice."

"It sounds like you guys really had it goin' on."

"I think we did," said Jim. "Some say we really messed things up with our attitudes about war, religion, sex, and politics, but at least we had the balls— Excuse me . . . At least we had the guts to speak out about things we thought were unfair or unjust. I hate to say it, but I haven't seen that from your generation."

Brenda pondered that comment and said, "You're right. I guess my generation hasn't done all that much, but I think we're more accepting of the differences in people than your generation."

"I agree, and that gives me some hope for the future," Jim replied. "We did what we could do. I hope your generation takes the baton and runs with it."

Brenda left, and Jim and I finished our beers. Before I headed out the door to go back to get dressed, he said, "Pick me up, and we'll go to the Serenity sign together."

"Right on, brother."

Chapter Thirty-Three

I got dressed and stood in the bathroom, admiring my outfit. The Afro wig I purchased on Amazon gave me big hair, reminding me of the look Sly Stone sported when he and the Family Stone took the stage at Woodstock. My T-shirt had GIVE PEACE A CHANCE printed across the chest, and a peace symbol necklace dangled from my neck. I had taken Clayton up on his offer to hunt for party-appropriate clothes at Goodwill, and he'd found the faded and torn bell-bottom jeans and the sandals I was wearing.

I wanted to avoid running into the others. I'd already breached the agreement to keep our outfits a surprise by visiting Jim earlier in the day. I quietly closed my apartment door and tiptoed to his apartment. His door was open, and he was waiting for me. I pushed him out of the building to the Serenity sign, where we positioned ourselves to have a good view of the entrance and sidewalk. Jim reached into the large pocket of his cut-off field pants and pulled out his iPhone and tapped Video, then we waited.

Motioning to the entrance doors, he said, "Oh my God,

check this out." He started recording. "Ooh la la, a real-life flower girl."

As Kathleen approached, I unconsciously breathed, "Wow!"

She walked with the poise and elegance of a model. A crown of fresh daisies accentuated her wig's shoulder-length blond hair. She smiled and waved when she spotted us. She wore Jackie Onassis sunglasses with large, round lenses, a beautiful yellow peasant dress with a tiny white peace symbol pattern, and a faded blue jean jacket. She was barefoot and carried her sandals and a small overnight bag.

Jim hit the Pause button.

Kathleen was bubbling with excitement. "You guys look fantastic! This is so much fun!" She bent over and gave Jim a quick hug. When she finished hugging him, she stood erect and looked at me. I was in awe of her beauty. "The sixties were all about treating people equally, right?" she asked. Before I could respond, she moved over to me, put her arm around me, and gave me a firm hug that seemed to last a little longer than a casual hug between friends.

I liked it.

"You look fantastic!" I said.

Smiling broadly, Kathleen said, "Thank you. It was fun pulling all this together. I can't wait to see what the others are wearing."

"You're about to," said Jim as he began filming Clayton and Charlie coming toward us.

Kathleen bobbed up and down as she hooted and yelled, "Right on, brothers!" Clayton responded with an enthusiastic fist pump, and Charlie raised an arm over his head and made a peace sign.

Jim giggled. "I don't think Charlie's outfit would have cut the cake at Woodstock." Charlie's daughters-in-law must have watched sixties video clips from Johnny Carson for inspiration. The result was an upwardly mobile, capitalist, "just got off the golf course" look. He wore a dark Beatles haircut wig, a navy-blue Nehru blazer over a white T-shirt, bright-red plaid pants secured at his waist with a wide white belt, and white buck shoes. He carried a gym bag.

Clayton walked toward us with confident strides. His long, kinky gray hair—no longer restrained in a hair tie—was in full display, hanging over his shoulders and down his back. The breeze occasionally blew it across his face in spite of a red, white, and blue star-spangled headband. One sustained gust wrapped the hair across his eyes like a blindfold, causing him to step off the sidewalk, lose his balance, and nearly fall. He recovered, stepped back on the sidewalk, and glared at the edge of the pavement as if it was responsible for his stumble.

The phone in Jim's hand was shaking as he tried to control his laughter. "I can't wait to play that in slo-mo," he said.

Unfazed, Clayton stopped, tipped his head back, used both hands to gather his hair, and then gently laid it back in its original position. The two continued their stroll.

"I nominate Clayton for the best costume," said Jim as he continued filming. Clayton wore a light-brown cowhide vest over a sunburst-patterned, tie-dyed T-shirt in bright orange and blue. The unbuttoned brown vest was trimmed with long fringe. The black straps from the backpack containing his overnight items were around his shoulders. His tie-dyed blue jeans were tucked into soft, knee-high brown leather boots—also trimmed with fringe.

"Woodstock 2019, baby!" Clayton yelled as he and Charlie received welcoming hugs from Kathleen and exchanged high fives with Jim and me.

We'd been talking for a few minutes about our clothes and the party when Kathleen asked, "Wait. Where's Abbie?"

"I'll call her," said Jim. She came out just as he began dialing her number. He hung up and began recording. She spotted us and waved.

There were streaks of blue in her wild, unkempt hair. She wore bright-red lipstick, long fake eyelashes, and large hoop earrings. The gold sequins on her sleeveless shirt sparkled and glimmered in the sunshine.

"What does her shirt say?" asked Charlie, squinting to read the message printed in bold black letters across her chest.

"'Groovy girl,'" I said, reading it for him.

"I don't remember seeing any hookers at Woodstock," whispered Clayton. Jim gave Clayton a stern look to remind him he was recording.

"Knock it off, Clayton," whispered Kathleen, who was trying to keep from laughing. "Great outfit!" she yelled as Abbie got closer.

Realizing Jim was recording her approach, Abbie abruptly stopped and let go of her walker. She put her right hand behind her head and her left hand on her hip, then began gyrating like a hula dancer. Clayton encouraged her by yelling, "Shake that thang!"

Abbie's gyrations continued as she slowly turned her back to reveal skintight black leather pants that she'd somehow managed to pull over her ample posterior. On her feet were black high-topped Converse basketball shoes.

Clayton saw the incredulous look on my face and burst out laughing. His laughter made Abbie laugh, and she hammed it up more by spanking herself twice. By the time she turned around and retrieved her walker, she was laughing so hard that she was snorting and gasping for air. Her snorts triggered a cascade of laughter from the rest of us. Jim stopped recording when she reached us.

Abbie was greeted with hugs and high fives. Referring to her leather pants, she said, "I greased my legs up with two sticks of butter I stole from the dining room to get these suckers on."

We talked and laughed until Clayton said impatiently, "Let's boogie."

"We have to have a picture first," insisted Kathleen.

"I'll take it," said Charlie.

"No, you won't. You need to be in the picture," she said. She looked at Clayton. "I thought you arranged for one of the nurses to take the picture."

"I did. But, obviously, she forgot." Clayton took out his phone and began punching in a phone number. He put it on speaker as it began ringing.

"Nurses' station, Serenity Assisted Living. This is Jackie. May I help you?"

Clayton smiled and said in a Southern drawl, "Yeah. What y'all doin', Jackie?"

"Who is this?"

"Yeah, my name is Richard, but some people call me Big Dick. Anywho, I gots to deliver me some tents, chairs, and shit—excuse me, *stuff*—to them hippies out by your sign there for some kinda marijuana celebration tonight, and they said to send the bill to y'all. So, what's yer billin' address, ma'am?"

"Wait. What are you talking about?"

"Ma'am, as I tol' ya, them hippies out by yer sign out there want me to send y'all a bill for the stuff I'm supposed to deliver for the marijuana party thing tonight. But I gots to have me a billin' address."

"What hippies? What are you talking about? This is an assisted living facility."

"Ma'am, fer the last time, I'm tellin' ya, them hippies out at the sign says y'all responsible for the bill. Can ya just give me yer billin' address, please?"

"Just a minute."

From the *clunk* that came over the speaker, I guessed that Jackie put down the phone, then went to a window to see us gathered around the sign. When she picked up, she said, "Okay, Richard. I see the people you're talking about. They are not residents here, and they have no business being on the property."

"You mean y'all ain't gonna give no billin' address?"

"No, and if you deliver anything, Serenity will not pay for it."

The line went dead. A few moments later, Jackie flew out the entrance doors and walked briskly toward us. "What is going—" Nurse Jackie stopped mid-sentence when she recognized our faces. "What are you people doing?"

"We're going to Amsterdam for the international love-in," said Clayton.

"Amsterdam? Did you clear it with your doctors?"

"Our doctors recommended we attend," said Jim. "They said it would be an excellent opportunity for each of us to get in touch with our inner child."

Nurse Jackie scowled. "You're lying."

Acting shocked, Clayton said, "How dare you insult us that way. That's elder abuse right there. Right, everybody?" We all nodded in agreement.

Nurse Jackie backpedaled. "You're not going to have tables delivered or have a marijuana party on Serenity grounds?"

Clayton indignantly replied, "Of course not. Who would have told you such a ridiculous thing?"

Nurse Jackie did not answer, but she carefully looked us over. "Did you notify your families?" she asked.

"We all wrote letters that will be dropped in the mail tomorrow," said Abbie. "We agreed it would be better to let them know after we've left the country. That way, they won't worry as much."

Nurse Jackie obviously didn't know what to do. As she stared at us, Kathleen put her phone in Jackie's hand and said sweetly, "Jackie, honey, would you mind taking our picture?"

We squeezed together before she could react. She aimed the camera, Clayton said, "Stinky cheese," we smiled, and the picture was taken. Nurse Jackie stood frozen and speechless as Kathleen retrieved her phone, thanked her, and joined us as we headed toward the Mothership.

Chapter Thirty-Four

My neighbor, snoopy Glen, was blowing grass clippings off his driveway with a leaf blower when Clayton turned into my driveway. Jacked up with excitement, Clayton yelled, "Party time!" and gave a blast of his horn.

By the time we got out of the van, the leaf blower was quiet and Glen was standing in his driveway, staring at us. Abbie saw him too and waved at him, yelling, "Come to Mama for a little sixties lovin'. Check it out." Giggling, she turned and wiggled her rear. Glen dropped his blower and ran into his house. Still giggling, Abbie said, "I bet he'll have some bad dreams tonight."

We heard a honk as we made our way into the house. A small white bus with "Little Sunshine Day Camp" printed on the side pulled into the driveway behind the Mothership.

"What the hell?" said Clayton. The thumping of loud music was coming from inside the bus.

"It's my boys!" said Charlie.

Behind the wheel was a man with long dark hair, a red

bandana headband, and dark sunglasses. There were other unrecognizable people on the bus who were waving vigorously. The bus was turned off, and the side door opened to disgorge the occupants.

Rose and Karen leaped out of the bus and danced to the music blaring from a large boom box Rose held. They were dressed in matching lime-green long-sleeved blouses, lime-green-and-white plaid miniskirts, and white go-go boots almost up to their knees. Clayton, Bud, and Charlie hooted and hollered as they watched the women gyrating.

When Tony and Dean exited the bus, Abbie and Kathleen let loose with catcalls and whistles in rebuttal to the reception the men gave Rose and Karen.

Rose and Karen had dressed their men to look like two brothers from 1969 who'd heard about Woodstock, jumped in their Volkswagen bus, and headed to Max Yasgur's farm in New York for a weekend of sex, drugs, and rock 'n' roll. They wore the same thick, shoulder-length wigs, except Dean's was blond and his bandanna was turquoise. They wore T-shirts with a picture on the front of a Woodstock musician playing an electric guitar. Rose had selected Jimi Hendrix for Tony, and Karen went with Carlos Santana for Dean. They wore bell-bottom jeans, dark belts, and boots.

Kathleen nudged me with her elbow and motioned with her head toward Glen's house. "Check it out," she said.

I looked and saw Glen in his driveway, watching us while talking on his cell phone. He was animated and speaking loudly.

Chapter Thirty-Five

I turned on the stereo for Clayton and Jim after the first round of drinks had been distributed. Clayton smiled mischievously at Jim and me as he pulled a CD out of his backpack.

"This first tune will rock your face off. Are you familiar with the MC5? They were a Detroit counterculture band in the late sixties. If I remember right, they were on the cover of *Rolling Stone* in 1969."

"Did they do 'Kick Out the Jams'?" Jim asked.

"Yes, siree! They were crazy loud and super up-tempo. Almost punkish. Ever heard the live version?"

"Is that the one where the lead singer starts the tune by yelling, 'Kick out the jams, mother effers'?" Clayton's grin confirmed that it was. "I don't know, Clayton," said Jim. "Do you really think you should play that? Kathleen won't be impressed."

I shared Jim's concern.

"It's Woodstock, man," Clayton said. "This ain't no Carpenters concert. Kathleen will just have to . . . adjust. Who knows? Maybe she'll like it."

Jim laughed. "I kinda doubt that." He turned and glanced around the room. "What was that? Was that a knock?"

I didn't hear anything, but I broke off our conversation to check the front door. If someone was there, it was probably Glen being snoopy.

As I opened the door, the introduction for "Kick Out the Jams" exploded into the faces of two Bloomfield Hills public safety officers, who staggered backward as if they'd been hit by a hurricane-force wind. Rapid heavy metal guitar licks followed, drowning out the officers' voices.

The music stopped abruptly. I learned later that Kathleen had forced her way between Clayton and Jim and turned down the volume. Then they'd huddled out of sight along the kitchen wall and listened to my conversation with the officers.

"I'm very sorry about that," I said to the two men on my porch. "We're just starting a party, and my friends didn't know you were at the door."

The officers looked me over. Suddenly aware of my costume, I pulled off my Afro wig and said, "We're celebrating the fiftieth anniversary of Woodstock, and we all got dressed up for it."

"I see. What's your name, sir?" said the young officer, who appeared to be in his early twenties. He was holding a small notepad and pen. Standing quietly behind him was an overweight officer who appeared to be in his fifties. I thought he looked vaguely familiar. I glanced at the officer's name tag: J. Bacon.

Oh my God! I thought. It was the same officer Clayton had lied to about his leg.

"Bud Livingston," I answered.

"Whose house is this?" the young officer asked.

"Mine. Is there a problem?"

"Is the owner of that van inside the residence?" asked Officer Bacon.

I nonchalantly glanced down the hall toward the kitchen, where I heard my friends moving around. I didn't want to dime out Clayton, but I also didn't want to make things worse by lying. "Ah, yes, sir. He is."

"I'd like to talk to him when we're done with you," said Officer Bacon sternly.

"Okay, but what's the problem?" I asked.

"We had a report of some prostitutes coming to this house. One of them reportedly solicited a neighbor," said the young officer.

"So, my neighbor Glen called?"

"The identity of the complaining party is really not the issue, Mr. Livingston."

"Now, just wait a minute! That's a bunch of bullcrap!" said Abbie as she pushed her walker toward me, followed by the other women. "Are you sayin' we're prostitutes?"

"Yeah, what's up with that?" said Kathleen. Rose and Karen nodded in agreement.

The ladies' assertiveness seemed to put the officers on their heels. Officer Bacon peered around me and said, "We're just following up on a complaint, ma'am. That's all."

Abbie moved forward and positioned herself next to me at the door's threshold. "Let me tell you something, Officer. That little twerp next door was staring us down, so I teased him with an offer of a little sixties lovin'. It was just a joke. It's been so long, I wouldn't know what to do with a man, anyway. The equipment's all froze up, if you know what I mean."

"Yes, ma'am," said Officer Bacon, his face reddening.

"Now, for these three beautiful ladies who are here to

have some fun, it's damn near slanderous to imply they're prostitutes."

"We're not implying anything, ma'am. Just investigating a complaint, which obviously does not require any more action," said Officer Bacon.

Kathleen smiled and tried to calm the situation. "We understand, and we appreciate all you do. Would you like a soda?"

"No, thank you, ma'am," said Officer Bacon.

"I think we're done here now," said the young officer.

"Not quite," said Officer Bacon. "I need to speak to the owner of the van."

I called for Clayton, who slowly walked out of the kitchen with his head down like a child about to be disciplined.

When Officer Bacon spotted Clayton, he turned to his partner and said, "Yup, that's the guy I told you about."

Chapter Thirty-Six

Abbie and I moved aside, and Clayton stepped out on the porch. Clayton said, "Look, Officer Bacon, I'm sorry . . ."

Officer Bacon put his arm around Clayton's shoulders and said to the young officer, "This is the guy who cut off his leg with a pocketknife."

"The cave guy you told me about? You're kidding!" said the young officer. The young man extended his hand, and Clayton hesitantly shook it. "Everyone was talking about you at roll call the other day. God, that must have been painful."

"It was," said Clayton.

Not wanting to be party to his ongoing fraud, Abbie and I tried to separate ourselves from the conversation by looking down at the floor.

"I was so excited to introduce you, I interrupted. I apologize," said Officer Bacon. "You said something about being sorry."

"Oh, that . . . it was nothing. I just wanted to tell you I'm sorry about almost making you puke by telling you all the

149

details. That sawing through the tendon and the spraying artery stuff was unnecessary."

Officer Bacon laughed. "You almost got me to lose my lunch, that's for sure. But that's okay. I've seen a lot of things in twenty-seven years of law enforcement, but nothing compares to your story. It's good to see you again." He extended his hand, and Clayton shook it.

"It's a real honor to meet you," said the young officer, who vigorously shook Clayton's hand again. "Well, I guess we should shove off. You folks enjoy your party. Try to keep the noise down, or your neighbor will probably call us again."

When they turned to leave, Clayton looked at Abbie and me and winked. The officers were walking away from the house when the young officer stopped and turned back to face Clayton. "What's the deal with your license plate?"

Abbie quickly answered, "He wrote 'Up Yours.'"

"The stadium tune? You're kidding! You wrote that? I love that tune."

"It's played all over the world," said Abbie proudly.

"Wow! Can I have your autograph?" the young officer asked Clayton.

"Me too," said Officer Bacon.

"Sure," said Clayton. The officers returned to the porch, and the young one handed Clayton his notebook and a pen. Clayton looked at both men thoughtfully and asked, "Officer Bacon, what's your first name?"

"Jason."

Clayton leaned forward and squinted to read the younger officer's name tag. "Schwartz?"

"Yes, sir. Logan Schwartz."

Clayton wrote a note for the officers, praising their hard work, dedication, and public service. On each note, he signed his name in large, looping letters. He returned the notebook to Officer Schwartz, who smiled as he examined the notes. "Thank you so much," he said.

"You guys have a great day," said Clayton.

"Have a great party," said Officer Bacon.

The officers then turned and were walking down the sidewalk toward the driveway when Clayton yelled, "Hey, Officers!" When they looked back, he gave them a thumbs-up and said, "Up yours forever!"

"You betcha!" said Officer Schwartz.

"For sure," said Officer Bacon.

They waved, got into their patrol car, and drove away.

"Wow, Clayton, you were pushing your luck with that last comment," I said as I closed the door.

He grinned. "What comment?"

"You know what comment. Telling the officers 'up yours forever.'"

Smiling, Clayton said, "Shame on you, Bud. You think I said that as a clever way of sticking it to the man?"

"Yeah."

Acting offended, Clayton replied, "Why, I would never do such a thing! I was simply suggesting that the spirit of 'Up Yours' remain alive for generations to come."

I laughed. "Sure you were, Clayton."

Chapter Thirty-Seven

We gathered in the kitchen, and the conversation quickly turned to Abbie's solicitation of Glen, Clayton's previous run-in with Officer Bacon, and his parting words to the officers. Kathleen generously distributed a fruity, alcohol-laden concoction Abbie prepared in the blender, and I filled two pitchers from the keg and topped off the beer drinkers' mugs.

Finishing my host duties, I sat next to Kathleen at the kitchen table, where she and the other women were talking and laughing. I noticed Karen and Rose looking at the décor, and I suggested they take a look around. Kathleen said she'd join them, and the three got up and headed down the hall, leaving Abbie and me sitting across from each other. We were soon joined by Clayton, who sat next to me. He took a sip of beer and looked at Abbie, who seemed to be lost in thought.

"What's going on, girl?" he asked.

"Oh, nothin'. Just wondering where the time went."

"Yeah, I know. I can't believe it's been fifty years since Woodstock," said Clayton.

Abbie sighed. "When you're young, it seems like time moves so slowly. Like in high school, I felt like it took forever to go from my freshman year to senior year. Then you graduate, get married, the kids come along, and the next thing you know, you're older than shit."

"I know what you mean," said Clayton. "When I was a kid, a year seemed like eternity. Now a year is nothing. It's the blink of an eye. Tony and Dean and their families are on the life treadmill and looking forward to good things ahead, like graduations, weddings, getting together with friends, and stuff like that. We kinda left that stuff behind but can't stop looking forward. People our age get into trouble when they only look backward."

"That makes sense," said Abbie. "All the more reason for us to keep doin' what we're doin'."

I agreed. "We're kinda in the twilight of our lives," I said.

"Yup," said Clayton. "We're probably about 90 percent dead, according to the mortality tables."

Abbie and I laughed. "Now, that's a nice way of putting it!" she told him.

"Like that? Kinda cuts to the chase, doesn't it? But I know what you mean. With every year that goes by, you're one year closer to being gone. It gives you a different perspective about life and what's important. Some people call that wisdom."

"Yeah, I've told my doctor son, Brian, many times that he needs to slow down and smell the roses," said Abbie. "I don't want him to be our age and regretting he didn't spend more time with his family."

Clayton took the last gulp from his mug of beer. "That's good advice. You're always going to have some regret when you get old, but the less regret, the better."

"You guys have regrets?" said Abbie. "Seems like you've had pretty good lives." Looking at me, she said, "You were married to a doctor, lived in this beautiful house, and have successful kids. And we all know Clayton's story. What could you two possibly regret?"

I was a little put off by Abbie's directness and the assumptions she was making, but I knew she meant no harm. It was her "bull in a china shop" nature. And with all she'd been through with her addict son, she probably thought a rock star and a stay-at-home dad married to a rich doctor wouldn't have a care in the world. I'd made similar judgments about people—assuming that outward success meant inner peace. I remember struggling to understand why comedian Robin Williams took his own life a few years ago. He seemed to have it all—immense talent, adoring fans, and great wealth. It's hard to reconcile that image with someone burdened by worries or regrets, and I realized that was how Abbie perceived Clayton and me.

Clayton and I had shared our regrets during our van ride the first time we visited his mother in the nursing home, and I'd told Jim about my disappointments when we had a drink in my apartment after his birthday party. I decided it was time to let Abbie know that Bud Livingston didn't have a perfect life.

"Abbie, this probably isn't the best time to talk about it, but I have a lot of regret. I regret that Sharon and I drifted apart. I regret that the problems between us affected the kids. I regret that my kids barely speak to me." Realizing this was getting too deep, too fast, I said, "But we're at Woodstock, where we're supposed to be liberated from regrets and worries."

"I'm so sorry, Bud," she said. "I should have known from

a few of the comments you made about Sharon and the house. I didn't mean to—"

She stopped when I reached over and gently patted her hand. "It's okay, Abbie. Clayton once told me we all have stuff, and that's mine. Believe me, we're good." I looked her squarely in the eyes. "You know that, right?"

"I do."

Clayton was gazing out the window as if he had detached himself from my conversation with Abbie. I suspected he was thinking about his regrets—losing Candace, the love of his life, and never meeting his daughter, Marie.

"You okay, Clayton?" asked Abbie.

He smiled. "I'm jim-dandy! Abbie, my biggest, all-time regret is that I don't have another beer in my hand."

She smiled.

Clayton slid his chair back and stood. "My big thing lately is thinking about my legacy. What have I done for my brothers and sisters in the world? I'd like to think I'll be remembered for something more than 'Up Yours.'"

Abbie took Clayton's hand and said, "Don't worry about that. You will."

He thanked her, grinned, and began cracking his knuckles. "Bud, when was the last time anyone played that piano in the living room?"

"Gosh, I remember a guy tuning it around five years ago, just before Sharon got sick. She had plans for a party, but it never happened. Other than that, I don't have a clue when it was played last. Maybe thirty years."

"Well, it's time to change that." Clayton grabbed a pitcher off the counter, filled his mug with beer, and headed down the hall into the living room.

Chapter Thirty-Eight

C layton turned off the stereo, and we gathered around as he sat at the piano and loosened up his fingers by rapidly playing parts from familiar melodies. He paused and picked up his backpack. Then he pulled out some sheet music and asked me to distribute it.

"Remember when Numbnuts cut us short during your birthday celebration, Jim?" he asked.

"How could I forget that? My fifteen minutes of fame, gone forever."

"Well, Jim, we're gonna make up for that tonight. The sheet music is for the four songs I wasn't able to play."

With that, Clayton began playing "California Dreamin'" by the Mamas and the Papas, and we enthusiastically joined him in singing. When he finished playing, everyone clapped and complimented him. He smiled proudly, enjoying the attention and camaraderie. Glasses were refilled, and the singing continued as Clayton played the remaining three tunes. After that, we barraged him with requests, and he did his best to play the music. But he had to rely on others to supply the lyrics. Everyone was enjoying the "live karaoke," as Dean described it, when Clayton abruptly stopped playing.

"What's wrong?" asked Kathleen.

"It's Woodstock. I need to dance."

Karen and Rose, who had gotten noticeably louder and more animated, agreed.

"Yes! We want to learn some dances from the sixties," said Rose.

"You got it!" replied Clayton. "Hey, you guys, you should order the pizzas while I teach these youngins a thing or two about dances from the sixties. Grab your drinks, people! Let's go!"

While Kathleen and I were ordering pizzas and before the music started, we heard Clayton giving the young people an enthusiastic tutorial on the swim and the mashed potato, with Jim, Charlie, and Abbie providing occasional input.

"Now, there's a shitload of other dances from the sixties," said Clayton, "but you'll have to learn those on your own. The dance most popular at Woodstock, and my all-time favorite way of dancing, is freestyle, which means do any damn thing you want. There are no rules. Just shake it, jerk it, twist it, move it, and groove it. Whatever the music commands you to do."

"The pizza has been ordered!" said Kathleen as we returned from the kitchen.

I topped off all the men's mugs with beer except for Tony's. He declined, explaining that he'd volunteered to be the designated driver. Kathleen filled the women's glasses with punch.

Just as I was about to put down the beer pitcher, Kathleen raised her glass. "Fill 'er up, mister," she said, and I filled her mug. Then she looked at Clayton. "Hey, Clayton. You're the sound guy. Let's get the dance party started!"

"Yes, ma'am!" He reinserted the CD, set it to the second tune, turned up the volume, and hit Play. "Nobody but Me" by The Human Beinz blared from the speakers and immediately energized everyone in the room. Kathleen grabbed my hand and pulled me out to the center of the floor to dance. Abbie stood and rocked back and forth with her hands on her walker. Jim was clapping to the beat. Clayton was twisting and flailing as if he were possessed, and Charlie was doing the swim and the mashed potato with his sons and their wives.

The music ended. Charlie was breathing hard, as if he had run a marathon. "I'm gassed," he said.

"That sure was fun!" said Kathleen.

"That tune brought back some great memories," Abbie offered.

"I need to start working out," I said as I was trying to catch my wind.

The next tune was "Mony Mony" by Tommy James and the Shondells. Kathleen sprang to her feet and grabbed my hand, yelling, "Come on! I love this tune."

Abbie and Charlie smiled and moved to the music as they watched us freestyle in a dancing circle while singing. We all joined Tommy James in singing the chorus, and we sang every "Yeah" and every "Mony Mony" with increasing enthusiasm and volume.

Kathleen yelled in my ear, "I think I heard a knock at the door. It must be the pizza guy."

I yelled back, "Wow! That was fast! I paid the tip online."

"What?"

"I already paid the tip."

Kathleen gave me a thumbs-up and headed toward the front door. Just then, Rose positioned herself in front of me and encouraged me to join her in doing the swim. I pointed down the hall toward the front door and said, "I have to help Kathleen." She nodded and slid over by Clayton, who was continuing his wild freestyling.

I saw Kathleen reaching for the front door when I heard a loud and forceful knock. She said, "Geez, hold on. I'm coming." I looked out the window to see if the police had returned. April's car was parked behind the bus.

"Oh shit!" I yelled, "Turn the music down!"

Chapter Thirty-Nine

Kathleen opened the door, and I heard April's voice.

"I'm sorry. I can't hear you," said Kathleen. "Just a minute."

The music abruptly ended.

Then I heard "Who the hell are you, and what the hell are you doing in my house?"

I stepped in front of Kathleen. "Don't you dare talk to her that way, April. And what is this BS about this being your house?"

"What the hell is going on here, Dad? I got a call from the neighbor, who said the cops were here." She looked at my outfit and peered into the house. Clayton, Abbie, and Rose were standing in the hallway leading to the kitchen. Clayton waved and winked at her. "What kind of freak show is this?"

"That's it! You're not going to insult my friends. You need to leave. Please go."

"Dad, what are you doing?"

160

"We're assisting each other in living. Good night, April."

I closed the door. A moment later, I heard the screech of tires and a loud bang. I opened the door and saw the rear of April's car pressed against the front of a small, rusty car with a Domino's Pizza sign on the roof. April was standing beside her car, yelling at the young pizza deliveryman. She was accusing him of ruining her $60,000 car and illegally parking in her driveway. The deliveryman seemed to be trying his best to ignore her while talking on his cell phone and inspecting the damage to the front of his car.

When April yelled, "My attorney will have your ass," the delivery man pulled the cell phone away from his ear and angrily responded, "Tell that to the cops when they get here."

I closed the door and continued watching through the living room draperies. A police car arrived with two officers, who talked with April and the pizza guy. April appeared to be smiling a lot and talking animatedly, almost as if she was flirting with the officers. One officer returned to the patrol car while the other remained talking to April, who was becoming increasingly agitated. She had the same look she'd get as a teenager when things weren't going her way. Her voice was getting louder. She stamped her foot, turned, and marched a few steps to her car. Then she turned to make one last remark to the police officer before she got into the driver's seat and slammed the door.

A tow truck appeared and loaded the damaged pizza delivery car while April remained in her car. While the car was being loaded, the deliveryman sauntered up to the house with one pizza box. He acknowledged that I had ordered three large pizzas but explained that two of them ended up on the floor of his car. He promised to talk to his manager about giving me a credit on my card. He walked back to the street and got into the passenger side of another Domino's car, which had just arrived. He waved to the officers. The car sped off with the tow truck following.

The officer who had been in the patrol car emerged, had a quick word with his partner, and approached April. He knocked on the driver's-side window. She lowered the window, and the officer handed her a piece of paper, which I surmised was a ticket. The officers went back to the patrol car and left.

A minute or two later, April started her car, slowly backed down the driveway, and was gone.

Chapter Forty

Kathleen passed out paper plates, and we each took a slice of pizza. After we finished eating, Charlie's sons and their wives stood, stating that they had to get up early to help a relative move.

I felt awful about what occurred with April and the pizza, and I apologized profusely. They assured me that they'd had a great time in spite of it all and warmly exchanged handshakes and hugs with everyone before leaving the house and climbing onto the bus. Charlie, Kathleen, Clayton, and I stood on the front porch, waving as the bus moved down the driveway and onto the street. Tony gave a toot of the horn as he pulled away.

We went back to the living room, where Abbie was nodding off in the recliner and Jim was paging through a magazine. Seeming to sense that the party spirit was starting to wane, Clayton grabbed his backpack and pulled out a colorful cookie tin.

"We're not done yet," he said. "There's no way in hell we're ending our celebration of the fiftieth anniversary of Woodstock by going to bed at 8:30."

"What's in the tin?" asked Kathleen.

"Brownies made from scratch."

"I'm impressed! My grandma used to make brownies that were out of this world. I've never been able to duplicate her recipe."

Clayton smiled. "These brownies may be a little different from the ones your grandma made. Hey, Bud. Got any coffee? Nothing better than a good cup of joe with a brownie."

"Comin' right up!" I went to the kitchen and started brewing a pot of coffee. Soon, the smell of coffee floated through the house.

Abbie stirred in the recliner. "What the hell time is it?"

"Time to party," said Clayton. The coffee finished brewing, so I went back to the kitchen, put the pot on the serving tray with some mugs, and returned. Rubbing her eyes, Abbie sat upright and yawned. The coffee was poured and distributed, and we waited for Clayton to open the tin and distribute the brownies.

Clayton cleared his throat. "Okay, everyone knows who Pete Townshend is, right? The lead guitarist for The Who? Anyway, shortly after Pete arrived at Woodstock, someone gave him a cup of coffee spiked with acid." Clayton looked at Kathleen, who flinched. "Not acid like hydrochloric acid, but LSD—lysergic acid diethylamide. Pete realized he'd been burned after he began hallucinating, and he was really pissed. I didn't blame him one bit. That was bullshit."

"I'm not taking LSD," said Kathleen sternly.

"Relax, my child. This isn't about taking LSD. It's about full and fair disclosure. It's about honoring a person's right to choose, which wasn't done with good, old Pete."

"Are these what I think they are?" asked Jim, grinning.

"Indeed," said Clayton.

"Awesome!"

"What are you guys talking about?" asked Kathleen.

"I added some extra spice to the brownies," said Clayton.

"Like what?"

"Marijuana. They're marijuana brownies, Kathleen," I said.

Kathleen blushed, "Oh my goodness. I had no clue."

"So, here's the deal," said Clayton. "When we first started talking about this party, I figured we had to have Mother Nature's finest to celebrate the fiftieth anniversary of Woodstock. I didn't want to bring a bunch of joints and stink up Bud's nice house, so I figured an edible would be perfect. I don't want anyone to feel pressured. Whether you partake or not, no judgments either way. Like at Woodstock, we are here in the spirit of love and togetherness." He opened the tin, looked at the squares of brownies, and grinned. "Who wants one?"

"I'm sorry. You guys know I led a kind of sheltered life, so forgive me for asking questions," said Kathleen.

"No problem. Shoot," said Clayton.

"Well, I'm kinda scared and intrigued at the same time. So, if I eat a brownie, I'll get stoned, right?"

"Affirm tomato," said Clayton emphatically. "It'll be great!"

"Is it like being drunk? I was drunk a couple times, so I know what that's about."

"Let me tell you about the first time I got stoned. The cops said I was the most violent and assaultive child they'd ever encountered. It took years for my parents to pay for all the damage I caused to the playground equipment."

Kathleen stared at Clayton in disbelief . . . until he

165

cracked a smile. "Damn it, Clayton," she said. "I asked you a serious question."

"I'm sorry. I couldn't resist. For me, being stoned is better than being drunk because I'm not inclined to do crazy-ass things when I'm stoned. When I was on the road during my drinking days, it was not unusual for me to trash some poor guy's motel or get in a fight. Marijuana relaxes me and makes me think about things differently."

"Explain that to me—about thinking differently."

"It's different for everybody, but when I'm stoned, I have a better appreciation of the beauty of the world and the miracle of nature. Like, I might be amazed at the colors in a flower bed or the shapes of clouds. Those same things I might not even notice if I wasn't stoned."

"That sounds kind of neat," said Kathleen. "That's a much different experience than I expected. The stereotypical stoner in the movies is spacey and laughs a lot."

"It's true about the laughing," Clayton said. "When I'm stoned, ordinary things sometimes strike me as being really, really funny. A couple weeks ago, I was standing at the base of one of those big oak trees at Serenity after I smoked a joint. There was a squirrel up in the tree, and he wanted to get down in the worst way. But he didn't have the balls to come all the way down because I was standing there. He moved in little spurts toward me, and with every spurt, he squeaked. He'd get closer and closer, then chicken out and scoot back up the tree to his original starting spot. He did this over and over for at least ten minutes. I laughed my ass off. Just me and Mr. Squirrel, having a little fun."

Kathleen looked at me for reassurance.

"It's been over forty-five years since I was stoned," I told her. "But what Clayton says is accurate. That's the way I remember it."

"Are you going to do it?" she asked.

"After all that happened this evening, I could use a little boost."

"Now that's the spirit!" said Clayton enthusiastically. "Jim?"

"Shit, yes!"

"Charlie?"

"As long as no one tells my boys."

"Abbie?"

"You guys know how much I hate drugs. And they say that for some people, marijuana may be a gateway drug that leads to harder shit. But I'm at Woodstock, and I figure a brownie is probably less harmful than half the crap the doctors prescribe. So, the hell with it. I'm in."

"You don't have to do it, Kathleen," I said. "There's no pressure at all. So you don't feel like the odd person out, I won't have one if you don't."

"Who said I don't want one?" she said. "Will you make sure I don't do anything stupid?"

"Absolutely."

"Okay, then," said Clayton as he removed a brownie and put it on his paper plate. He cut it in half with his fork and said, "We should go halfsies because this stuff is way more potent than it was fifty years ago." He put half the brownie back in the tin and passed it to Abbie.

The tin was passed from person to person until it was returned to Clayton. He put it down, picked up his brownie, and grinned. "We're quite the motley crew, aren't we?" He took a bite and, as he was chewing, said, "But I'm sure glad our paths crossed."

We concurred and ate our brownies.

167

Chapter Forty-One

While sixties folk music played softly in the background, I told them stories about my neighbor Glen and the problems he had caused in the neighborhood. Abbie and Kathleen wanted to know more about April, and I told them how adept she was at manipulating people with her charm and good looks. We talked about Charlie's sons and daughters-in-law and how fun it had been to have them at the party.

Kathleen was sitting on the floor with her eyes closed, swaying to the music. She opened them, giggled, and looked around as if she was afraid a stranger was eavesdropping. "I've got an idea!" she whispered.

Clayton winked at me.

"I think we should call Serenity and ask for Clayton. When they say he's not there, we'll call back and ask for Jim. When they say Jim's not there, we'll call again and ask for Abbie. We'll keep it going until we cover everybody. It'll really mess with them. I think it'd be great!"

"Boy, I don't know, Kathleen," I said.

Clayton laughed. "I like it! Do it!"

Grinning, Kathleen said, "Wait. You want me to do it?"

"Hell yeah! It's your idea. You do it!" he replied.

Eager to apply pressure, Abbie quickly scrolled through her cell phone. "Here it is!" Then she read the number out loud.

"I don't know. Should I?" asked Kathleen.

Clayton began chanting, "Do it, do it, do it," and the others quickly joined in.

"Okay, okay, I'll do it!" We all cheered as Kathleen picked up her cell phone. "What was that number again?"

Between giggles, she hit the number display on her cell phone as Abbie slowly recited the ten digits. Her eyes widened when the phone rang. "One ringy dingy." She giggled. Then she said, "Hi, may I talk to . . ." Kathleen looked blankly at me. "Ah . . . Clayton Davis. May I speak to Clayton Davis, please?" She listened for a few seconds. Then she said, "Oh, sorry . . ." She began laughing. "I guess I dialed the wrong number. Bye." She tossed the phone to me like a hot potato as she continued laughing. "I almost forgot what to say."

"Wouldn't know a thing about that," said Charlie, who was also laughing.

I smiled at Kathleen. "Maybe we shouldn't be making phone calls tonight."

"Okay," she said as her attention immediately shifted to Clayton, who had pulled a package of Double Stuf Oreos out of his backpack. "Oh my God! May I have one of those?"

Clayton glanced at me and smiled. He carefully opened the Oreo package and handed it to Kathleen. "Knock yourself out."

She took the package, removed an Oreo, studied it, then bit into it, oblivious to the crumbs tumbling down her shirt and onto the floor. Clayton started laughing, turned away, and put his hand over his mouth. But he was unable to stifle his laughter, as evidenced by his shaking shoulders. That started me laughing, and I completely lost it as I watched her savoring another bite, her daisy crown on her head askew and Oreo crumbs decorating her mouth and shirt.

"What? What's so funny, you guys?" she kept saying as she wiped her mouth with her hand and grabbed another cookie.

When I finally got myself under control, I said, "You really like Double Stuf Oreos, don't you?"

"Oh. I sure do," she said as she bit into another. I studied her face as she closed her eyes and said, "Mmm." Even with cookie crumbs at the edges of her mouth and lacking the poise and control I was accustomed to, she was still adorable. I imagined being with her over fifty years ago when we were young and just out of high school. I snapped out of my moment of reverie when Jim said, "Hey, Bud."

"What?"

"I heard what you said to your daughter out there, and I thought that was amazing."

"What'd I say?"

"Something like 'We're assisting each other in living.' How'd you come up with that?"

"I was so pissed, I don't even remember saying it."

"But it's so true, man," said Clayton. "Think about it. We could be somewhere stuck in a room waiting to die, but we're not doing that. We're livin', man. And that's cool."

"That's for sure," said Jim.

"Sometimes, I wonder where I would be without you guys," said Charlie. "But then I forget what I was wondering about." He smiled, and everyone laughed.

"I have a question for you living assistants," said Abbie.

She stopped to look in the direction of a faint *ping, ping, ping* sound. "What's that?"

I looked under the shade of a tall lamp next to the couch. "It's a moth. It must have flown in when we had the door open."

The moth was inside the shade and flying around the light bulb. Over and over, the moth hit the light bulb, flew around, bounced off the shade, and then hit the light bulb again.

"Stay away from the light, little friend," said Charlie as everyone watched the moth going around and around the light bulb.

"Please set him free, Bud," pleaded Kathleen. "And don't hurt the little guy."

I put my open hand up to the light. When the moth landed on it, I closed my hand, walked to the front door, opened it, and set the moth free.

"My hero," said Kathleen dramatically as I walked back into the living room and sat down.

"You said you had a question for us, Abbie. What was it?" asked Jim.

"It's about the drug court thing."

"Should I stay or should I go? Great tune by The Clash," said Clayton. "That's your question, right?"

"Huh?"

"You want to know if we think you should go to your son's drug court deal."

Abbie nodded.

"Absolutely, 100 percent, no-holds-barred, you should go," Clayton said. "Think about this, Abbie. Why did that moth keep banging into the light bulb? He was attracted to it. He couldn't help himself, even though the light bulb was hot. He would have kept going around and around that light bulb until he was dead. But Bud gave him an opportunity to live, and now he's out there happily flying around, trying to find a date."

Clayton took a sip of his coffee. "Abbie, I've been around a lot of people with drug problems, and many of them are dead. Over and over, they kept going back to the drugs. They couldn't help themselves. The drugs were their light bulb. The drug court is giving your son an off-ramp, just like Bud did for our friend Mr. Moth. Your son has a chance to live, and we should be there for him."

There was not a sound for several moments as we all thought about what Clayton had said. Kathleen stared at him in open-mouthed awe. "Wow, Clayton. That was an amazing analogy. You're quite the phil-o-siff . . . I mean phil-lop . . ."

"Philosopher?" I said.

"Right. Philosopher."

"Clayton, sometimes you say some pretty bizarre shit. But you really nailed that one, brother," added Jim.

"Then you'll go with me?" asked Abbie.

"For sure!" responded Clayton.

Abbie smiled. "Thanks. That's a big relief." She looked at Kathleen, who was clutching the Oreo package in her lap and blissfully munching on a cookie. "Kathleen, I'm ready for an Oreo."

Fueled by the brownie, I found myself obsessing about the moth I had freed and its significance to Abbie's question about attending the drug court graduation. "Isn't it something that the moth got in the house, found the light, and became the topic of Clayton's sermon?" I said. "Without that moth, the whole conversation would have been different. Was that chance? Or was there some greater force that directed that moth in here so Clayton would be inspired to talk, we would agree to go to the drug court graduation, and Abbie would be comforted?"

"Now, that's some heavy shit, dude," said Clayton. "I need another halfsie to get my head around that." He picked up half a brownie and took a bite.

Charlie was smiling and seemed to be staring at some unseen thing on the ceiling. "May the greater force be with you, my friends." His serious tone and deadpan delivery cracked everyone up, and that led to animated reminisces about watching the first *Star Wars* movie, released in 1977.

"You probably never heard of him, but John Williams is the musical freak of nature who wrote the *Star Wars* theme, which may be the most recognized tune ever written," said Clayton. "I met him in LA in the early seventies. Even then, he was widely recognized as a music-writing powerhouse. He told me he liked the 'energy' of 'Up Yours.' He didn't mention the music or lyrics, so I was never sure if he actually liked the tune or was just blowing smoke up my ass. Speaking of music, I bet all this mellow sixties stuff we're playing drives you nuts, Bud. Songs about peace, love, and togetherness aren't your thing."

"I like the music. Why would you say that?"

"Because you're a big Kiss fan! You like the glitter, pyrotechnics, and big hair stuff. And there's absolutely nothing wrong with that."

I laughed. "You're an ass, Clayton. You know, that damn poster scared the crap out of me my first night at Serenity."

Kathleen began giggling. "This is really funny."

"How so?" asked Clayton.

"Well, a lot happened that day. April dumped me off, and I was tired and nervous about going to dinner with a bunch of people I didn't know."

"Okay, so what happened?" asked Clayton eagerly.

"So I went into the bathroom to get ready for dinner. I closed the door and began running hot water in the sink. I held a hot, wet washcloth over my face. I just needed a calming, relaxing moment before dinner, which turned out to be my fart machine initiation dinner with you clowns."

Charlie began laughing. "That was hilarious! Bud, I can still see the look on your face after that first fart, when Clayton scowled and accused you of farting."

"His face turned beet red," said Jim. "Remember that, Clayton?"

Clayton giggled. "I do. I definitely do. I thought his head was going to explode." They all laughed.

"Yeah, that was a real treat," I said. "What I remember most vividly is that second fart, when Clayton leaned forward in his chair and said so seriously, 'If you're going to fart, I wish you would do it away from the dinner table.'"

Giggling, Kathleen slapped Clayton on the knee. "Shame on you, Clayton!"

When the group quieted, I added, "And, of course, Jim piled on. He said something like 'Where I come from, it's not good manners to fart at the table.'" While everyone was laughing, I said, "At that moment, I could have crawled under a rock."

When the laughter subsided, Clayton said, "Getting back to the poster, what happened with that?"

"Right. Okay. So, I was holding the washcloth over my face and trying to relax. As I pulled the washcloth off, I looked in the steamed-up mirror and saw him standing there behind me."

"Boom!" said Clayton, then he and Jim laughed loudly.

"Who was standing there?" asked Abbie.

"Gene Simmons, Abbie," said Jim. "Well, I mean,

Clayton put a life-size Gene Simmons poster on the bathroom door before Bud moved in."

Abbie laughed. "That's a hoot!" She took a bite of her Oreo and turned to me. "Did you really think someone was behind you?"

"Damn right! I spun around like a top to face my attacker."

"Hold on, man! Back up," said Clayton. "Jim, you just said I put the poster on the bathroom door. Don't go pinning all the blame on me! You were the brains behind the operation."

Jim laughed. "Okay, maybe I had a minor role."

"Minor role, my ass," responded Clayton. "It was your idea! You're the one who insisted we buy the poster. And come to think of it, you came and got me when you realized the housekeepers hadn't locked the door."

"I want to talk to my lawyer," said Jim, causing more laughter.

Giggling uncontrollably with a partially eaten Oreo in her hand, Kathleen looked at me and said, "Tell 'em . . ." Her giggling continued until she blurted, "Tell 'em . . . what you told me."

"What? That I damn near wet myself?"

Jim and Clayton howled with laughter, and the others joined in.

I interrupted their laughter and added, "Wait. There's more! So, I figured the poster was left behind by the former tenant, right? I asked Kathleen who that was, and she told me it was Sister Mary Katherine. I wondered what kind of a weird-ass nun would have a Gene Simmons poster on her bathroom door."

Clayton laughed until tears ran down his cheeks, Jim

was doubled over in his wheelchair, and the rest of the group was laughing along with them.

Clayton took a deep breath and tried to contain his laughter. He rubbed his eyes and said, "Now, that's quite a story."

"Please pass the Oreos," said Kathleen. She pulled out a cookie and took a bite. "This is my sixth one." She smiled, revealing black cookie particles stuck to the gums around her front teeth.

I laughed.

"What?" she pleaded, then continued her ravenous chewing.

"Nothing." I looked at Clayton, who had been watching Kathleen. We burst out laughing again when our eyes met.

"What?" she asked again as she swallowed her last bite.

"Just enjoying the evening," I said.

"Right. Just groovin' at Woodstock," added Clayton.

Chapter Forty-Two

J im noticed Clayton stifling a yawn and looking at his watch. "You're not thinking about going to bed, are you, Mr. Fluffy Tart?" Jim asked. "My God, it's only 10:30! You said you wanted to party until midnight." He shook his head as if he was disappointed. "It's obvious you're nothin' but a big, old windbag."

Clayton's back straightened. "I resemble that remark! Jim, I'd be up until the crack of dawn if this were a normal Woodstock party. But this is no normal Woodstock party. Chaosstock is what it was. Yeah, that's right. Complete and total Chaosstock. Friggin' cops, an April tornado at the front door, the horrendous car accident in the driveway . . . All that shit sucked the life right out of me."

Abbie laughed. "And the beer and marijuana had nothing to do with it?"

"Well, maybe a little, but all that other stuff didn't help."

"You're so full of it, Clayton," said Abbie, "but I'm tired too."

We agreed it was time to wrap things up, so I guided

them down the hall to the bedrooms. Abbie and Kathleen were going to sleep in the master bedroom, and Charlie, Clayton, and Jim all had their own rooms. I claimed the living room couch.

After helping the men get settled in, I got a blanket and pillow and returned to the living room. It was a mess, and I couldn't ignore the clutter. I tossed the pillow and blanket on the couch and began picking up. I carried some coffee mugs and beer glasses into the kitchen, then grabbed a tray. When I returned to the living room, I heard a distinct *thump*. I listened for a moment and could faintly hear what sounded like crying.

I walked down the hall and found that I hadn't heard crying. Kathleen and Abbie were laughing hysterically. I smiled, listened for a few moments, then returned to the living room and continued picking up. I carried a tray of items into the kitchen and placed them on the counter, unaware Kathleen had left the bedroom and was stealthily trailing behind. As I turned around, she said, "Boo!"

I flinched and she giggled.

"I thought you said we would pick things up in the morning," she said.

"I did, but I didn't want to feel like I was sleeping in a landfill."

"Did you hear us?"

"I did. Sounded like you were having some fun. What was that thump I heard?"

"You should have seen it." Kathleen giggled. "Abbie couldn't get her leather pants off, so I had her sit in that chair with the arms." She giggled again. "Our plan was for her to push on the arms of the chair with her hands to raise herself while I pulled on the bottom of her pants until they slid down over her butt. We tried a bunch of times. I pulled on one leg, and then the other, but we didn't seem to be getting anywhere. I'm not kidding you, Bud. My arm was getting tired, and I thought we were going to need your help. Anyway, she kept lifting herself up, and I kept pulling, and when the pants finally came free, I fell on my butt. I sat there, looking at Abbie sitting in that chair in her red underwear with her leather pants at her ankles, and she said, 'I think you got 'em,' and I just lost it. It just struck me so funny."

"That must have been quite a sight."

Apparently realizing the story was funnier to her than it was to me, Kathleen said, "Well, I guess you should have been there." She moved toward the refrigerator. "I came out for a bottle of water. Are there any left?"

I got a bottled water out of the refrigerator and gave it to her.

She took it, smiled, and said, "Great, thanks. Good night."

As she turned to leave, she hesitated, spun back around, and gave me a quick kiss on the cheek. "Thanks for the great day."

Before I could react, she was heading down the hall to the master bedroom.

Chapter Forty-Three

The next morning, Clayton walked into the kitchen while I was preparing the coffee.

"Top of the morning to ya, brother!" he said. "The others are up and will be with us in a few minutes. How ya doin'?"

"I'm all right."

"Whaddya mean 'all right'? Saying you're all right is like saying you're fair to middlin'. You should feel better than that. What's goin' on?"

"I don't know, Clayton. I just feel like Woodstock was a flop. It didn't go the way I expected. All that planning—"

"Hold the phone, chief! Flop my ass! It was a shindig of epic proportions and one I'll never forget. We made the best of what was thrown at us, just like we did at the real Woodstock when it rained for three frickin' days. We were together, we had some laughs, listened to some good music, danced, and got a little buzzed. Trust me, it was a far better day than most people our age had."

"I suppose you're right."

"I know I'm right, brother! No more of that nonsense!

180

We all owe you a debt of gratitude for having us over and letting us live. It was fucking great!"

"Good morning, guys," said Kathleen as she and the others entered the kitchen, wearing their usual street clothes.

"That brownie really kicked my ass, Clayton," said Abbie.

"You're welcome, milady."

The coffee was distributed, and, for much of the morning, we talked and laughed about all that had occurred. Clayton told stories about the real Woodstock. He said he vividly remembered when Graham Nash, David Crosby, Neil Young, and Stephen Stills arrived in a helicopter. He partied with them in John Sebastian's tent and said they were nervous about playing because it was only their second gig. When it came time for them to play, he claimed he assisted them in setting up and did his best to help them feel relaxed and confident.

"Wait," I said. "Are you saying you were on the stage with Crosby, Stills, Nash and Young at Woodstock?"

"Yeah, the stage was totally chaotic, and they asked me to make sure everything was good to go. Maybe they wanted some support too. I kept telling them not to worry—that things would be fine. But when I saw the crowd from the stage, I got nervous too. Seeing all those people and feeling their energy blew me away."

Charlie's jaw dropped. "So, you really know those guys?"

Clayton casually took a sip of coffee. "I did. Did a lot of studio stuff with them in LA."

Charlie persisted. "Who did you know the best?"

"Graham Nash, for sure."

The discussion gave me an opening to remind Clayton

that Nash was playing in Royal Oak at the end of the month and suggest we attend the concert. Everyone was immediately on board except Clayton.

"I suppose we could," he said, "but it wouldn't be the same without the others."

I looked quizzically at Jim, and he rolled his eyes.

Chapter Forty-Four

We disembarked from the Mothership and slowly made our way up the sidewalk to the Serenity entrance. I held the door open and entered the building last.

As we started down the hall toward our rooms, Brett came storming out of his office and said, "Where the hell have you guys been?"

Taken aback by his aggressiveness, we stopped and exchanged wary looks. Clayton finally responded, "Amsterdam."

"That's a bunch of bullshit, and you know it. But it's typical for a pathological liar," snarled Brett.

His insult and hostile tone stirred feelings of resentment and indignation I hadn't experienced since my days of protesting the Vietnam War in the late sixties. I remembered people trying to provoke us by questioning our patriotism and lambasting us with all sorts of colorful profanities. The police were always quick to arrest the protestor and not the provocateur. Back then, I tended to turn the other cheek.

Not today.

I looked at my friends and smiled. "You're right, Brett. We weren't in Amsterdam." He nodded approvingly, thinking I was going to come clean. "We were in Katmandu."

"You obviously didn't heed my warning when you moved in," said Brett angrily.

"What warning?" asked Clayton.

"Tell you later," I said.

"Excuse me, Bud. I think you're mistaken. It was Hong Kong," said Jim, causing Abbie to giggle.

Brett stared at Jim and Abbie as if he was getting ready to pounce.

Abbie defiantly stared back at Brett and said, "I disagree, Jim. It was Berlin."

Charlie quickly answered, "It was not! It was Paris."

"That's enough! Shut up!" yelled Brett.

Very calmly, Kathleen said, "I don't appreciate your hostility and tone. We're entitled to come and go as we please. We're not children."

"I had a full staff here, but you took off without telling anyone where you were going. You missed your meals and medications, and a couple of you—" He glared at Abbie and Jim. "—are supposed to have help getting tucked in at night. You may not be children, but you sure act like it."

"Up yours!" said Kathleen.

He glared at her as his face went flush with anger. "What did you say?"

Smiling, she said, "You heard me, honey."

Brett stared at her for a couple seconds. But she stood still and straight, like a military officer, and stared back at him defiantly. Clayton, Charlie, and Jim were grinning, and

Abbie looked scared. I don't know how I looked, but I was feeling a mixture of astonishment and pride.

"I've had it with you people," said Brett. He turned, walked back into his office, and slammed the door.

I looked at the hall camera and hoped he wasn't watching us as we laughed and teased Kathleen about kicking his ass.

Upon entering my room, I tossed my overnight bag on the couch, turned on my laptop, and began searching the internet for some of the people Clayton had mentioned before and during the Woodstock celebration. I discovered that one of them was employed by Warner Records as a session musician. His email address was posted on the company website. I decided to shoot him an email. When I finished writing, I laughed to myself and signed off with a name that wasn't my own.

Brenda came to my apartment later in the afternoon and told me she felt terrible about a conversation she'd had with Clayton. She said she'd asked him how his mom was doing because she'd heard that the nursing home called a few times looking for him. She speculated that his mom was taken to a hospital, but she wasn't sure because the calls had been routed to Brett. She said Clayton was very upset and had left in a panic. I assured her she did nothing wrong and that I'd reach out to him to find out what was going on.

Later that evening, Clayton responded to my text message and wrote that his mom had pneumonia and had been admitted to Beaumont Hospital in Troy.

Chapter Forty-Five

I t had been three days since Clayton had gone to be with his mother. Finally, he called and said his mom was conscious and communicating but very sick. He said he needed to stay with her and wouldn't be able to drive us to Mark's drug court graduation in the morning.

Abbie had been apprehensive about attending the graduation anyway and didn't seem disappointed when I told her Clayton couldn't drive. She said it was not a big deal and muttered something about sending Mark a nice card.

I joined Kathleen and the others in insisting we attend the graduation as planned, and I arranged for an Uber van to pick us up.

We were ready and waiting the next morning when the Uber arrived at the front entrance. With assistance from Jim's aide and the driver, everyone got into the van for the drive to the courthouse in Warren. Abbie seemed unusually pensive and quiet along the way.

As we emerged from the van, we noticed a steady stream of people walking toward the courthouse entrance.

We followed until Abbie stopped near the entrance and pulled her walker off the sidewalk.

"What's wrong?" asked Kathleen.

"I don't know if I can do this," said Abbie, her voice quaking.

"Why?" I asked.

"I'm just so scared," she said as she took a tissue from her pocket and wiped the tears from her eyes.

"Scared? Scared of what?"

"Scared of feeling hope. Every time I've had that feeling about Mark, I've had my heart broken. I just can't deal with that again."

"Abbie, listen," I said. "Anyone in your place would feel the same. We just have to trust that Mark wouldn't be graduating if he wasn't ready. Maybe this a new beginning for both of you."

"I know you're right, Bud. I'm really trying hard to pull it together. Just give me another minute."

A nice-looking, well-dressed man approached us. He seemed to be looking for someone, stopped a few feet away, and said, "Mom?"

"Brian! Oh, Brian," cried Abbie as she started toward her oldest son. They embraced, and she said through her tears, "I'm so glad you're here. Why didn't you tell me you were coming?"

"I figured you didn't get an invitation because you didn't say anything, and I didn't want to upset you by letting you know I got one. Why didn't you tell me you got an invitation?"

"I don't know, Brian. I guess I was afraid to even talk about it. I wasn't sure I was going to come anyway. But my friends made me realize I needed to be here, and they wanted to come too."

Brian looked at his watch. "We really should get in there, Mom. The place is filling up." Abbie introduced us, and we headed toward the entrance.

We entered the courtroom and walked down the aisle, looking for a place for six people to sit. Near the front, a man who appeared to be in his mid-sixties and a woman about the same age smiled and slid down the bench seat to make room for us. I put Jim's wheelchair and Abbie's walker in the corner of the courtroom and sat next to Kathleen at the end of the bench seat next to the aisle.

The courtroom furniture had been moved in preparation for the graduation. The two ornate tables and matching chairs for attorneys and their clients had been pulled aside. Five chairs were placed directly in front of the judge's bench. To the right of the chairs was a lectern positioned to face the audience.

At eleven, the door leading to the judge's chambers opened. A court officer came out and loudly commanded the audience to stand as he stood next to the door like a sentry. A moment later, the four graduates—two men and two women—walked out, followed by the judge, who was dressed in a traditional black robe. The graduates stood in front of their waiting chairs as the judge, a very tall man in his mid-forties with short-cropped gray hair, walked to the lectern, smiled, and directed everyone to be seated.

I concluded that the older man dressed in gray slacks and a light-blue short-sleeve shirt was Mark. He was considerably thinner than Brian but was about the same height. And his hairline and facial features were similar. The other man had dark eyes and a shaved head, and he wore a long-sleeve shirt that did not fully conceal the tattoos on his arms and around his neck.

One of the women had stylishly cut short hair and

appeared to be in her mid-thirties. She wore a floral-print dress with shoes that nicely complemented her outfit. She didn't look like a person with a drug problem. I was unable to estimate the other woman's age. There was a hardness in her face that probably came from years of addiction. She was as tall as Kathleen but much thinner, and the blue dress she wore hung loosely on her slender frame.

The audience and the graduates sat. The judge smiled again and said, "Welcome to the Thirty-Seventh District Court. I am Judge Chad Coggins. Thank you for being here on this very special day, which may be the most significant day of our graduates' lives. Today marks a new beginning for them after months of hard work.

"Believe me, graduating from drug court is not easy. We've actually had people who wanted to quit drug court and go back to jail or prison because they couldn't handle being rigorously supervised and held accountable. Drug court participants are randomly and frequently drug tested, are required to attend individual and group counseling and self-help meetings, and meet regularly with their assigned probation officer and the case manager. If they don't follow the rules, they are subject to a variety of sanctions, including jail time. At the appropriate time, they are expected to secure and maintain employment and become self-sufficient. In some ways, drug court is like boot camp, and getting through it takes courage, determination, and resiliency. That is why we are here to celebrate this important day.

"Drug addiction is a disease caused when powerful substances hijack the soul of a person. When that happens, the addict's existence is centered on finding and using. It's as if they're being directed by a demon living in their brain who needs a steady supply of drugs to exist. He snips the morals-and-values circuitry in the brain so the host person will do whatever is necessary to obtain drugs without reservation or guilt. That's when the lying, cheating, stealing, and manipulating begin. That's when relationships with friends and family members are strained or broken.

"But the good news is that the demon often overestimates his own power and underestimates the power of the human spirit. He thinks he's in complete control. But with many people, he can't snuff out their longing to be free of him. They remember the life they once had, the people who love them, and the things that could have been. But their desire to break free often isn't enough. They need help. The demon does not give up easily, and the road to freedom is really, really hard. There may be setbacks and failures. And sometimes, it may seem easier to quit. But the ones who persevere are worthy of our respect. And that is why they deserve to be recognized and honored today.

"These four—Madison Benzeni, Sydney Hadel, Larry Stanton, and Mark Miron—have persevered, and I am proud to be standing here with them. Please join me in giving them a round of applause."

The audience clapped. Several people hooted and whistled. When everyone quieted down, the judge explained that one of the traditions of graduation was that each graduate must provide a brief testimonial documenting their recovery journey. The judge requested applause be withheld until the testimonials were completed.

Madison Benzeni stood and walked confidently to the lectern. She smiled at a man and two boys seated in the front row. She described herself as a typical thirty-five-year-old soccer mom who got addicted to Vicodin after she injured her knee playing softball. She explained how she had hidden her addiction from her husband and two young boys for over three years—until she nearly killed herself in a car accident. Madison said her addiction almost ruined her marriage, and she regretted the turmoil she had put her family through. She tearfully thanked her sons and husband for standing by her while she was in drug court, and she vowed to be the mother and wife God wanted her to be.

Sydney Hadel got up next and approached the lectern with some typewritten notes in her hand. Seeming nervous, she put down her notes, introduced herself, and said she was twenty-five years old. She read how she had been a cheerleader and honors student in high school when her father died of an overdose of legally prescribed medication. She was unable to cope with his loss and turned to marijuana and alcohol to numb her pain. Within a year, she had lost most of her friends, and her grades had plummeted. She began hanging out with the wrong crowd. One night, someone convinced her to shoot heroin. She was afraid to do it. So she stuck out her arm, and her friend injected her. After that, she was hooked and did just about anything to support her habit. Thanking the police officer who arrested her and members of the drug court team who assisted her, she proudly stated that she had been clean for 426 days. She had just completed her first year of college and made the dean's list. She smiled and gave a thumbs-up to the couple sitting next to Abbie before she returned to her seat.

Larry Stanton, the man with the tattoos, stood at the lectern and eloquently and emotionally described how he had been abandoned by his mother and placed in foster care, where he was physically and sexually abused. By the age of seventeen, he had dropped out of school, joined a gang, and made money selling drugs and stolen firearms. He got addicted to fentanyl and eventually went to prison on gun charges. When he was paroled, he relapsed and was caught with a small quantity of fentanyl. Instead of sending him back to prison, the judge ordered him to complete drug court. Larry said drug court saved his life, and he thanked God for loving him in spite of all the bad things he had done. Now he was working as a union ironworker, and he and his fiancée were saving to buy a house. His involvement in a community drug outreach program was giving him the opportunity to tell his story to high school students.

Walking back to his chair, Larry looked at Mark and nodded, signaling that Mark should go to the podium. But Mark was frozen in his seat. His head was lowered, and his hands rested in his lap, clutching a few sheets of paper. Larry gently wrapped his muscular, tattooed arm around Mark's shoulders and whispered something in his ear. Mark nodded, slowly got up, and walked to the lectern. He put the papers down and ran his hand across them a couple of times, as if to smooth out the wrinkles. Reaching into the breast pocket of his shirt, he pulled out some half-reader glasses and put them on. He cleared his throat, looked down, and began to read.

"My name is Mark Miron, and I'm forty-five years old. I've been a drug addict for twenty-three years. I was raised . . ." He looked at Brian and Abbie and said, "I can't do this." He put his hands on the sides of the lectern and looked down. After a few moments, Larry jumped from his seat and put his arm around Mark. They talked in whispered voices while the audience watched. I heard Larry say, "Just forget about the notes. Go with your heart, man. You got this." Larry gave Mark a reassuring pat on the back and went back to his seat.

Mark took off his glasses and placed them on the lectern. He wiped his brow with his hand, took a tissue out of his hip pocket, and wiped his nose. Then he put the tissue back in his pocket, took a deep breath, and looked at Brian and Abbie.

"Brian wrote me a letter and told me he was coming to the graduation, but I never expected to see you here, Mom. After all I've done to our family, I wouldn't have blamed you if you hadn't come." Mark paused and swallowed. "I know I put you and Dad through hell. I let you down over and over again. You cared enough about me to send me to rehab three times, and each time, I went back to using. It must have felt like a kick in the gut every time I failed. Only now do I realize the hurt and disappointment you must have felt after each failure."

Mark's jaw was quivering as he looked at Abbie and tried not to cry. "I'm so sorry. Everyone wrote me off as a loser, yet you were there for me, and I took advantage of you. I lied over and over again. I stole from you. And . . . this is really hard to say. Mom . . . in spite of my years of denials, I did steal your rings and pawn them downtown for drugs.

"The tough thing about recovery is that the more clear-headed you become, the more you realize how much damage you caused. Mom, I know I caused you years of pain and heartache. I'm sure the financial and emotional strain I put on Dad contributed to his death, and my stealing from you robbed you of the comfortable retirement you deserve. Sometimes, the guilt is almost unbearable, and I have to lean on God to help me.

"I loved Dad. He was a good and honorable man. I disrespected you, our family, and his memory by showing up high at his funeral. You were right in throwing me out and telling me we were done, that you never wanted to see me again. You and Dad loved each other very much, and I know you were hurting when he passed away. I should have been there to comfort you in your grieving, and I wasn't. I will regret that every day of my life.

"After we had those words at the funeral home, I drifted down to Ohio, thinking I could con Brian into giving me some prescription medication that I would either use or sell. I figured my brother the doctor would help me out. He didn't, and that's when I realized I had no one. And the sad thing is that, at the time, I didn't really care.

"I lived wherever I could after that, always looking for ways to get my next fix. I made my way back to Michigan, and that's when I got arrested again for heroin possession. I can't remember if I contacted one or both of you about getting me out of jail. I was really sick from withdrawals.

"As my head began to clear, I thought about my pathetic, wasted life and concluded the world would be better off without me. I had burned every bridge. I had no friends, no home, nothing. That's when I hit bottom. That's when I thought about ending it all.

"So I took a plea, fully expecting to go to prison. But the judge sentenced me to drug court. With the help and support of all these good people, I've been clean for twenty-three months—the longest stretch in twenty-three years. I'm taking care of myself, Mom. I have a full-time job that pays the bills and a little apartment in Hamtramck. I even have a girlfriend I met in church. I think you'd like her.

"I don't expect you to welcome me back with open arms. I'm sure you're afraid of getting burned again. That's understandable. I just hope that we can have a cup of coffee someday and talk like we used to. I've missed you, Mom and Brian. You're all I have. I hope you will someday find it in your hearts to forgive me."

The courtroom was unusually quiet. Mark picked up his papers, turned, and began walking back to his chair.

Larry met him halfway and gave him a firm hug. When they sat, Judge Coggins reached over and tenderly patted Mark on the shoulder. Many of the people across the aisle to my right had tears in their eyes. I glanced at Kathleen and noticed that her eyes were red from crying. Brian had his arm around Abbie as she wept.

The silence was broken when someone in the back of the courtroom began clapping.

Chapter Forty-Six

I glanced over my shoulder and was surprised to see Clayton standing in the middle of the last row with people sitting on either side of him, proudly clapping and looking unconcerned that everyone else in the courtroom was quiet. At that moment, a man sitting on the same bench stood and joined Clayton. Two women a few rows ahead stood and joined in, and soon, everyone in the courtroom, except the graduates, was standing and enthusiastically applauding.

The graduates exchanged glances and smiled. Judge Coggins stood next to them, clapping and smiling like a proud father. I looked at Abbie, who stood motionless, seemingly mesmerized by the outpouring of energy and emotion.

As the applause diminished, Judge Coggins directed everyone to sit. He moved back to the lectern and told some lighthearted stories about the graduates and their numerous drug court accomplishments. He asked the graduates to join him at the lectern, where he shook their hands and presented each one with a certificate and gift card. He thanked the audience for attending. Before asking for a final round of applause, he encouraged everyone to visit with the graduates in a conference room down the hall, where soft drinks and snacks were being served.

As we sat talking about the ceremony and waiting for the aisle to clear, Clayton appeared next to me with the wheelchair and walker I had stashed earlier. "Good morning, fellow blue-hairs," he said.

"What's goin' on, man? You told me yesterday you couldn't make it," I said.

Clayton smiled. "I did tell you that. But when I got thinking about it, I figured they'd have free food and soft drinks. So I couldn't pass it up."

"Were you here the whole time?" asked Kathleen.

"Well, I heard the first three graduates, but then I got a text message from my online astrologist and had to go out in the hall and deal with that."

"Are you kidding?" said Kathleen indignantly. "You missed Mark's testimonial for an online astrologist?"

Clayton smiled. "How Venus and Mars are aligned is important to my spiritual health."

She rolled her eyes. "Okay, now I know you're kidding. You're such a BS'er, Clayton Davis. I'm surprised your nose isn't three feet long."

"How's your mom doing?" I asked.

"She's very sick, but she's holding her own," said Clayton.

"What's wrong with your mom?" asked Charlie.

"She has pneumonia, Charlie. She's in the hospital."

"Oh, I'm sorry. Should I have known that?"

"You may have been told that before, but that's okay." Clayton patted Charlie on the back. "Thanks, buddy."

Abbie and Brian were the last to leave their seats and

join us in the aisle. She grabbed Clayton's hand as he slid her the walker. "Thanks for coming. It means a lot," she said.

"I woke up this morning and knew my mom would want me to be here, so here I am. My only complaint is that I must be allergic to something in the courtroom. My damn nose was running, and my eyes were watering the whole time."

Abbie smiled. "Mine too. We must be allergic to the same thing." She squeezed his hand. "Thanks, Clayton."

After Abbie introduced Clayton to Brian, we headed down the aisle, out of the courtroom, and into the hall, where a sizable crowd had gathered near the conference room entrance. I went ahead to see what was going on, and the others waited. I saw Judge Coggins and the four graduates in a large conference room in an informal reception line, shaking hands and talking to the attendees. Mark excused himself and walked toward me.

"You were with my mom, right?" he asked.

"Right. I'm Bud."

"Nice to meet you, Bud," said Mark, shaking my hand. He seemed nervous and preoccupied, and he kept looking down the hall toward the people gathered there. "I really don't know how to say this, Bud, so I'll just ask. Do my mom and Brian want to see me? I mean . . . I won't be offended if they don't."

"Of course they do, Mark. You want to see them, don't you?"

"I do."

He and I walked a short distance down the hall until I spotted Abbie and Brian, who had their backs turned and were talking to Charlie and Kathleen. I pointed them out.

Mark looked at me as if he was seeking my approval,

then walked slowly toward Abbie and Brian. Kathleen appeared to notice him and smiled. Abbie turned and was face-to-face with Mark.

"Mom, I—"

Abbie gently put her hand over his lips. "Shhh. Don't say a word. You've said enough for today." They embraced, Brian threw his arms around them, and they all broke down in tears.

"I'm so sorry, Mom," said Mark between sobs.

"Not a day went by that I didn't think about you, honey," said Abbie. "I'm so glad to have you back."

"I'm really proud of you," said Brian. "What you did in there took a lot of guts."

We gave them space while they tearfully reunited. When they were finished, Abbie introduced Mark to her "great friends" and told him how we comforted her with friendship and humor. She pointed at Clayton, smiled, and said, "And that guy right there. Don't believe a damn word he says."

"Ouch!" said Clayton. "Mark, sometimes your mom doesn't appreciate my sophisticated sense of humor."

Abbie laughed, making Mark smile. "Clayton's idea of a sophisticated sense of humor is a fart machine taped under a person's chair. Right, Bud?"

"Don't get me involved in this!" I said. "Mark, all I can say is if you ever visit your mom at Serenity, be sure to check under your chair."

Eventually, we made our way to the conference room, where we met Judge Coggins and the other graduates. Abbie, Mark, and Brian ended up in a corner while the rest of us mingled and enjoyed the refreshments. As the crowd began to thin, Clayton reminded us that the Mothership was waiting to transport us back to Serenity.

"What about Abbie?" asked Kathleen.

Abbie seemed to sense we were getting ready to leave. She left her sons for a moment and approached us. She told us to go ahead without her and that she'd be spending the afternoon with her boys.

When we arrived back at Serenity, Clayton parked the Mothership near Brett's Mercedes convertible. He looked at the car and said it reminded him that he needed to talk to Corrine at the nursing home about what she told Brett when we were away celebrating Woodstock and his mom was sick and needing to go to the hospital.

While pushing Jim up the sidewalk toward the entrance, with the others following closely behind, Clayton nudged me and motioned with his eyes to an exterior security camera on the corner of the building. He asked me if I had ever noticed it. I told him I hadn't. He speculated that the camera was newly installed so Brett could keep an eye on his precious car.

Chapter Forty-Seven

A few days later, I was startled by a loud pounding on my door just before breakfast time. Thinking there was an emergency, I jumped up from my kitchen chair, scurried to the door, and opened it.

Abbie looked at me and barked, "Follow me."

I asked her what the hell was going on as she rapidly pushed her walker down the hall with me trailing behind. She said she saw a suspicious-looking man carrying a dark-colored briefcase walking up the sidewalk toward the entrance.

We turned the corner and spotted the man just as he entered the building and went into Brett's office. Irritated, I said, "I can't believe you rousted me out of my apartment for this."

I told her I was going to the dining room for breakfast, and she decided to join me. She gobbled up her breakfast in a few minutes, then said she was going back to see what was happening with Brett and his visitor.

I'd finished eating and was returning to my apartment when I saw Brett talking to Abbie. He was standing in the entrance doorway, appearing to block her from entering the building.

They were talking, but I couldn't hear what was being said. Brett turned, looked at me, said something more, then stepped out of the way. I heard him say, "Have a great day." He gave me a smug look, then went back into his office while Abbie approached.

Her face was beet red, and she seemed to be hyperventilating. "Don't say anything," she whispered. "Just come with me to Jim's apartment." I started to ask her what was going on, but she cut me off. "Shut up! He could be watching."

When we got to Jim's apartment, Abbie pushed her walker aside and plopped down on the couch next to him. Her hands were shaking, and she was still breathing hard, like she had just finished running a footrace.

Growing impatient, I said, "Abbie, what's going on?"

Between her gasps, she said, "I think . . . he . . . knows."

"Who? Knows what?" said Jim.

"Brett . . . I think he knows what I saw."

"What did you see?" I asked.

"Brett's visitor. He arrived with a dark-colored briefcase and left with a light-colored briefcase."

I looked at Jim skeptically, then asked Abbie, "Why were you outside?"

"When the guy left, something seemed odd. So I went outside and watched him walk down the sidewalk to his car. That's when I noticed he had a different briefcase. When I was coming in, Brett blocked my way and said I seemed awfully interested in his friend. He also said I always seem to be close by when he has visitors."

"You have been watching him a lot, Abbie," said Jim.

"Sooner or later, he was bound to notice. So what'd you say?"

"I told him that I'm a muscles-and-buns kind of gal, and he seems to have plenty of friends that fit that description. I apologized for gawking, and he told me I need to be more discreet."

"It sounds to me like he accepted your explanation," I said.

"I don't know, Bud. His eyes told me different." Her voice cracked, and her lip quivered. "I'm afraid . . . I'm afraid he may try and knock me off."

"Now, stop talking like that, Abbie!" said Jim. "Nobody is going to knock you off. Even if the guy had a different briefcase, it doesn't mean anything. You're overthinking this."

"No, I'm not! How come no one believes me?" She started to cry.

"I'm sorry," said Jim. "I believe you. The briefcase switch and Brett's confrontation with you were weird. It's been a couple of weeks since we agreed to keep requesting pills until refills were ordered. Let's check and see if any of the refill pills are missing."

She liked that idea and settled down. Jim took a deep breath, seemingly relieved he'd deescalated the conversation.

Abbie said she was going to lie low for the rest of the day, but she'd ask for a pill after Nurse Jackie and Brett went home in the afternoon. Jim said he'd do the same later in the evening.

Jim asked me what I thought after Abbie left. I told him that her suspicions about Brett seemed to be a stretch and that her theory that he was in cahoots with his partners at the other facilities seemed like something out of a dime novel. I said it was more likely that a nurse with a drug problem was stealing their pills. Jim agreed, but he shared Abbie's concern that if others were involved, the records might be altered to make everything look fine. The police would believe the records over our suspicions. We agreed that the best course of action was for Jim and Abbie to continue requesting pills.

My discussion with Jim reminded me that I had twenty-nine Vicodin the day I moved in and gave all my medication to Nurse Jackie. Since I hadn't taken any Vicodin, I thought it made sense for me to find out if I still had twenty-nine. Jim agreed and suggested I go to the nurses' station early in the morning and say I'd had a rough night of sleep because of the pain in my hip. He said they'd give me a Vicodin and that I should ask then how many I had left in case the pain persisted. I said I'd drop by his apartment after I found out.

Shortly before dinner, Jim and I received a text message from Abbie: *11 left out of 30. I'm not coming to dinner.*

Jim responded: *Okay. I'll be in touch after 8:00.*

I played cribbage with Kathleen and Charlie for a couple hours after dinner. My phone chimed shortly after I returned to my apartment. It was a text from Jim to Abbie and me:

13 left out of 30. Abbie was right about the stealing. Talk to you tomorrow.

Chapter Forty-Eight

As I was leaving my apartment early the next morning to go to the nurse's station, I saw Clayton coming toward me from the direction of the entrance. I knew immediately something was wrong. His eyes were red-rimmed, and his ponytail was partly undone.

"What's goin' on, Clayton?"

"Mom died a couple hours ago."

"Oh no. I'm sorry." I hugged him, and he melted into my arms and cried.

We let go of each other, and he wiped the tears from his eyes. "I knew it was coming, Bud, but it doesn't make it any easier."

"I know. What can we do?"

"Nothing. My mom didn't want a memorial service. She's going to be cremated. I just have to notify the few relatives she has."

"Why are you here now?"

"I came back to get my address book and some paperwork she gave me about being cremated. I'm not sticking around. I need to get back to the hospital."

"I'll let everyone know. Keep in touch."

"Thanks, Bud." We hugged again, then Clayton walked down the hall toward his room.

I changed my mind about going to the nurses' station and went back into my apartment, turned on my laptop, and began searching for the best seats I could find for the Graham Nash concert at the end of the week. It took over an hour, but I eventually found and secured fourth-row middle seats. I paid a lot of money, but I didn't care.

Checking my email, I was surprised to find a friendly response to the email I'd previously sent to the LA session musician. The man wrote that Clayton was one of the most talented musicians he had ever known. He provided me with a few leads for follow-up emails, which I decided I'd attend to after the concert.

When I finally went to the nurses' station, I told the nurse my aching hip had kept me awake half the night. When she gave me a pill, I asked if I should be thinking about a refill. She said that was a good idea because I only had nine pills left.

"Nine pills? You're kidding."

"Is there a problem?"

I realized I should have hidden my surprise. "No. I guess that makes sense when I think about it. Thank you."

I immediately went to Jim's apartment.

"What'd you find out?" he asked.

"There's nine pills left out of twenty-nine."

"And you haven't taken any since you got here?"

"Not one."

"Holy shit! If your pills are being stolen, they must be stealing from everyone with a prescription. We need to call

Abbie." When I didn't respond, Jim shot me a puzzled look. "You're holding back, Bud. What's going on? Is there something more?"

"Yeah. But it's not about the pills. It's about Clayton's mom. She passed away early this morning." I told Jim about running into Clayton and learning the bad news.

"I'm glad he ran into you, Bud. Is there anything we can do?"

"Well, I kinda took matters into my own hands. Since there isn't going to be a memorial service, I thought a nice way to support Clayton and celebrate his mother's life is to go to the Graham Nash concert on Friday. I figured I had to act quickly to secure a block of six good seats, so I got online this morning and bought tickets. I just hope Clayton's okay with it. He's given me mixed signals."

"I know what you mean, but I still think the concert is a helluva idea. What do I owe ya?"

"Keep your money, Jim. Clayton first brought up the Graham Nash concert back in June, and it's been on my mind since then. Buying the tickets was something I've been planning to do. What was that advice Sister Mary Katherine gave you?"

"Go out strong."

"Right. So, Friday will be one of those going-out-strong days for all of us. Let's call Abbie."

Chapter Forty-Nine

After we finished talking to Abbie, I looked for Kathleen and found her in the dining room. Her eyes filled with tears as I told her about running into Clayton earlier in the morning and learning that Marian had died. She stared across the empty room for a moment, dabbing her eyes with a tissue.

"Sorry," she said. "I'm thinking about what Clayton said when we went to see Marian—that she was everything to him. It's sad."

After answering her questions about my conversation with Clayton, I told her about purchasing the concert tickets. She smiled and told me I was a very thoughtful guy. She asked if Clayton knew what I had done. I said that he had no idea and that I bought the tickets online right after I saw him.

"I don't know what the deal is with him and that concert," said Kathleen. "The last couple of times we talked about it, he didn't seem overly enthused about going. Have you noticed?"

"Definitely. I'm sure he was at Woodstock, and he probably met other musicians. I've wondered if he overexaggerated his relationship with Graham Nash and that's why he seems reluctant to go. He's such a BS'er sometimes, you know?"

Kathleen laughed. "Yeah, he tells some whoppers, I'll give you that. It will be interesting to hear what he says when you tell him about the tickets."

I brought her up to date on the missing pills, Abbie's confrontation with Brett, and the plan to hold off calling the police. She looked concerned and listened intently.

When I finished, she asked, "Do you really think Brett would do that? Rip off the residents?"

I told her I believed pills were being stolen, but I wasn't buying Abbie's theory that Brett was at the center of it, or that there was some sort of criminal enterprise involving the whole Serenity organization.

She smiled and shook her head. "Wow! There sure has been a lot going on around here since June."

"I know. It's wearing me out. Too much action."

I expected another smile, but she seemed preoccupied. "Bud, I . . ." She cleared her throat. "You're a good guy. We're lucky you landed at Serenity."

I wanted to tell her I felt blessed to have met her, but I chickened out. "Being here is a slight improvement over sitting home alone and watching the grass grow. Now I can watch the grass and have a social life."

Kathleen laughed. "A man with everything."

I didn't feel good about sidestepping her compliment, and I wanted to say more. "It's funny how it all worked out. I didn't want to come here. My daughter pressured me into it."

"There's nothing worse than a daughter on a mission. I know how that goes."

209

"For sure. Kathleen, I didn't really know how lonely I was until I got here and began living again." She looked at me expectantly. "I . . . I feel blessed for the friendships I've made here . . . especially—"

"Can you believe that no-good son of a bitch is stealing our medication?" said Abbie loudly as she approached us. "I'd like to punch him in the throat."

Kathleen smiled at me. "You can always tell what's on Abbie's mind."

Chapter Fifty

On the morning of the concert, I printed the concert tickets, then studied my notes about Clayton and his connection to the sixties LA music scene. Just as I was about to follow up on a recent lead, there was a knock at the door.

"Door's open!" I called out.

Clayton walked in. He looked rested, and the color was back in his face. I closed the notebook and stood. "Clayton! I'm so sorry about your mom. How are you holding out, my friend?"

"I'm doing okay. My mom and I had some quality time together before she passed, and I'm grateful for that. I'm at peace. We had a good life together."

"I'm glad you had that time together. If you're at peace, then your mom is at peace too."

He reached in his pocket, pulled out a pack of gum, and offered me a stick. I declined. He unwrapped the gum, plunked it in his mouth, and began chewing. "Well, I'm not totally at peace." He seemed to be looking for a wastepaper basket.

I held out my hand, and he gave me the gum wrappers. "How so?"

"I'm at peace with my mom's death, but I'm not at peace with Brett. In fact, I'm really pissed off at him."

"Why?"

"Remember when we got back from Woodstock and Brett met us at the door?"

"How could I forget?"

"He knew my mom was in the hospital and didn't say anything. After we got back, I found out that someone from the nursing home called a couple of times looking for me and explained to Brett that Mom was really sick."

"Maybe there's more to the story," I said.

"Oh, I thought about that. So, after the drug court graduation, I went to the nursing home and talked to the nurse. She told me she spoke to Brett and told him that Mom's condition was very serious and she urgently needed to speak to me. That son of a bitch let us walk right by without saying anything. Plus, all of our cell phone numbers are on file, and he never called me or anyone else. He deliberately avoided telling me."

"That's terrible."

"Mom needed me those first twenty-four hours in the hospital, and I wasn't there, thanks to Brett. Thankfully, she didn't die while I was at Woodstock, or I would be thinking about murder. Mom and I had time together, and that was good. But Brett still deserves some payback for what he did."

"What do you have in mind?"

Clayton looked around suspiciously and whispered, "I hired a guy down in Detroit. His name is Guido. He's a hit man for the Mafia, and, believe it or not, he's Gordy Accordee's cousin. Remember Gordy? The accordion guy at Jim's birthday party? Small world, huh? Anyway, Guido heard about Brett firing Gordy and how we stroked Gordy with a little cash before he went out the door. Because of our generosity, Guido will shatter Brett's kneecaps with a baseball bat for free. Isn't that awesome?"

"Clayton, don't do that. You could end up in prison."

"Really?" He smiled. "Bud, you're so damn gullible! No one's going to hurt that turd. But I'm definitely going to do something. I'm just gonna take my time and come up with a plan."

"Let me know when you get it figured out. I may help you if we won't get arrested."

"You got it. Mind if I sit?"

Clayton sat on the couch, and I returned to my place at the table. "Want some coffee?"

"No. I'm good. Bud, Jim called me yesterday and told me you bought Graham Nash tickets. That was really thoughtful and generous."

"I thought it would be a nice way to end a difficult week."

He hesitated. "Thanks for doing that."

"Clayton, are you sure you want to go? Maybe it's too soon with your mom and all. I should have asked you first."

"No, no. I'd love to go. It'll be a good concert. It's just . . ."

"What?"

Clayton looked at me with a pained expression. "This is a little weird for me to talk about, Bud. I knew Graham Nash and the rest of the guys in the band, and so many others when they were starting out. They became superstars. I was a one-hit wonder who zoomed into obscurity. I think I had as much as or more talent than many of the musicians who made it big, but I got left behind. So it's kind of uncomfortable for me to go to a concert like this. It reminds me I fell short. Does that make sense?"

"Fell short? Are you kidding? You made a huge, significant contribution to sixties music. 'Up Yours' is played all over the world. People love that tune after fifty years, and it spans three generations. Grandpa and Grandma heard 'Up Yours' when it first came out in the late sixties, and now they're taking their grandchildren to stadiums where it's still played. That's an amazing accomplishment!"

"But I didn't have any staying power. Guys like Nash are still performing while I'm stuck in this place."

"You ever hear of Margaret Mitchell?" I asked.

"No."

"She wrote one novel. *Gone with the Wind.* It's a classic. She was one and done, but she's still recognized as a famous author."

Clayton smirked. "So, you're saying I'm the Margaret Mitchell of rock 'n' roll?"

"Sort of. My God, Clayton. Of all the music that's ever been created, there's probably ten tunes that are regularly played in stadiums, and yours is one of them. That's an incredible accomplishment! And beyond that, there's something far more important."

"What?"

"You said a few minutes ago that you and your mom had a good life together. Do you think you would have had that life if you had been on the road for months at a time, chasing fame and fortune? Maybe the cards you were dealt were to be a good son to your greatest fan until the end of her days. You did that, and you should feel good about it."

"But what about chicks?"

"What?" I asked.

"All the babes I could have had."

"Seriously?"

Clayton smiled. "No, Bud. Relax. I'm just kidding."

"So, we'll go to this concert tonight and have a good time, right?"

"Right."

"And you won't be thinking about what might have been?"

"Maybe a little, but not too much."

Chapter Fifty-One

As recommended by the concert website, I arranged for assistance with seating. We checked in at the will-call office, and a young attendant led us to our seats. Clayton and I helped Jim out of his wheelchair, and he followed Clayton down the fourth row to our assigned seats. Abbie gave her walker to the attendant and followed Charlie. Kathleen went next, and I sat next to her.

"I'm so excited!" said Kathleen. "I've never been to a concert like this. And so close to the stage . . . it's unbelievable!"

I looked down the row at the men and saw them laughing, talking, and pointing at the stage. Kathleen and Abbie were animated and giddy. This was going to be a good night.

There was an impressive amount of equipment on the stage. Two roadies scampered about, checking the microphones and amplifiers, while another checked the guitars to confirm they were in tune. I looked at the center microphone, where Graham Nash was sure to be. We were definitely close enough to see him. Would Nash be close enough to see us with all the stage lighting?

As the seats filled up with enthusiastic concertgoers, we talked about our lives in the late sixties, when Kathleen was a young mother living in Livonia, Abbie was single and working at the Ford River Rouge complex in Dearborn, and I was a student at U of M, protesting the war. Considering our different backgrounds and life experiences, I thought how weird it was that fate, luck, or maybe even divine intervention brought us together and how our friendship seemed to have given us all a second wind—a final burst of spirit to get across the finish line.

I looked around and noticed that all the seats were occupied and the audience seemed to be growing restless with anticipation. The lights were adjusted, and the audience grew quiet. A man dressed in jeans and a casual shirt walked to the center microphone and said, "Ladies and gentlemen, the Royal Oak Music Theatre is proud to introduce two-time Rock & Roll Hall of Famer and music icon Graham Nash."

We clapped and cheered with the rest of the audience as six men and two women walked onto the stage. Nash was recognizable from his black outfit and full head of silver hair. As his bandmates settled into their positions, Nash picked up his acoustic guitar, sauntered over to the center microphone, and said, "Good evening, everybody. We've got a bunch of songs for you." The audience cheered, and Nash and his band began to play.

For the next hour, he treated us to a variety of songs that spanned his long career. Between songs, he talked about his early influences and his work with the Hollies and Crosby, Stills, Nash and Young. His stories and quips were interesting and entertaining, and we were thrilled when he played songs we recognized from long ago. There was a moment when I thought Nash seemed to look at us and smile, but I thought nothing of it.

We stayed put at intermission while many of those around us stood and stretched or left to use the restrooms. I looked in Clayton's direction and saw a man at the end of the aisle trying to get his attention. Clayton was turned in his seat, talking to Jim and Charlie, and had his back turned toward the man. I cupped my hands over my mouth and yelled, "Clayton."

He looked, and I pointed at the man. Clayton turned, the man said something, and Clayton put his index finger on his chest, as if to say, "Me?"

The man nodded.

Chapter Fifty-Two

C layton looked back at us, shrugged, and made his way toward the man, requiring people in the row to stand up. The man and Clayton shook hands. They talked for a few minutes, then Clayton followed him toward the front of the stage and through a side door.

Jim looked down the row at me in wide-eyed astonishment and mouthed the words *What the fuck?*

Equally surprised, I cupped my hands and yelled, "I have no idea!"

"You don't suppose—?" said Abbie.

"That he really knows him!" said Kathleen.

"If he really knows him, I'll take everything back I said about Clayton being a bullshitter," said Abbie.

I wondered if one of the musicians knew Clayton and had invited him backstage. Abbie floated the theory that Clayton had set it up. A man behind us said his sister once was called out of a concert for a family emergency.

Lights were lowered, and people took their seats. The drummer walked out, sat, and began pounding out a familiar beat.

Boom ba boom ba boom ba boom!
Boom ba boom ba boom ba boom!
Boom ba boom ba boom ba boom!

Nash appeared on the stage. The audience cheered, the beat continued, and Nash clapped in time to the beat. "You know that beat?" he yelled in the microphone. "What's that beat?"

We yelled, "'Up Yours'!"

"Right on! What's that beat again?"

More people yelled, "'Up Yours'!"

Boom ba boom ba boom ba boom!

"Come on, Detroit, you can do better than that. What's that beat again?"

The audience screamed, "'Up Yours'!"

Nash laughed and nodded at the drummer. He stopped, and the audience became quiet. "I can play a whole song, and some people have no clue what they heard. My friend writes a song, and you can identify it before the first guitar lick." He laughed. "Something's wrong with that."

He continued. "I've had a wonderful surprise tonight. I was visited by an old friend I have not seen for over forty years. One of the most talented musicians I have ever known, he helped Crosby, Stills, Nash and Young immensely when we first started out. The guy can play anything and, by all rights, should be in the Rock & Roll Hall of Fame. Ladies and gentlemen, I'm proud to introduce you to my good friend, and the father of 'Up Yours,' Clayton T. Davis."

Clayton looked dumbfounded as he walked out on the stage. The audience erupted with applause. Nash paced back and forth across the front of the stage, encouraging everyone to stand. We stood, overjoyed that our friend was being honored this way. Jim and Charlie were high-fiving each other. Kathleen had her fingers in her mouth and was whistling so loud it hurt my ears. Abbie stood, looking dumbfounded, and kept repeating, "I don't believe this shit."

The applause continued, and Clayton looked like he was on the verge of tears. Nash said into the microphone, "This is the standing O you never received but richly deserve."

The audience responded, and the applause grew louder. Clayton stood at the microphone, seeming flabbergasted and enthralled by what was happening. At one point, he pointed at us and grinned, causing us to hoot, holler, and wave.

When the applause tapered off, Nash said, "Anything you'd like to say, Clayton?"

Clearly choked up, Clayton struggled to regain his composure. He cleared his throat and said, "I remember talking to Graham at Woodstock fifty years ago, after he arrived in a helicopter." He paused and smiled for effect. "And that's all I remember about Woodstock."

The audience roared, and Nash laughed and hugged Clayton. "This guy has the best sense of humor, and he's one helluva prankster. Tell them what you did to Crosby."

"Really? You want me to tell them that?"

"I do." When Clayton hesitated, Nash began chanting and fist-pumping, "Tell us, tell us, tell us," and the audience joined in.

"Okay, okay, okay," said Clayton, and the chanting subsided. "Crosby told me he hated snakes, so I bought a big rubber one. I put it in his kitchen cupboard and hooked it up with fishing line so when he opened the cupboard, the snake would rise up."

Giggling, Nash eagerly said, "Tell them what happened."

"Crosby opened the cupboard, saw the snake, screamed, and slammed the cupboard shut."

The audience laughed and clapped.

Like a parent trying to extract information from a naughty child, Nash said, "Tell them what happened next, Clayton."

"Well, the prank got a little out of hand." He turned to Nash. "You really want me to tell them the rest?"

"I do." Again, Nash encouraged the audience to join him in chanting, "Tell us, tell us, tell us."

"Okay." The chanting stopped. "Crosby ran into his bedroom, got his shotgun, and shot the cupboard three times."

The audience roared again.

Nash was laughing hysterically. He slapped Clayton on the back and said, "God, I've missed you. How about joining us on a few songs toward the end?"

Clayton, who was obviously taken aback by the request, said, "Well, I . . ."

Nash didn't wait for his answer. He yelled in the microphone, "Who wants Clayton to join us a little later on?"

The audience cheered loudly, Nash and Clayton shook hands, and a roadie guided Clayton off the stage.

Over the next hour, Nash and his band cranked out more songs and told more stories about people and things that had inspired the songs. Nash's voice was strong and clear, and the supporting music was perfect in every way. Some of the songs were well-known, and Nash encouraged the audience to sing along. I smiled as I watched my friends moving in time to the music.

Nash ended the set with "Just a Song Before I Go,"

which he wrote in a few minutes in the early seventies after a friend challenged him to write a song before they departed for an airport, where he was to catch a flight home. When the song ended, he and his bandmates went to the front of the stage, waved goodbye, and walked off the stage while the crowd screamed and clapped for more.

"What happened to Clayton?" asked Abbie.

"Yeah, I thought he was going to play," yelled Charlie.

"I think he'll be out for the encore," I answered.

After a couple of minutes, the band reappeared on the stage. Clayton, who was now wearing sunglasses, sat at the piano. I could see the pianist watching from the shadows just offstage.

"Do you want a little warm-up, Clayton?" Nash asked.

"Sure." His fingers raced up and down the keyboard as he played a quick compilation of boogie-woogie, ragtime, and rock 'n' roll. When he stopped, the audience cheered and clapped.

"Now, that's what I'm talkin' about!" said Nash. "Ready, Clayton?"

Clayton nodded and began playing "Our House," with Nash singing the lyrics. I sensed Kathleen was looking at me; I turned and our eyes met. She smiled. I was tempted to reach for her hand but didn't, unsure how she would react. I smiled back.

When they finished, Nash waved Clayton to the front of the stage while the audience applauded. Clayton got up from the piano and joined Nash. One of the band members handed him an acoustic guitar. Nash picked up his acoustic guitar, and they began playing "Teach Your Children Well." Nash and his bandmates handled the vocals while Clayton stood to Nash's left, strumming along and smiling as if he had played the song hundreds of times.

At the end of the song, Nash said, "So I'll be leaving you with an important piece of advice." He smiled. "Love the one you're with."

He looked at Clayton, who was beaming, and nodded. Then they began playing "Love the One You're With." The rest of the band joined in as the song progressed. I thought the title was spot on and wondered if Kathleen was thinking the same. After Nash sang, "And if you can't be with the one you love, honey," he cupped his hand to his ear. I joined the audience in responding, "Love the one you're with."

Nash and Clayton put down their guitars, and the rest of the band joined them at the front of the stage. Nash put his arm around Clayton's shoulders and said, "Thanks, everybody! We had a great time tonight!"

Some of the band members threw guitar picks into the audience; others slapped the hands of people close to the stage. Nash started off the stage. Then he stopped, blew kisses to the audience, and walked off with Clayton following.

Chapter Fifty-Three

We stayed in our seats, waiting for Clayton. The roadies came onto the stage and began disassembling and packing the equipment. Only a few concertgoers remained.

Kathleen smiled at me. "Thank you so much! This was an amazing evening. I can't wait to tell my girls about it."

"You're welcome. I knew it was a stretch, but I was secretly hoping somehow Graham and Clayton would see each other and talk. I never expected to see our friend up there on stage performing. It turned out perfectly."

"Why was he so reluctant to come in the first place?" Abbie asked. "I figured he was bullshitting and didn't want to look foolish if Nash didn't recognize him or refused to talk to him."

I shrugged. "He told me that being around some of his famous friends reminds him that he never made it to the top."

"That's ridiculous. The guy's song is played all over the world."

"We talked about that. But after tonight, I think he'll look at things differently."

"He should! The guy's a star! Even Graham Nash said he should be in the Rock & Roll Hall of Fame." Abbie paused and looked at the roadies working on the stage, then turned back to Kathleen and me. "I guess I need to apologize. He may be a bullshitter about a lot of things, but he was straight with us about Woodstock and knowing famous people. I'm going to tell him to write a book."

Charlie leaned forward and looked at me. "Why are we waiting?"

"Because Clayton drove, and he has the keys."

"Oh, that's right."

"Hey, Bud," Jim called from down the aisle. He gave me a thumbs-up and said, "Thanks, man. Great time."

The man who first contacted Clayton appeared and talked to Jim. Jim pointed at me, and the man walked down the empty row in front of us until he was in front of me.

"Are you Bud Livingston?"

"I am."

The man reached in his pants pocket and pulled out a set of keys. "Here are Mr. Davis's keys. He instructed me to tell you to take the Mothership home, and he'll return with an Uber."

"That sounds good. Thank you." The man did not leave, so I asked, "Was there something else?"

"Mr. Livingston . . . um . . . Mr. Davis would not let me come out here until I promised to give you something. And Mr. Nash insisted."

"What?"

The man walked out of the row of seats in front of me and came down the row where we sat.

"Okay, what are you supposed to give me?" I asked.

"Mr. Livingston, I apologize, but I think it would be better if you stood."

I stood.

"I'm sorry, this is a little awkward. I'm just following instructions," said the man as he gave me a firm hug.

Chapter Fifty-Four

The next morning, I poured a cup of coffee and surveyed the dining room. Charlie and his sons were sitting at a nearby table, engaged in lively conversation. Abbie and Mark were quietly talking at a table in the corner. Charlie saw me and waved me over. Soon, we were joined by Kathleen and Jim.

We talked excitedly about the concert and Clayton's reunion with Nash. Dean and Tony said they briefly talked to Clayton when they arrived a half hour earlier. They said he looked tired and hungover—and that he mumbled something about being "too old for this shit."

When the klatch ended, I told my friends I was going to skip lunch and spend the rest of the day napping and relaxing. I returned to my apartment, lay on my bed, and was asleep in minutes. I slept soundly until I was awakened by a soft knock at the door.

I got up, opened the door, and was surprised to see Kathleen holding a cribbage board and something wrapped up in a napkin. She looked lovely. Her emerald-green sweater complemented her dark eyes. I didn't remember her wearing the sweater or leggings at coffee. *Did she get dressed up to see me?* I dismissed that thought, figuring that she had probably worn the same outfit that morning and I hadn't noticed. I'd never been particularly observant when it came to women's clothing.

She smiled, and it looked like a part of her front tooth was missing. "I thought you might be hungry, so I brought you a sandwich." She handed me the sandwich, and I invited her in.

I was embarrassed by the clutter in my little living room and apologized as I hastily picked up newspapers and some of the stuff I'd printed about Clayton. She watched with an amused look on her face, and I hoped she didn't think I was a slob.

We sat, and as she smiled a lot and talked animatedly about her morning activities, I saw her tooth wasn't missing or broken—there was a chunk of something black stuck to it. I wanted to mention it, but she was always so poised and attentive to her appearance. I knew she'd be mortified if I mentioned it. I tried to ignore it by looking her in the eyes as she spoke, but, apparently, my gaze kept shifting from her eyes to her mouth. After a few moments, she said sternly, "Why are you looking at me like that?"

"Ah . . . you've gotta . . ."

She began giggling. "What?" She smiled broadly, fully exposing the black thing. Her giggles turned into a roar of laughter. "It's a raisin, Bud! I stuck it there just before I knocked."

Watching her was funnier than the prank, as she carried on, clapping her hands and bouncing up and down on the couch like an excited kid. When she regained her composure, she tore off a piece of the napkin that was around my sandwich and wiped her tooth. She smiled broadly again and asked, "Did I get it?"

"You did." I laughed. "At first, I thought you'd lost a tooth. When I realized you had something stuck there, I didn't know what to do."

"The look on your face was priceless! I can't believe you didn't say anything. Were you just gonna ignore it?"

"Of course not! I was about to suggest we have some tea and floss our teeth. It's my standard line when I have company."

She laughed and challenged me to a game of cribbage after I ate the sandwich, and I eagerly accepted. As we played, we talked about our past and present lives, and I was surprised by how comfortable I felt being alone with her. I won the game, and Kathleen challenged me to a second. Our conversation continued as we moved our pegs up and down the board. She accused me of trash-talking as I gloated over the good cards I was getting, and she playfully reminded me of that when she came from behind to win.

Finally, she glanced at the clock on her smartphone and said, "Oh my God! I've got to run. My grandson is coming over soon."

We stood, and, for a brief moment, we were close, facing each other. I felt like a teenager on a first date. I wanted to kiss her but just couldn't bring myself to do it. A handshake seemed ridiculous. Thankfully, she solved the dilemma by giving me a firm and sustained hug and a gentle kiss on the cheek. She released me and said, "Thanks for playing cribbage with me."

"I've enjoyed the afternoon. Thanks for coming by." I opened the apartment door and said, "I'll see you at dinner. Have fun with your grandson."

"One of these days, I'll have to introduce you," said Kathleen as she departed.

"I'll look forward to that."

I gently closed the door, leaned back against it, and said, "Wow."

Chapter Fifty-Five

A few minutes later, Clayton sauntered in, eating from a bag of potato chips. He plopped onto the couch and said with a devilish grin, "Kathleen said at lunch she was planning to see you, and I just saw her leave your apartment. So are you guys . . ."

"Clayton! We're just friends."

"I'm calling bullshit on the 'just friends' part, Bud. Doing his best Forrest Gump imitation, he said, "You and Miss Kathleen are like 'peas and carrots.'" He leaned back on the couch, casually ate another chip, and folded his arms. "You think she's attractive, right?"

"Definitely."

"And she's got a great personality?"

"For sure."

"Then what the hell are you waiting for, brother? You guys seem perfect together."

"What are you suggesting I do? Borrow the Mothership and take her to a movie?"

"The Mothership would work." Clayton leaned forward and whispered, "There's a drive-in movie theater about forty miles south of here, and the back seats in the van fold down."

"Knock it off, Clayton. I'm serious. I'm seventy-three years old. It's a little late in the game, don't you think? And frankly, I'm a little gun-shy after all I went through with Sharon."

"Listen to yourself, Bud. You're boxing yourself in." Clayton poured the crumbs from the bag into his mouth. In a whining voice as he chewed, he said, "I'm too old for romance and excitement. I prefer playing bingo and talking about bowel movements." He rolled up the empty potato chip bag, threw it at the garbage can, and missed. He shrugged, brushed the crumbs off his hands and lap, and, with a heavy sigh, said, "Look, Bud. Remember what my mom said about Kathleen. She's a keeper. Don't let her slip away. Remember?"

"Yeah."

"Well, that was damn good advice. I told you about Candace, my keeper, and there isn't a day that goes by when I don't regret letting her slip away. You only get one shot at this, brother. There are no do-overs."

"I know, but . . ."

"But what?"

"I don't know. I've got scars from things with Sharon and the kids. I'm just nervous about getting close to another woman."

"The Sharon-and-the-kids ship sailed, dude. You turned the page when you landed here. Bud, we see you for who you are. A good man." He smiled and added, "And longtime Gene Simmons fan. It's okay if your family didn't like your obsession with a bass guitarist who paints his face and sticks his tongue out. But if they were too fucked up to see the good person you are, then that's their problem. Fuck 'em.

You need to offload that shit and deal with the here and now. It's clear to all of us that Kathleen has a thing for you. Embrace it, man! You won the lottery! I'd give anything to be in your shoes and have someone who could fill the hollow spot I've been carrying around all these years."

"I just don't want things to get weird."

"What do you mean?"

"Clayton, I value what I have here and don't want to mess it up. If things don't work out with Kathleen, it will throw a wrench into our group friendship. I'd hate for that to happen."

"You're a half-empty guy, my friend. You gotta change that attitude. Things don't always go down the swill hole. Life is a big adventure, man. Climb aboard and live it! If you and Kathleen end up hating each other, I'll still talk to you, but I'm not sure about the others."

"That's comforting," I said.

"You know I'm kidding. Getting to know her better may be the best decision you've ever made. You two deserve each other. Let go of the cautiousness and hesitation. That's how old people think, and we're not there yet."

"I suppose you're right."

"Hell yes, I'm right. Just promise me one thing."

"What's that?" I asked.

"I'll be the best man."

"Get the hell out of here."

Chapter Fifty-Six

Jim had just finished telling me about his upcoming appointment at the VA when we learned that Clayton was in bed with flu-like symptoms. Jim asked me if I'd be willing to drive him to the VA in a couple of days if Clayton wasn't feeling better. I said I'd be happy to take the Mothership on a road trip.

On the day of Jim's appointment, an aide reported that Clayton was on the mend but still a bit lethargic. Jim sent Clayton a text message asking if we could borrow the Mothership, and a short time later, the aide presented him with the keys.

We decided to leave early. One of the nurses told us we were likely to run into traffic delays caused by road construction. Jim gave me the keys and insisted on riding shotgun, so I helped him get out of the wheelchair and into the front passenger seat.

When we were underway, Jim said, "You're probably surprised to learn that I'm not the healthiest guy on the planet."

I smiled. "Gosh, I never would have known."

"They check my blood and run a few tests every three to four months. That's usually it. But today, I want the docs to look at my right leg. It's really sore and has been bothering me since the concert."

"Is it bruised?"

"No, but Brenda checked it this morning and said it looked swollen."

"I'm glad you're gonna get it checked."

As we turned onto the highway, Jim continued, "Yeah, I know. Every time I have a checkup, I expect them to tell me I've got something that's gonna kill me."

"Why would you say that? Because of Agent Orange?"

"Right. The VA says it's linked to fourteen diseases, and some of them are fatal. My messed-up legs, heart disease, skin cancers, and prostate cancer are all related to Agent Orange, so I figure it's only a matter of time before one of the biggies gets me."

"Don't say that. If you were going to have one of the biggies, it probably would have shown up by now."

"I hope you're right." For a few moments, Jim stared out the passenger-side window, then said, "Whatever happens . . . I'm at peace with it."

"That's good," I said.

He laughed. "I'm a slow learner. It only took fifty-plus years to get there."

"How'd you get there, Jim?"

"It wasn't easy. As I told you after my birthday party, the war really fucked me up. War is glorified in movies, but killing and seeing people being killed scars you for life."

"I'm sure it does."

"The war we fought wasn't popular, but we were doing our damnedest . . . and then to come back from that hell and have people treat us like the enemy was hard to take.

So many people died for nothing, and nobody seemed to care."

I began to wonder if I'd really understood the war before getting caught up in the protests. It occurred to me that I never thought about soldiers like Jim, who were honorably serving the country and sacrificing so much while I was living comfortably and attending anti-war gatherings. Why weren't the soldiers on my mind at the time? Why didn't I think about their suffering? Why didn't I honor them when they returned home? I'd pushed aside the guilt I felt for many years, but getting to know Jim brought those feelings to the surface with an intensity that shook me.

After a few moments, Jim said, "The mental stuff was bad enough, but learning that my cancers and physical problems were caused by Agent Orange really sent me. I felt like the army and the country stole my life from me and that no one gave a shit."

I didn't know what to say.

"I was a bitter and angry son of a bitch for a long time. At one point, I tried to end it all. Do you want to know what happened?"

"Only if you're okay talking about it."

"Bud, I couldn't handle the pain any longer, so I began considering ways to do it. Using a weapon seemed too violent, hanging seemed too Wild West, and I couldn't be sure taking a bunch of pills would do the job. I decided to do the sure thing."

"What?"

"It was 1979. I went to the mall and bought what I needed. I got home, closed the blinds, popped a beer, and wrote a note. That took a long time. There's a lot to think about when you're ready to check out."

"I suppose there is."

"Anyway, after I finished the note, I sat there for hours, trying to get my courage up. What lay ahead was going to be very unpleasant. I pounded another beer, took a deep breath, and picked up the bag containing the little gift I'd bought for myself. I remember my hands shaking as I slid it out of the bag. I stared at it for a while, then said, 'Fuck it,' and put it on the turntable."

Chapter Fifty-Seven

"Turntable? I'm not following."

"This is really hard to say, Bud." I glanced at Jim, who was looking out the passenger window. "I tried to commit . . ." I waited, thinking he was overcome with emotion. He cleared his throat. "Bud, I tried to commit . . . Bee Geeicide."

"Bee Geeicide? What are you talking about?"

Jim erupted in laughter. "Your wife was a doctor! I can't believe you don't know about Bee Geeicide! It's when a rock 'n' roll purist intentionally listens to disco for the purpose of making his head explode. It's an incredibly painful way to go, Bud."

"Good grief. You've been around Clayton too long!"

After a couple minutes of sporadic giggling, Jim composed himself and said, "Bud, the scars on my wrists remind me of the lowest point in my life and how far I have come since that day. I'm just glad I wasn't successful."

"Me too, Jim. Very glad."

"Even after years of counseling and therapy, I was still a complete mess when I arrived at Serenity two years ago. I

239

had all that crap weighing on me—bitterness about the war, my health problems, and feeling like I was abandoned by my country and God. I couldn't see the good in anyone or anything. I planned to sit in my room and wait around to die. I hoped I wouldn't have to wait too long."

"It's hard for me to picture you like that, Jim. What changed?"

"Sister Mary Katherine saved my ass. When I arrived at Serenity, I didn't want to talk to anyone. I ate alone, and I came back to my apartment and stayed there. One day, she came to my door. She wanted to talk. I didn't, but she was incredibly persistent and came by every day. Gradually, we began having two-way conversations, and those grew into long talks about life and living. She was really smart and such a good listener. After a while, she'd heard my whole story. She didn't push religion, but I could feel her love and spirituality. She opened my eyes, Bud."

"I wish I could have met her. Everyone speaks so highly of her."

"You and Sister Mary Katherine have a lot in common."

"Like what?"

"Good with people, compassionate hearts, and a strange fascination with Gene Simmons."

"Very funny."

Jim chuckled. "Sister Mary Katherine made me realize I had a choice to make. I could wallow in bitterness and self-pity or go out strong by making the best of the time I have. She used to say that the essence of life is loving and being loved. That's what I try to live by. Goin' out strong seemed a lot more fun anyway. She introduced me to Clayton and the others, and I began to realize that living could be fun. If my number came up tomorrow, I'd be goin' out strong. It's all good, Bud. I'm the happiest I have been in over fifty years,

and I feel like I've been a part of something very special—
like a family or . . ." Jim smiled. "A gang."

"Gang is right. The Serenity Gang."

"And you're an important member of the gang, Bud.
Don't know where we'd be without you."

"Thanks, Jim. I'm glad to be part of the gang. I'm also
the happiest I've been in a very long time."

The traffic slowed to a crawl as I navigated the Mothership through a construction zone, where heavy equipment
was moving around and flagmen were directing traffic.
Thinking about Jim's life made me profoundly sad. He was
right. The life he could have had was stolen from him.

"Jim, until I met you, I'd never had a friend who served
in Vietnam."

He smiled. "Lucky you."

"I've had a lot of time to think about the Vietnam
years . . ." I shook my head in disgust. "I'm ashamed that I
was living well and protesting the war on the streets of Ann
Arbor while you were fighting to stay alive."

"You were just a kid, Bud. We all did things when we
were young and stupid that we might later regret."

"You're right. I was an idealistic kid who thought he had
all the answers. But I didn't know shit. I was caught up in a
movement that blinded me to your patriotism and suffering.
When the country called, you responded. When the
country called many of my friends, they fled to Canada.
What you did was noble and much harder. I respect you for
answering the call."

The traffic had come to a standstill. I looked at him and
said, "I know I'm over fifty years late in saying this, Jim, but
thank you for all of your sacrifices, and . . ." My long-
suppressed guilt nearly overwhelmed me, but I was determined to finish what I'd started. I swallowed and wiped a

tear from the corner of my eye. "I'm really sorry for all of the things you and so many others went through." I paused, looked ahead, then looked back at Jim. "I'm honored you are my friend."

"Bud, that's the nicest thing anyone has ever said to me." He reached over and patted me on my shoulder. "Thank you, brother."

Chapter Fifty-Eight

I pushed Jim into the John D. Dingell VA Medical Center in Detroit, and we made our way to the internal medicine department. After checking in, we waited several minutes in a small lobby until a nurse came out a side door, confirmed Jim's identity, and pushed him into the office interior. He returned almost three hours later.

"I thought you escaped," I said. "What's going on?"

Jim sighed and shook his head in disgust. "They want to admit me overnight for observation. The doc sent me down to imaging because he suspected a blood clot. Turns out he was right. They gave me a shot of something and told me to go to admitting. This is the shits."

We found the admitting office, where Jim met with a cranky woman who had him fill out a number of forms and sign paperwork. When their business was done, she looked at me and said, "Can you take him to the nurses' station on the fifth floor? They'll show you his room."

We left admitting, found an elevator, and made our way to the fifth-floor nurses' station as directed. The nursing supervisor, who introduced herself as Lindsey, led us to

Room 514 and asked me to step into the hall while she helped Jim remove his clothes and put on a gown. In a few minutes, she came out of the room and told me I could go in.

He was dressed in a gown and lying on his back on the bed. A compression stocking was on his right leg, which was elevated with two pillows. I sat in a chair next to the bed, and we made small talk until his dinner tray arrived.

I checked the time on my cell phone.

"You thinking about heading out?" asked Jim.

I stood. "Yeah, now that you're all settled in, I think I'll get out of your hair and let you eat in peace. I'll be back here tomorrow morning by eight. Maybe Clayton will come along if he's feeling better. Need anything?"

"I'm good. I should be out by tomorrow, and I'm sure Lindsey can fix me up with some toiletries to get me through the night."

"Okay." I patted Jim on the shoulder. "Good night, my friend."

He extended his right hand, and we shook. "Bud, what you said today . . . it meant a lot. Thanks."

Chapter Fifty-Nine

I sent a text message to Clayton before I left the medical center parking lot to update him on Jim's hospital admission. I asked him if I could use the Mothership in the morning to return. He responded that he was feeling better and would like to go along. We agreed to meet in the lobby in the morning. He said he'd let the others know Jim was spending the night in the hospital.

The next morning, Clayton and I arrived at the medical center and took the elevator to the fifth floor. We walked past the nurses' station and down the hall to Room 514. The door was open, and the light was on. A woman from housekeeping was mopping the floor. I asked her where Jim was, and she said to check at the nurses' station.

I looked at Clayton and shrugged, then we walked back down to the nurses' station. A nurse was sitting there, staring into a computer monitor.

"Excuse me," I said. The nurse looked up. "We're looking for our friend, Jim Rogers, who was in Room 514. Where is he?"

"You'll have to excuse me for a moment." The nurse

245

stood and walked down the hall to an office. She briefly looked back at Clayton and me, knocked twice on the closed door, then entered. After a couple of minutes, she emerged with another nurse, and the two walked toward us. The nurse who had been at the nurses' station returned to her chair and resumed her computer work.

"Hi, I'm Lindsey," said the nurse who had come out of the office. She looked at me and said, "You were with Mr. Rogers yesterday, right?"

"Right. I'm Bud Livingston, and this is Clayton Davis. Jim's a good friend of ours."

"I see. Would you gentlemen mind stepping into my office?"

Lindsey's sober manner made me uncomfortable. We followed her into the office, and she motioned for us to sit in the chairs in front of her desk. We sat, then she walked around the end of her desk and sat in a padded office chair across from us.

"Do you know Sister Mary Katherine Medoza?" She opened a manila file and looked at some papers. "Mr. Rogers listed her as his emergency contact. We've been trying to reach her since early this morning."

"She died a few months ago," said Clayton.

"I see," said Lindsey sadly.

"What's going on?" I asked.

She shifted in her chair. "I'm sorry. There's no easy way to say this, so I'll just say it. Mr. Rogers died early this morning. I wasn't here at the time, but I understand the emergency team did everything they could. I'm so sorry."

I looked at Clayton, who was holding his hands over his face. He quickly stood, said, "I have to get out of here," and walked out.

Stunned, I struggled to respond. "I was just with him. He seemed fine. What happened?"

"Apparently, it was a pulmonary embolism."

"What's that?"

"The blood clot in his leg broke loose, went into his lung, and restricted his blood flow."

"But they gave him a shot! I thought it was supposed to make the clot go away."

"That's true. I can only speculate that the clot was big. The heparin didn't have time to work. Mr. Rogers also had a weakened heart, and that may have contributed to things. I'm truly sorry."

I tried to process everything that had happened. Twelve hours earlier, Jim was in good spirits. And now he was gone. The guilt was nearly overwhelming. I should have stayed longer and not been so quick to get back to Serenity. I might have been able to detect a problem. Or Jim might have told me he was in pain, and I could have reported that to the nurse. The thought of Jim dying alone without friends or family at his side made me feel nauseous.

"I should have been here. I'm so sorry, Jim," I said to myself before I covered my face with my hands and began to cry.

"Mr. Livingston . . . Mr. Livingston."

I wiped the tears from my eyes and looked at Lindsey, whose eyes were also watery. "Is there anything I can do for you or Mr. Davis? Would you like to talk to the hospital chaplain?"

I pulled a tissue from the box on her desk and blew my nose. "No thanks. Where's Jim now?"

"His body was moved to the mortuary. They're trying to track down a sister he listed as his next of kin. Would you like to leave your phone number so she can call you, assuming we find her?"

I gave Lindsey my phone number.

"Do you have any other questions?"

I shook my head and left the office. I saw Clayton several doors down the hall, leaning against the wall. His eyes were red, and his face was flushed. It appeared he had aged in those few minutes.

He asked me about my conversation with Lindsey. I told him about the blood clot letting loose and going into Jim's lungs. "I should never have left him," I said.

He put an arm around my shoulders, saying, "Don't take that on, brother. There's no way you could have known."

Chapter Sixty

On the way to the Mothership, I asked Clayton if he knew Jim had a sister. He said Jim had mentioned his sister a couple of times, but they weren't close. I explained that Jim had identified her as the next of kin and the hospital was trying to reach her.

We were quiet on the way home. I found myself staring ahead, grappling with guilt and sadness. Clayton seemed deep in thought and was probably thinking about all the good times he'd had with Jim—and the void he would have in his life without Jim's quick wit and warm presence.

When we pulled into the parking lot, we decided to ask Abbie and Kathleen to come to my apartment, where we would tell them the bad news.

We went into the building and were relieved that Brett didn't come out of his office and talk to us. I sent Kathleen and Abbie a text when we reached my apartment: *We just got back from the hospital. Clayton and I are in my apartment. Mind coming down?*

Sure. What's up? responded Kathleen.

I didn't reply.

Abbie answered, *I'm just hiking my pants up. Be right there.*

I tried to remain even-keeled when Kathleen and Abbie entered my apartment, but I had a hard time making eye contact with them. Clayton didn't say anything. Kathleen looked at me, then at Clayton, and back at me, and the color seemed to vanish from her face. "What's wrong? Something is wrong, I just know it."

"Oh God, please don't tell me something happened to Jim," cried Abbie. "Please tell me he's okay."

Clayton stood and wrapped his arms around her. "Jim died early this morning."

Kathleen buried her head in my chest and cried. I wrapped my arms around her and stroked her hair while Clayton held Abbie tightly as she wept.

After the crying stopped, my friends sat on the couch while I made coffee. My cell phone buzzed as I was describing what happened the day before. I didn't recognize the number and said, "Maybe this is Jim's sister." I took the call.

I heard a female talking, but her words were drowned out by other voices and commotion in the background. I wondered if she was calling from a bar. After telling her twice that I couldn't understand what she was saying, she yelled, "Shut up, you guys," and the background voices quieted.

The woman introduced herself as Brandy, Jim's sister. She explained that someone from the hospital gave her my number.

She seemed unmoved by my condolences and more interested in picking up Jim's "stuff." She said she was coming to Michigan from Youngstown, Ohio, in a couple of days and wanted directions and advice about the size of the trailer she'd need.

When I asked about a funeral service, she said, "We ain't doin' that." I tried to convince her that Jim deserved a service, but she wasn't interested and eventually hung up as I pressed her to change her mind.

The phone still in my hand, I looked at my friends in disbelief. After I told them about the conversation, Abbie described Brandy as "trailer trash," and I couldn't disagree. Kathleen was more diplomatic and pointed out that people grieve differently. She speculated that Brandy might not wear her feelings on her sleeve.

"No way!" said Clayton. "She's a douchebag, and that's why Jim wasn't in contact with her. Do you really think he'd have distanced himself from her if she was sweet and lovely?"

"You may be right, Clayton. But things happen in families that can strain relationships," Kathleen said. Abbie and I looked at each other and agreed that she had a valid point.

"Well," said Clayton, "whether she's an unemotional, grieving sister interested in Jim's stuff or a trashy douchebag, she's decided there won't be a memorial service. So we need to do something about that."

Recognizing that Jim wouldn't want us moping around, we decided to celebrate his life in Kathleen's apartment immediately after dinner the following day. Kathleen said she'd make a list of the things she'd need, and Clayton and I agreed to pick them up at Walmart in the morning.

The final piece of business involved Charlie. He was at work and unaware that Jim had died. I said I'd talk to him when his son dropped him off before dinner.

Chapter Sixty-One

S hortly before dinner, I went outside, sat on a bench, and waited for Dean or Tony to drop off Charlie. It wasn't long before I spotted Dean's pickup truck coming down the driveway. I stood and waited for them.

Charlie saw me and waved as Dean stopped the truck in front of the building. "Not every day I have a greeter to welcome me when I get back from work," he said as he climbed out of the truck. "Are you practicing for a job at Walmart?"

I tried to muster a smile. "I wanted to catch you as soon as you arrived." We waved to Dean as he drove off. "You mind if we sit down?"

"I don't mind." We sat next to each other on one of the benches.

"What's up?" he asked.

"I've got some bad news, Charlie." I had never delivered sad news like this, and I didn't realize how difficult it would be. I looked at him, and there was fear in his bright-blue eyes. "Jim died early this morning at the hospital."

"Oh no. What happened?"

"The blood clot in his leg got into his lungs."

Charlie clasped his hands and stared at the ground. "Jim was a good friend. He never got impatient with my memory lapses. I'll always be grateful for that."

"I agree. Jim was a good man."

Charlie looked up at the sky and said, "I really had fun with him at the concert." He looked at me. "How are the others holding up?"

"Everyone is pretty sad, but since there's not going to be a funeral, we've decided to celebrate Jim's life tomorrow at Kathleen's."

"That's a great idea, Bud. I know Jim would appreciate that. I guess we'll just have to pull together. Thanks for letting me know."

I motioned toward the entrance. "Want to head in?"

"Why don't you go ahead, Bud. I want to sit here on this beautiful day, think about Jim, and pray for a while."

I patted him on the shoulder and walked into the building. Then I decided to drop in on Kathleen. When I reached her door, I looked farther down the hall, toward Jim's apartment, and noticed that the door looked ajar. I walked closer, then slowly opened the door and said, "Hello?" No one responded. I walked into the apartment and again said, "Hello?" No answer. The bathroom door was halfway closed, and the light was on. I thought I heard the medicine cabinet open and close, then a drawer. The door opened. The bathroom light went off, and Brett walked out.

"What are you doing here?" I asked.

"I could ask you the same thing."

"You didn't answer my question, Brett. Why are you in here, and what are you doing in the bathroom?"

"Oh, that. Well, his sister called. She'll be coming up from Ohio this Friday morning to move his stuff. I just wanted to make sure there weren't any drugs in the bathroom. You can't be too careful these days."

"I thought all the drugs are kept at the nurses' station."

"They're supposed to be, but I've found over the years that some of our residents, particularly the unhealthy ones, don't turn them all in. When they pass, there's a risk other residents might steal them."

"Really, Brett? Other residents stealing medication from their deceased neighbors and friends? Gimme a break."

"Listen, Bud, I don't appreciate your tone. I've been in this business long enough to know that prescription drugs are abused by all sorts of people, including people in assisted living facilities. You should just mind your own business."

"Jim was my friend. His business is my business. I think you need to get out of this apartment."

"Don't tell me what to do. I'm responsible for Jim's apartment now that he is no longer with us, and I'll do whatever is necessary to safeguard it until his sister gets here. So let's both leave before I call the police and have you arrested for trespassing."

I reluctantly walked out of Jim's apartment, with Brett following. He locked the door and, with a smirk, said, "Have a good night, Bud."

Chapter Sixty-Two

The next morning, Clayton and I went to the Walmart camera department to pick up some photographs of Jim that Kathleen arranged to have duplicated. As we waited for the clerk, Clayton grabbed an abandoned cart while I looked at Kathleen's shopping list.

We meandered around the store until we found the party favors aisle. I glanced at Kathleen's list and put a package of red, white, and blue streamers and some balloons into the cart. I looked around and didn't see Clayton. I waited for a moment, then began pushing the cart toward the grocery section.

Someone grabbed my butt cheeks. I turned and faced Clayton, who was wearing a latex Donald Trump mask.

"Oh, excuse me. I thought you were a woman," said Clayton, imitating the president's voice. Continuing his impression, he said, "You know, Bud. Nobody knows butts the way I do. Butts are really amazing and terrific, and when you're famous like me, you can grab anyone you want." I laughed. Clayton pulled off the mask and looked at it admiringly. "I'm getting it." He tossed it into the cart.

"What are you going to do with it?"

"I don't know. I collect masks and other funky stuff. Did I ever tell you I have a full gorilla costume?"

"No. You never mentioned that."

"You know Brett is a big Trump fan, right? I mean, he's got a picture of him in his office."

"Yeah, I saw that when I moved in."

"I'll figure out a way to use the mask to drive him nuts. Let me think on it."

We picked up apples in the produce department and then went searching for cinnamon and sugar. We were cutting down the candy aisle when Clayton abruptly stopped and picked up a package of six giant Tootsie Rolls. As I was examining the package, I asked, "You like Tootsie Rolls?"

"Yeah, sometimes." He tossed the package in the cart.

When we found the spices, Clayton again vanished while I located the cinnamon. Walking farther down the aisle, I picked up a small bag of sugar. Clayton reappeared with a single can of whole-kernel corn, which he dropped in the cart.

"What's that for?" I asked.

"Every once in a while, I get a craving for corn," he said. I wasn't sure if Clayton was bullshitting but decided to let it go. We picked up booze and went through the checkout.

We were passing a strip mall on our way back to Serenity when Clayton pumped the brakes. "Oh man, we gotta stop at the new Reptile World," he said. Then he turned around and headed back to the store parking lot.

"You like reptiles?"

"Hell no. I just wanna see what they have. I partied

with Alice Cooper during his drinking days. He's from Detroit, you know. He told me he's always on the lookout for props for his concerts. The dude goes to reptile stores, casket factories, and all kinds of freaky places. It's his thing."

We walked up and down the aisles, looking at lizards, turtles, and snakes. There were many different species of snakes in all sorts of sizes and colors. We stopped in front of the display for pythons and boa constrictors.

"Could you imagine owning one of those?" asked Clayton.

"Not at all. They give me the creeps."

"I think it's in our DNA to be afraid of snakes," he said. "They're so primitive and unpredictable, like dinosaurs."

I agreed.

After a few minutes, he said, "Okay, I've seen enough. Let's roll."

When we got back to Serenity, we looked through the Walmart bags and pulled out Clayton's mask, Tootsie Rolls, and can of corn. He stuffed them in his backpack.

We delivered the party supplies to Kathleen's apartment. She and Abbie looked through the bags to make sure we got everything on Kathleen's list.

"I'd invite you guys in, but Abbie and I have work to do," Kathleen said.

"All that running around today, and this is what we get," said Clayton facetiously. "Thanks a lot."

"Quit your bellyaching and get the hell out of here," said Abbie.

Clayton and I laughed as we walked out the door.

Chapter Sixty-Three

After dinner, we met in Kathleen's apartment, which was all decked out in honor of Jim. Red, white, and blue streamers and balloons hung along the tops of the living room walls. On the kitchen table were framed photos of Jim taken at the Graham Nash concert, Woodstock, the Fourth of July, and his birthday.

The smell of baked apples and cinnamon hung in the air, and Kathleen suggested we have dessert first. As she was passing out bowls of warm apple crisp topped with ice cream, she apparently heard me tell the others about the snakes we had seen at Reptile World.

"There were all kinds of snakes there," I said. "Big ones, small ones, and colorful ones. Why would anyone want to own a snake?"

"We're always finding snakes in the junk buses out at Motor City Bus Repair," said Charlie. "They're disgusting."

"Did you see the big one in the corner of the store named Jumbo?" asked Clayton. "It had to be ten feet long. I wonder what they feed it."

"No, I didn't, thank God," I said. "I'd be dreaming about it tonight."

"I wouldn't want to handle a big snake like that," said Kathleen. "But snakes don't bother me. My grandpa taught biology in high school and always had snakes in his class-room. We used to play with them all the time. My kids used to keep a garter snake in an aquarium."

"You'd actually pick up a snake? Eww," said Abbie.

"Sure," replied Kathleen. "As long as it wasn't poiso-nous or big like Jumbo."

Clayton grinned. "You just don't seem like the snake-lover type."

"Snakes get a bad rap," said Kathleen. "They don't bug me at all. You just have to know how to handle them."

When we finished eating dessert, Abbie poured herself a glass of the fruity vodka drink she had created, took a sip, then poured Kathleen a glass of wine. The men wanted beer, so Kathleen grabbed one can at a time and passed each one to Abbie, who gave them to me for distribution.

I stood and said, "I propose a toast to our friend, Jim. We're drinking to celebrate you. We are blessed that you were our friend, and we're glad you found peace and happi-ness before you died. You went out strong, Jim, and we intend to follow your lead. God bless you."

"Right on," said Clayton. After we clinked the drinks we were holding, he added, "And I hope you and Sister Mary Katherine are continuing your conversations and listening to a lot of Kiss. Right, Bud?"

When are you ever going to let that go?" I asked.

Clayton smiled. "Never."

For the next hour, we laughed and talked about Jim and the time we'd spent with him. While the beverages flowed freely, the conversation turned to Brett's snooping in Jim's apartment.

"That no-good son of a bitch was looking to see if Jim had any drugs," said Abbie.

"It sure seems that way," said Kathleen.

"This has got to end," I said.

I turned to Abbie. "You've made a believer out of me. There's something going on with Brett, and it could be what you suspected all along. I think it's time we call your son, Brian. He'll know what to do."

Abbie frowned and ran her hand through her tangled hair. There's no way to reach him. He's in Africa doing volunteer work in some godforsaken place. He won't be back until the end of next week." Her frown turned to a look of concern. "What are we going to do without Jim? He was an important witness."

"We're not waiting for Brian," said Clayton. "It's payback time for that piece of shit. We have to do it for my mom and Jim. I promise it will be fun, no one will get hurt, and no one will get arrested. Who's in?"

"What do you have in mind?" I asked.

"I can't reveal that now, or I'd have to kill you." Clayton looked at Kathleen and laughed. "I'd love to get a photo of you with that look. The caption would be, 'Oh my God, now what?'"

"I can't get kicked out of here," she said.

"Don't worry about it. We'll be fine. Tomorrow is Friday, and it's supposed to be unseasonably warm, with a high in the low eighties. A perfect day for giving Brett a little how do you do. I'll give you the details when we leave the parking lot tomorrow afternoon. Once I give you the details, you can stay in the Mothership if you don't want to participate."

"Wait!" said Charlie. "I have to work tomorrow."

"I know. We'll meet you at work."

"Let's bust that little weasel's balls," said Abbie eagerly.

"I'm in," I said.

Kathleen seemed surprised by my enthusiasm and wary of Clayton's plan. "Nobody gets hurt, right?"

"Right," said Clayton. "It's just a simple way of demonstrating our profound affection for a total asshole."

"And nobody gets arrested, right?" she asked.

"Of course not, Kathleen. But if we do, I promise I'll post your bond so you won't spend too much time in the clink."

Kathleen frowned. "Not funny, Clayton."

"C'mon, you know I'm just kidding. I guarantee we won't get caught, and we won't get kicked out."

Kathleen rubbed her hands together, looking nervous. "And this will be like a prank and not against the law?"

"Exactly," Clayton said. "It'll be a piece of cake. Bingo, bango, bongo!"

"Well, I guess I'm in then," she replied.

We all cheered.

"Tomorrow, the Serenity Gang strikes back," said Clayton.

And we all cheered again.

Chapter Sixty-Four

After breakfast, I returned to my apartment to watch the news and see if anyone had responded to the emails I'd sent using the leads the LA session musician provided. As I turned on my computer, my phone buzzed. I checked it and found a photograph and a text message Abbie sent to me and the others.

The photo was taken at the Serenity entrance. A heavy woman appeared to be talking to Nurse Jackie. She had bleached blond hair and was wearing skintight chartreuse yoga pants and a sleeveless shirt. Next to her was a man about her age with a long gray goatee and do-rag. Two young men stood behind them. One had a shaved head and tattoos all over his arms, and the other was shirtless and had a mullet.

Below the photo, Abbie wrote, *The Beverly Hillbillies just arrived in a piece-of-shit pickup with a junky cap covered in Trump stickers and a U-Haul trailer. Am I judging? Yes, I am! They're a motley crew. Don't like 'em already.*

Kathleen responded, *Let's meet them. Maybe we'll be pleasantly surprised.*

Clayton added, *Or not!*

I heard talking in the hall and knew Brandy and the others had entered the building. A few minutes later, I received a text from Kathleen advising that Nurse Jackie had opened the apartment and gone back to the nurses' station.

As I walked down the hall toward Kathleen's apartment, I noticed that Jim's door was wide open. I stopped when I heard two people arguing.

"Bullshit, I get the TV."

"Fuck you! I called it first."

Then there was a thump and the sound of breaking glass.

"Now look what you've done, you idiots! That was a nice picture. Probably worth a hundred bucks," said a female voice. Jim had some nicely framed pictures of landscapes hanging in his living room, and I assumed one of them had just broken.

"He pushed me, Ma!"

"Just shut up and start helping Mike."

I knocked on Kathleen's door, and she invited me in.

"I just heard them arguing over Jim's TV," I said. "I think the boys got in a scuffle over it and one of Jim's pictures got broken."

"You're kidding."

"No, I'm not. No wonder Jim didn't keep in touch with them."

Undeterred, Kathleen said, "They're Jim's family, and we need to meet them."

I picked up the tray she'd prepared and followed her out of the apartment and down the hall to Jim's apartment. I saw Clayton walking toward us and nodded.

Steve Parks

Kathleen knocked on the open door and said, "Good morning."

A male voice said, "Ma, someone's here."

A woman appeared. "Yeah?"

We introduced ourselves, and the woman said she was Jim's sister, Brandy. She looked at the tray I was holding and said, "Whatcha got there?"

Kathleen smiled and said, "I made you some coffee and cookies to give you a little energy this morning."

"Good deal," said Brandy as I handed her the tray. She looked at me. "You the dude I talked to on the phone?"

"I am."

"Thought so." She looked behind her and yelled, "Jake!"

"What?" he screamed back.

"Get out here! And bring my smokes with ya!"

The young man with the tattooed arms appeared. He'd removed his shirt to reveal a mural of tattoos all over his chest and stomach. His lower lip was bulging with tobacco. He handed Brandy a pack of cigarettes and a lighter. She gave him the tray, which he carried into the apartment. He returned a moment later with one of the Styrofoam cups that had been on the tray. Kathleen cringed when he spit in it.

Brandy pulled out a cigarette and put it in her mouth.

"Brandy, I don't think you're permitted to smoke in here," said Kathleen.

She struck the lighter and lit her cigarette. "Whatever." She took a long pull on her cigarette and blew out the smoke. "I got a couple of questions. We didn't bring no boxes, and I was wondering if you had some we could use."

"I might have one or two in my closet," said Kathleen. "I'll get them." She rolled her eyes at me and went to her apartment.

264

"Sorry. I don't have any boxes," I said.

"I don't either," said Clayton.

"Also, do you guys know if Jim had any deposit boxes or one of them rented storage garages?" asked Brandy.

"We heard he might have some guns," said Jake.

"Shut up about that," said Brandy.

Jake snickered. "Heard he liked knives too."

Brandy smirked. "Go help your brother." He spit in the Styrofoam cup, then turned and walked away.

I was sure the remark about Jim liking knives referred to his suicide attempt years ago. The punk kid was mocking his own uncle, and Jim's sister went right along with it. I looked at Clayton, who was red-faced and clenching his fists. I knew he was thinking the same thing.

"Don't know of any safe deposit boxes or storage units," I said. "Hey, Clayton. Let's help Kathleen look for those boxes." I looked at Brandy and added, "We'll talk to you later."

"Later," she said, then the door slammed shut.

Clayton and I exchanged disgusted looks, then walked the short distance to Kathleen's apartment. There was a knock at the door a few moments after we arrived. Before any of us could respond, the door flew open and Abbie entered.

"What's goin' on?" she asked.

"The human tattoo just insulted Jim big time," said Clayton.

"It's true. I heard it," I said. "And the sad thing is that Brandy seemed to think it was funny. It really pisses me off."

"What'd he say?" asked Abbie.

"They said they heard Jim might have guns," I told her.

"They asked if we knew if he had a safe deposit box or off-site storage."

"Then the kid smirked and said he heard Jim liked knives too," said Clayton.

"And Brandy kind of smiled when he said it," I added.

"You're connecting that to the scars on Jim's wrists?" asked Kathleen. I nodded. "God, that's awful."

"I knew they were no good from the moment I saw them," said Abbie.

"I'm not letting these pieces of human garbage insult one of my best friends," said Clayton.

"Clayton, we're too old to go toe to toe with a couple punks and their mom's boyfriend," I cautioned.

"I agree. That's why Kathleen and I are going for a ride."

"We are? Where are we going?" she asked.

"Reptile World."

Chapter Sixty-Five

Kathleen was impressed by the sizes and varieties of the snakes at Reptile World. There were snakes from all over the world, ranging in size from six or seven inches to Jumbo, the huge python Clayton had mentioned. Like a kid in a toy store, Clayton walked a few steps ahead of Kathleen, excitedly bouncing from one enclosure to another and talking about the snakes and how one of them would be chosen for his "special mission."

Kathleen stomped her foot. "Clayton, stop! Can you please hold still for just one minute?"

He froze. "What?"

"After dragging me here, the least you can do is tell me what you have in mind."

"Sure. Okay." He pointed at all the snakes. "We're going to send one of these lucky buggers back to Ohio with those assholes."

"If you want to scare them like you did David Crosby, why don't you use a rubber snake?"

Clayton shot her a befuddled look. "Duh? I used a fake snake with David because he was the only target. A live snake is always recommended when there is more than one target."

"Really?"

"I can't believe you didn't know that! There've been several articles written about it in *Prank Magazine*."

Kathleen laughed. "Sorry, I don't subscribe to that one."

You should! I'll get you a subscription for Christmas."

She put her hand on her hip. "Tell me how you're gonna do it. How are you going to send a snake home with Jim's relatives?"

Clayton shook his head. "Oh, Kathleen. You're always focused on the details. Didn't anyone ever tell you the devil is in the details? There are times when the details are unknown and one must be creative and resourceful to create a masterpiece. When I wrote 'Up Yours,' all I had was an introductory drumbeat and a title. I had to fill in the rest. The tune just evolved. So just relax and let the prank evolve. I've got this."

"Come on, Clayton. Okay. Why'd you bring me here?"

"I need your help in picking out a nice snake to send home with Brandy and the crew."

Kathleen sighed. "You didn't need me to pick out a snake. Why am I here, Clayton?"

"Ah . . . well . . . I just need you to handle the snake."

"What do you mean *handle*?"

He smiled. "Why are you so damn edgy? All you have to do is coax it out of the box and put it where I tell you."

"Clayton, I told you last night I don't want to get kicked out of Serenity," snapped Kathleen. "I don't have anyplace to go."

"You won't get kicked out. No one will ever know we did it."

"I don't know. Someone could see us. I'd be too nervous. I'm nervous just thinking about it."

Clayton patted Kathleen on her shoulder. "Nothing to worry about, girl. With Bud and Abbie helping, we can pull it off. No problem. If you don't feel comfortable helping with the prank, at least you can help me pick out a snake. There's no harm in that."

"I'll help you pick out a snake," said Kathleen sternly. "But why can't Bud or Abbie help you put it somewhere?"

"You heard them last night. Everybody hates snakes except for you."

"Come on, Clayton. You're putting a lot of pressure on me."

"No pressure at all. I'll figure it out if you don't want to be involved. It's okay. Just help me pick out a snake. I'll spend up to $300. This will be the mother of all pranks!"

They agreed they needed to pick a snake that wasn't native to North America so Jim's relatives wouldn't recognize it. Clayton was adamant the snake had to be at least three feet long for shock value. They eventually settled on one, and Clayton happily paid $250 and some change.

When they were on their way back, Clayton pulled into a 7-Eleven parking lot. He put the Mothership in park and told Kathleen he'd be right back. He got out of the van, went into the store, and returned a few minutes later carrying a brown paper bag.

"What's that?" asked Kathleen as Clayton climbed in.

"A six-pack of Pabst Blue Ribbon—liquid gold for rednecks."

Chapter Sixty-Six

"The prank gods are with us today!" said Clayton as he pulled into the Serenity parking lot. "Brett must be gone. His car isn't here. I just hope he's back by late this afternoon, when we take our little ride with Bud and Abbie."

They sat in the Mothership for a few minutes, watching the front entrance. Clayton turned and looked at the nondescript box on the floor behind the front passenger seat. "Think our little friend is doing okay?"

"I'm sure he's doing just fine."

They noticed that the U-Haul trailer had been detached from the truck and pushed close to the entrance. The pickup was parked a short distance away in the circular drive.

"I'll be damned," said Clayton. "They're loading the trailer. Here they come."

Brandy walked out, followed by the older guy and the two boys. They were all carrying big bundles, which they put into the back of the trailer. A cigarette was dangling from Brandy's mouth as she pointed and appeared to be shouting directions.

"Looks like they're wrapping Jim's stuff in bedding and towels and carrying it out to the trailer," said Kathleen.

"Can you believe those morons didn't think to bring boxes?" replied Clayton.

She slapped her hand to her mouth. "Oh my, I never gave her the boxes I promised."

"Don't worry about it. Looks like they're doing just fine."

Brandy carefully laid her cigarette on the concrete next to the trailer, and they all went back inside. Clayton picked up the bag containing the six-pack, then he and Kathleen got out of the van. The snake would stay put for the time being.

As they walked up the sidewalk toward the entrance, Clayton noticed that Jim's bed, mattress, coffee table, and end tables were already packed in the trailer. Brandy and the others were packing bundles of Jim's property around them. Clayton was surprised by the progress they had made since he and Kathleen had left for Reptile World.

Just as they reached the front door, they saw the two boys carrying Jim's couch out. Brandy was on their heels, barking directions.

"Now, put that on the grass over by the truck. We'll load it after we finish loading the trailer. You can sit on it on the way home."

Brandy picked up her cigarette, took a puff, and looked at Kathleen. "Weren't you gonna get me them boxes?"

"I had to run an important errand, but I will get them to you in a few minutes."

Brandy and the boys went back into the building.

Clayton looked at Kathleen and smiled. "Can you believe it? Delivered on a silver platter!"

"What are you talking about?" she asked.

"The couch! They're going to put that in the back of the pickup, and the boys are going to sit on it on their way home. The plan is already coming together."

"So, what is it?"

"I go over to the couch, take off the cushion, and cut a hole where the cushion sits. We put the snake in the hole, put the cushion back on, and the boys load it in the truck. The snake goes special delivery back to Ohio and eventually emerges to remind them that nobody gets away with insulting our dear friend Jim."

"I don't know, Clayton. What if somebody is looking? What if they come out while the snake is being put in there?"

"We need a diversion . . . or two. Let's talk to Abbie and Bud."

Chapter Sixty-Seven

W e sat at Kathleen's kitchen table to discuss Clayton's plan.

"Here's the deal," said Clayton. "We have a three-foot boa constrictor in the Mothership."

I looked at Kathleen, then back at Clayton. "What?"

"Kathleen insisted I buy it."

"Did not! You said you wanted a snake about three feet long, and I saw that one. You're the one who decided to buy it."

"Who cares!" Abbie said, then giggled. "What's the plan, Clayton? This is going to be great!"

"We're going to give those Ohio hicks a special, lasting memory of their trip to Michigan to ransack Jim's apartment," said Clayton.

"How?" I asked.

"This will have to be perfectly coordinated to be successful. We'll have to communicate by text messaging to be sure everyone is in place." Clayton ran his hand through his hair. "We'll need a double diversion."

Sometimes I wish Clayton would just get to the point. "What are you talking about?"

"Jim's couch is on the lawn by the truck. That is what we will use for the snake's new home. I'll go out there, lift off the right-side cushion, and cut a hole in the fabric that's covering the springs so the snake can go inside. I can do that in thirty seconds or less. I'll replace the cushion, nonchalantly walk to the Mothership, and get the snake. I'll send you a text when I have the snake and am ready to return to the couch. This is the beginning of the double diversion."

"Where are we when you're doing this?" I asked.

"Right here."

I looked at Kathleen. She seemed nervous. "Are you okay?"

"I'm fine."

"What next?" Abbie asked Clayton eagerly.

"Implementation of the first diversion. When I text you that I'm ready to return to the couch, Abbie will take this sixy of Pabst Blue Ribbon and go to Jim's apartment to keep the Beverly Hillbillies entertained. It's really getting hot out, and they'll go for that PBR like flies going to sh—" Clayton stopped himself and smiled at Kathleen. "Honey. I'll put the snake box on the couch's left cushion and head for the dining room."

"Why are you going to the dining room?" asked Kathleen.

"For the second diversion. I'll go directly to the piano, and when I sit down . . ." He paused. "Wait a second. Kathleen expressed reservations about doing this, and I want to be respectful of that." He looked at Kathleen. "No pressure whatsoever. We'll modify the plan if we have to."

"You haven't said what you want me to do," Kathleen said. "Tell me what you're thinking, and I'll decide."

"Okay. After I put the box on the left cushion, I'll go to the piano in the dining room. I'll text you when I sit on the piano bench. That's the signal for you and Bud to begin walking out to the couch. Right after I text you, I'll begin playing to distract the attention of staff and the residents. They'll be drawn toward the music, and no one will be looking outside. When you reach the couch, Bud will remove the right cushion, open the box, and put the box on its side near the hole I made. You, Kathleen—our resident snake lover—will encourage the snake to crawl into the hole. The snake crawls into the hole, Bud replaces the cushion, then delivers the box to Brandy." Clayton smiled. "She said she needed boxes, right? Easy peasy."

"So, all you want me to do is make sure the snake goes into the hole?" asked Kathleen.

"That's it! Simple!"

She looked at me. "You'll be with me, right?"

"Of course."

"My kids can never find out. They'd disown me."

"My lips are sealed. Are you up for it?" I asked.

Kathleen closed her eyes and rubbed her forehead. She stopped, looked at her friends, and said, "Okay. I'm doing it for Jim."

They all high-fived, and Clayton stood.

"Where are you going?" asked Abbie.

"To cut a hole in the couch. It might be a little while. I'll have to wait until the coast is clear. Just stay here and keep an eye on your phones. One more thing," said Clayton. "Kathleen, you told Brandy you might have a couple of boxes. You wanna check on that?"

"Sure." Kathleen stood, walked to the closet, and opened the door. "Here they are."

Clayton walked to the closet and pulled out two

medium-size boxes. "I'll put these at Jim's door," he said. Then he smiled and looked at us. "Jim would be all over this, wouldn't he? Damn, I miss him." He took a breath, said, "Let's do this," and left.

Chapter Sixty-Eight

Clayton left Kathleen's apartment, put the boxes on the floor outside Jim's apartment, and stood in the hallway listening. He could hear muffled voices. He decided to sit on one of the benches at the front entrance of the building and wait until Brandy and the gang brought another load out to the trailer.

After a few minutes, Brandy came through the door carrying a bundle of things wrapped in a blanket and slung over her shoulder like Santa Claus carrying Christmas presents. She was followed by the human tattoo, who was carrying a floor lamp and a toaster. They'd apparently taken the legs off Jim's kitchen table. Mullet boy was carrying the tabletop, and the older guy was carrying the table legs in one hand and a pillowcase that appeared to be stuffed with kitchen items in the other. They loaded their haul into the trailer and headed back into the building.

It was time for Clayton to make his move. He reached in his pocket and pulled out a small jackknife and a quarter. He discreetly opened the knife. With the knife and the quarter in his right hand, he walked slowly toward the

couch as if he were strolling in the park. When he reached
the couch, the entrance doors flew open, and two children
ran out, followed by a young woman. One of the children
stopped, looked back, waved, and yelled, "Bye, Grandpa."

Clayton casually walked past the couch and pretended
to look at the flower beds as the children ran down the sidewalk toward the parking lot with the woman following.

When they reached their car, Clayton turned around
and walked back toward the couch. He went to the front of
it, where he stood with his hands on his hips, looking at it
like a prospective buyer. He reached down and pulled off
the right cushion, acting as if he were checking out the
condition of the fabric and quality of the springs.

He dropped the quarter on the surface and held the
open knife in the palm of his right hand. Then he bent over,
put both hands on the fabric, and pushed a few times.
While he was doing that, he held the knife between his
index finger and thumb and cut a slit in the fabric. He gave
the slit a pull with the tip of his index finger to rip it open a
little wider. After rolling the knife back into the palm of his
right hand, he picked up the quarter with his left hand and
put the cushion back in place. Finally, he stood erect and
held the quarter up in the air to appear to be examining it.

"Must be your lucky day," said a voice behind him.

Startled, Clayton quickly turned and faced Don
Durman, an avid walker who lived on the other side of the
building.

"I guess so. Probably Jim's last quarter."

"Too bad about Jim," said Don. "He was a good guy."

"He sure was," replied Clayton.

Don was not in a hurry, and he talked to Clayton about
the lovely warm weather and the people moving Jim's stuff.
Clayton didn't want to be standing next to the couch when

Brandy came out again, so he said, "Don, you'll have to excuse me. I've got to get my heart medication in the van."

"I understand," said Don. "I've got some ticker issues myself."

Don had started to turn toward the entrance when Clayton said, "Oh wait." Don looked at him. "In a few minutes, I'm going to play the piano in the dining room. I have some new stuff I want everybody to hear. Be sure to let everyone know."

"That'll be great! We'll see you in there."

Clayton was walking down the sidewalk toward the Mothership when he heard Brandy scream, "Damn it! I told you to tie those bundles better." He turned around and saw the human tattoo bent over, picking up clothes that had spilled out of the bundle he had been carrying. His brother and the older man stood watching while holding the boxes Clayton had dropped off. Brandy screamed, "Quit standing around and put that shit in the trailer."

Clayton reached the Mothership and opened the sliding side door. He was greatly relieved the snake had not escaped from the box. He texted Kathleen, Bud, and Abbie: *Couch job completed. At the Mship. Waiting for Brandy and the rest to go back inside. Will be in touch.*

The human tattoo finished picking up the items that had fallen on the ground, carried them over to the trailer, and threw them in. He and the others talked for a couple minutes, then went back into the building.

When Clayton figured they had reached Jim's room, he picked up his phone and texted: *I'm leaving the Mship with our friend and going to the couch. Time for Abbie to rock 'n' roll.*

Chapter Sixty-Nine

A bbie looked at her phone and saw Clayton's message. She stood and said, "It's showtime." Then she wrapped the plastic bag with the beer around one of the handlebars of her walker and headed out the door to Jim's apartment. By the time she reached it, Clayton had walked from the Mothership to the couch, placed the box on the left cushion, walked through the entrance doors, and was en route to the dining room.

Abbie reached in the bag, pulled out a can of PBR, opened it, and knocked on the door.

"Just a minute," yelled Brandy. The door opened a moment later.

Abbie took a swig of beer. "You guys have been working so hard, I thought you might like to take a beer break."

"For sure," said Brandy. "Come on in." Then she yelled over her shoulder, "Time to take a break, boys."

Abbie handed Brandy a beer as she pushed her walker past her into the apartment. It smelled strongly of sweat, cigarettes, and marijuana. The men walked into the room, and Abbie gave them each a beer. She noticed they had moved out most of Jim's stuff.

"What's your name?" asked Brandy.

"Abbie." Pointing to the human tattoo and mullet boy, Abbie said, "And who are these handsome boys?" Mullet boy smiled, revealing a missing front tooth.

"These are my sons, Jake and Zach."

"Wow! They could be models," said Abbie.

She looked at the tattoos all over Jake's stomach, chest, and arms. "I love your tattoos. So beautiful! Hey, I see you've got your name tattooed on your chest there. That's a good idea in case you ever forget who you are. You know, I've been thinking about having my date of birth and Social Security number tattooed on my hand 'cause they're always asking me for them things when I go to the doctor. I could just look at my hand, and I wouldn't have to think about it. Good idea, don't you think?"

Jake nodded.

Pointing to the older man, Abbie said, "This your husband?"

"This is Mike. We ain't married, but we've been together for over four years."

"How lucky you are," said Abbie. She took another drink from her beer and said to Brandy, "So what's your connection to Jim? I didn't really know him. Too bad he died."

"I'm his sister," said Brandy. "I hadn't seen him for years. I didn't even know he was here until the hospital called. It's pretty cool I ended up with his stuff. Didn't expect that."

* * *

As soon as Clayton sat on the piano bench, he was joined by Don Durman and a few other residents, who stood waiting for him to launch into his first tune. He smiled at them and said he'd start as soon as he finished sending a friend a text message. He wrote, *Bud and Kathleen, I'm sitting on the piano bench and ready to go. I gotcha covered. Good luck!* Then he hit Send.

Clayton began his routine warm-up, which started slow but ended with his hands racing up and down the keyboard. People were already gathering around him when he broke into his first song, "God Bless America," and encouraged the audience to join him in singing.

Chapter Seventy

K athleen showed me Clayton's text.

"Are you sure you're good with this?" I asked.

"I'm not sure, but let's go before I change my mind."

We left the apartment and walked down the hall toward the front doors. We could hear the piano and singing coming from the dining room. When we slid out, we saw the box sitting on the couch as planned. We walked to the couch, and I looked around to see if anyone was in sight.

I hesitated, and Kathleen whispered, "Go for it."

When I removed the right cushion, I saw the hole. I opened the box and laid it on its side. Kathleen peered over and looked in the box. She slowly reached into it and gently eased the snake out. Its tongue flicked in and out as it tasted the fresh air. She carefully put her hand behind the snake's head and pointed it into the hole. The snake seemed to understand what she wanted and slithered into the hole and out of sight.

She looked at me and smiled; I picked up the box and put the cushion back in place. We walked back into the building, heard Clayton playing, and decided to go to the dining room. There, we saw Clayton surrounded by residents and Serenity employees, who were enthusiastically singing "This Land Is Your Land" as he banged out the tune on the piano.

He looked at us, and Kathleen smiled and waved excitedly. He winked back and smiled.

Chapter Seventy-One

Back in Jim's room, Abbie asked, "Got one brewski left. Who wants it?"

"Mike and me will split it," said Brandy. She opened the can, took a long drink, and handed it to Mike.

"So, where you from?" asked Abbie.

"Youngstown, Ohio," said Brandy.

"Youngstown! I was there once and never again."

"Why's that?" asked Brandy.

"It was the most awful day of my life. My husband got bit by a snake."

"Oh my God, how terrible!"

"Yep. We were stayin' with some friends kinda out in the country—lots of fields and woods around. Pretty nice, but never guessed there'd be snakes there."

"So what happened?"

"During the night, my husband got up to go to the bathroom, and a snake bit him on his Achilles tendon. That's the tendon that goes from your heel up the back of your leg."

"What kinda snake?" asked Zach.

"I don't know. I think it was called a copper-back or

silver-head or something. All I know is that it was big and real aggressive."

"Man, that would have freaked me out," said Jake.

They had taken the bait. Now it was time to set the hook. Abbie put on her best sad face and said, "My husband was rolling around on the floor in pain, and that damn snake bit him again—excuse me for sayin' this—right on the balls." She hung her head. "The poison made them swell up like a couple of balloons, and we never did have sex after that 'cause of the internal damage."

Abbie looked at Mike, who was rubbing his crotch with a very pained look on his face.

"That must have hurt real bad," said Jake.

"They carted him off to a hospital, where he stayed for almost ten days," said Abbie. "The docs said some snakes, by instinct, just go right for the balls."

"What happened to the snake?" asked Zach.

"It disappeared into a hole in the wall next to the closet and got away. Our friends told us the next year that the house got condemned because there was a big family of them snakes living in the walls. So that's my deal on Youngstown. The place where my sex life ended." She finished her beer and said, "I best be shovin' off. I wanna watch NASCAR this afternoon. You folks have a safe trip back to Ohio."

"Yeah. Thanks for the beer," said Brandy. "Nice meetin' ya."

Abbie heard the men carrying on about being bitten in the balls by a snake as she left the apartment and headed down the hall.

She smiled.

Chapter Seventy-Two

C layton was still playing when Kathleen and I decided to go back to our apartments. When we reached the front entrance, we watched Brandy slowly back up the pickup truck toward the trailer. We could see the couch in the bed of the pickup, under the cap.

After the trailer was secured, Jake and Zach climbed over the closed tailgate and sat on the couch.

"Can't say I'll miss them," I said as the truck and trailer began moving. I put the snake box I was carrying on the floor next to a trash bin.

"I definitely won't." Kathleen smiled. "But I sure would like to be a fly on the wall when our little friend reveals himself. Hey, let's go talk to Abbie and see how things went for her."

At lunch, everyone was upbeat and giddy as we talked about the Beverly Hillbillies and our parting gift to them. Abbie described the time she spent with them and her story about the Youngstown snake biting her husband in the balls. It made us laugh uncontrollably. I noticed that people around us who hadn't even heard Abbie's story were smiling in amusement, watching the antics at the table.

"This is going to be one helluva day!" said Clayton. "And we're just getting started! Meet me at my apartment at 1:30. I've got to run. Need to get things ready."

"When are you ever going to tell us what we're going to do?" asked Kathleen.

"On the way there."

"On the way where?" asked Abbie.

"To Motor City Bus Repair."

"What are we going there for?" asked Kathleen.

"You must have patience, my child." He stood and headed toward his apartment.

I was the first to arrive at Clayton's place. While we were talking near his kitchenette, I noticed a piece of wax paper on the counter with what appeared to be a glob of melted chocolate and a couple kernels of corn.

"Cooking today, Clayton?"

"Just put together a special treat. It's in the freezer. No big deal."

"I never thought of corn and chocolate going together."

"Are you kidding me? You never heard of chocolate corn fritters? They're the best."

"Is that what you were making?" I asked.

"Something like that."

When Abbie and Kathleen joined us, Clayton said, "We need to get the show on the road. Charlie's expecting us." He reached into the freezer, grabbed something, and quickly stuck it into a duffle bag that was already bulging with unseen items. Then he picked up the duffle bag, and we left.

As we were walking to the Mothership, I said I hadn't seen Brett's car for a couple of days and speculated that he was on vacation. Clayton said Brett was meeting with his partners in Traverse City but was due back soon. He grinned and added, "Which is perfect for us."

"How do you know that?" I asked.

"I also noticed that Brett hasn't been around, so I went to the nurses' station and made some subtle inquiries." He glanced back at Kathleen, who was walking with Abbie. He whispered, "I told them Kathleen had been talking to sweet little Brandy, and Brandy mentioned she was coming back to the facility late in the afternoon to talk to Brett. Nurse Jackie spilled the beans and told me where Brett was and when he'd be back." He grinned. "I used my patented information extraction method called 'bait and bullshit.' The CIA knows all about it."

I looked at Kathleen, who was too busy talking to Abbie to notice. "Why'd you mention Kathleen?"

Clayton shook his head. "Come on, Bud! You know the answer to that. Brett thinks I'm a pathological liar, and Nurse Jackie probably thinks the same. Kathleen, on the other hand, is Snow White. Everybody knows Snow White doesn't lie. I do, but she doesn't."

Chapter Seventy-Three

W e left the Mothership in the Motor City Bus Repair parking lot, then departed in a bus Charlie loaned to us and drove back to the Serenity parking lot. I climbed out of the bus, executed our plan with a little spontaneous ad-libbing, then jumped back on the bus for the return trip.

Brett's convertible was still there when we returned late in the afternoon.

"Okay, gang. We're just getting back from running errands," cautioned Clayton. "Be casual. Brett may be watching on the surveillance camera."

"I'm really nervous," said Kathleen.

"We're fine. Don't be nervous," I said.

Clayton and I went to the sliding side door and helped Kathleen and Abbie out of the van. Then we went up the sidewalk toward the entrance.

"What a gorgeous early September day!" I said. "It's got to be in the seventies." Kathleen seemed deep in thought and didn't respond.

I admit I was also a bit nervous as we entered the building. I glanced in Brett's office and was relieved to see him sitting with his feet on his desk, talking on the phone. Kathleen had mentioned more than once how Brett's anger during Jim's birthday party scared her, and I was sure she was afraid he'd jump out of his chair in a rage and confront us. He stayed put as we passed.

We took our time walking down the hall to our apartments, trying not to appear hurried or anxious in case Brett was watching. As we approached Kathleen's door, she whispered, "I need a drink. How about happy hour in my apartment in ten minutes? Bring your own stuff. We'll go to dinner a little bit late."

We thought it was a great idea and said we'd be back shortly.

Chapter Seventy-Four

As soon as she entered her apartment, Kathleen kicked off her shoes and filled a wineglass almost to the top. She took a sip, sat down, picked up the remote, and turned on the TV. She didn't care what was on. She just wanted to watch something to help get her mind off the events of the afternoon.

Oh my goodness, she thought. *What has gotten into me?*

She kept thinking her kids would be mortified if they ever found out what she'd done. Then she smiled as a strange feeling of satisfaction came over her. She took another sip of wine just as there was a knock on her door.

"Come in," she called.

But the door didn't open.

Is it locked? she wondered. Kathleen put down her glass and walked to the door. She opened it and smiled, expecting to see one of her friends.

"Hi, Kathleen," said Brett.

She felt her face flush and her heart pound. "What?" She started. Then she cleared her throat and tried to control her breathing. "What can I do for you?"

"Are you okay? You seem a little flustered."

"I . . . I . . . I just found out my granddaughter is pregnant!"

"That's great! Congratulations."

"Thanks. I'm really excited."

She decided that Brett's casual demeanor and upbeat tone revealed he didn't know of their afternoon activities.

"The reason I stopped by is that Nurse Jackie told me Jim's relatives might come back this afternoon, but nobody ever showed up," he said. "Did you hear anything about them coming back? I've got to leave shortly. I have a tee time at 6:15."

"No. I only briefly spoke to them," Kathleen replied. "When they pulled away, I had the impression they were going back to Ohio."

"Okay. Thanks. Sorry to bother you."

"No problem."

Kathleen closed the door and bounded over to the couch, where she picked up her wineglass and took a big gulp. She was standing there watching the latest Geico commercial when, again, there was a knock on the door.

Chapter Seventy-Five

Kathleen seemed rattled when she opened her door and let us in.

Clayton whispered, "What the hell was Brett doing here?"

Abbie explained to Kathleen that she had seen Brett at her door and texted Clayton.

"He knows what we did," said Kathleen in a serious tone.

"What? How's that possible?" asked Clayton.

"Charlie called him from the shop and asked him if he knew when we were coming back with the bus. Someone told him about seeing the bus in the parking lot, and he checked into it."

"Oh my God!" said Clayton. "I knew I should have talked to Tony or Dean."

As Clayton carried on about Charlie messing things up, I noticed that Kathleen had cracked a smile.

"Kathleen, shame on you!" I said. "You're fibbing!"

She smiled. "Maybe a little."

"You damn near gave me a stroke!" said Abbie.

"That wasn't funny!" said Clayton.

"You deserved that after all the stuff you've pulled on me!" said Kathleen.

Clayton laughed. "Now *I* need a drink!"

He and I popped a beer and plopped down on the couch. Abbie pushed her walker into the small kitchen and pulled out a glass from the cupboard. Then she put some ice in it, poured a healthy shot of vodka, and returned to the living room.

Clayton lifted his beer. "To the Serenity Gang, Jim, and Mom."

At the moment we clinked our beverages, I heard the voice of TV 6 news anchor Ross Bluestone say, "There was a freak accident on the Walter P. Reuther Freeway this afternoon involving four residents from Ohio. Let's go to reporter Danielle Roberts, who is at the scene. Danielle, what can you tell us?"

Danielle, an attractive woman in her mid-twenties, was standing on the shoulder of the highway. In the background, we could see the Beverly Hillbillies' pickup truck and U-Haul overturned in a ditch. The truck tailgate was open, and a portion of the couch was visible under the damaged cap.

"Oh my God! Look, you guys!" I said.

Kathleen, Abbie, and Clayton stopped talking and looked at the TV.

Kathleen put her left hand to the side of her face. "Oh no! I hope no one got hurt."

"Ross, the investigating officers tell us the truck, driven by Brandy Rogers of Youngstown, Ohio, was headed west on the freeway when her two sons, who were sitting on a couch in the bed of the pickup, were surprised by the sudden appearance of a snake. They panicked and screamed, causing Ms. Rogers to lose control and go into the ditch. Thankfully, no one was seriously injured."

"I understand there were some arrests. Can you tell us about that?" asked Bluestone.

"Yes, all four occupants are being detained pending extradition to Ohio. Brandy Rogers is being sought by Ohio authorities for felony welfare fraud, and her two sons, along with another man, are wanted on multiple home invasion charges in the Youngstown, Ohio, area and are alleged to be part of a northeast Ohio theft ring."

Bluestone smiled. "And the snake?"

Danielle smiled. "Ross, the snake was a three-foot boa constrictor—a baby, actually—and I'm happy to report that he was not injured and is currently residing at the Oakland County Animal Shelter."

"Great story, Danielle. Thank you," said Bluestone.

Kathleen picked up the remote and turned off the TV. We stared at each other in disbelief, not knowing whether to laugh or be grateful no one was hurt. As I took a drink of beer, Clayton said, "I wonder if he bit anyone in the balls."

I laughed as I was swallowing, causing beer to come out my nostrils. I grabbed a napkin from the coffee table and covered my mouth and nose while the others roared.

When the laughter subsided, Abbie said, "I wonder if Brett's found our afternoon surprise."

"Let's check it out," said Clayton.

We peeked through a crack in the curtains. The car hadn't moved since we'd returned.

Chapter Seventy-Six

B rett locked his office door, walked outside, and hurried down the sidewalk to his convertible in the parking lot. He barely had enough time to drive to the golf course.

He opened the driver's-side door and said, "Son of a bitch!" Then he turned away from the car in disgust, pulled his cell phone out of his pocket, and called Nurse Jackie, who was working second shift. She recognized his number and picked up.

"Hello?"

"Tell Connie in housekeeping to get her ass out to the parking lot *stat* with a bucket of water, cleaning solution, disinfectant, scrub brush, and a towel."

"Why? What's going on? What happened?"

"Some sick son of a bitch took a big dump on my car seat!" Brett yelled.

"What? Are you serious?"

"I'm tellin' ya, some sick son of a bitch took a huge shit on my car seat! Now, get Connie out here! It's oozing down my leather seat! Tell her to hurry. I have to be on the golf course at 6:15."

"Oh my God! That's awful. I'll call her right away."

"And Jackie."

"Yes?"

"Go to the kitchen and find out when corn was last served."

"What?"

"Do I have to paint you a fucking picture? Find out when corn was last served!"

"Okay."

Brett hung up without saying goodbye and waited for Connie. He kept glancing at his watch as Connie cleaned up the mess in his car. Realizing he was going to be late for his tee time, he called his partner and asked him to stall until he got to the golf course. He was in a foul mood when he arrived. He played horribly and lost over $200 betting with his partner and the two men who accompanied them. Tomorrow would be different. He'd start by finding the bastard who crapped in his car. The newly installed surveillance camera pointing in the direction of the parking lot would reveal the culprit.

Chapter Seventy-Seven

Brett pulled into the parking lot and parked next to a pickup truck with *Motor City Bus Repair* printed on the doors. As he walked up the sidewalk, a car with an Uber sticker passed him and went up the driveway to the building entrance. A thin man he had previously seen visiting Abbie got out of the car and entered the building.

Brett unlocked his office door as Clayton walked by on his way to the dining room. They made eye contact but said nothing. Brett sat in his office chair and turned on his computer. While it was coming to life, he looked out his windows to see if anyone was around. Seeing no one, he opened his safe, pulled out a rolled-up sandwich bag, and put it in the breast pocket of his blazer.

He logged into his computer, gaining access to the camera surveillance system. He scrolled through the descriptions of the camera locations until he found the camera for the parking lot. He then commenced a search for the time period between three o'clock, when he arrived on Friday, and 5:45, when he discovered the mess on his car seat. He clicked on Fast-Forward, causing images of cars using the driveway and people walking here and there to fly across the screen. He saw something strange at 3:21 and stopped the fast-forwarding.

An old yellow school bus pulled up, blocking the view of his car. He paused the video to study the bus. Most of the markings on it had been painted over, and the only visible word was *Church*.

He hit Play. He saw light shine into the right side of the bus as the passenger door opened and a dark figure went down the steps and off the bus toward his car. After a few moments, the figure moved toward the front of the bus. Brett could see he was wearing a cowboy hat. The figure hesitated, then walked out in front of the bus, where he was fully exposed to the surveillance camera.

Your ass is mine now, Brett thought. The figure wore jeans, leather riding chaps with fringe, a denim shirt, and a bolo tie. He paused the video and zoomed in on the person's face, which he immediately recognized.

It was Donald Trump.

That son of a bitch wore a mask!

Brett hit Play again. Donald Trump raised his arms and made peace signs, turned his back to the camera, dropped his pants, and displayed a full moon. He pulled up his pants, buckled his belt, casually went around the front of the bus, and entered.

Brett hit Pause again. He zoomed in on the driver, who appeared to have black hair. He hit Play, then Pause, then Play, then Pause, making the driver move in little spurts until he looked out the window.

Gotcha! He leaned forward to closely examine the image and realized he was looking at a gorilla head. *Damn it!*

Brett saw two figures in the middle of the bus who

appeared to be standing in the aisle. He pressed Play for a couple of seconds and then hit Pause. The bus was leaving and jumped forward a few feet. The two figures remained in the middle of the bus, but he couldn't see them clearly. He clicked Play again. The bus resumed its forward motion, and the movements and close proximity of the two figures suggested they were doing something together. Suddenly, a large white butt was pressed against the window. Brett hit Pause.

A couple rows down from the butt, the other figure appeared to be leaning toward the window. He clicked Play. The bus moved forward, and the figure appeared in the window. He hit Pause, zoomed in, and saw a person with long black hair and a pig mask holding their arm out the window. He pressed Play, and the person with the pig mask waved as the bus looped through the parking lot and headed back out to the highway.

Brett slammed his hand down on his desk and yelled, "Fuckin' bastards!" He pressed Fast-Forward and continued watching the video as people and cars flew in and out of the screen and the video time in the corner of the screen rolled. He stopped fast-forwarding at 5:16, when Clayton's van pulled into the parking lot. He watched Clayton and his passengers exit the van and walk toward the building.

He remembered his long-standing feud with Clayton, his recent confrontation with Bud in Jim's apartment, and Abbie's habit of snooping around his office. There were four people in the bus, and four people returned in the van. They obviously knew where the surveillance camera was located and wore masks so they wouldn't be recognized. They taunted him, knowing he would review the video.

"He's a fucking dead man!" screamed Brett as he bolted from his office and went to the dining room.

Chapter Seventy-Eight

When Kathleen, Clayton, and I walked into the dining room, I spotted Abbie and Mark sitting at a table with Charlie and his two sons. Abbie seemed to be doing much of the talking, and whatever she was saying had everyone laughing. Abbie motioned for us to join them. We bypassed the coffee station and walked over.

"Good morning," said Charlie. "She's telling us about the Beverly Hillbillies."

"Yup, just the Beverly Hillbillies," said Abbie, signaling that she wasn't talking about our prank on Brett.

"A snake in the couch! That's hilarious!" said Dean, smiling at Clayton. "You cooked that up?"

"Yes, sir. They were bad news, man. They deserved it."

"Where'd you get a three-foot boa constrictor?" asked Tony.

"The place where every smart shopper does their reptile shopping. Reptile World." Kathleen jumped in. "Did Abbie tell you they were all arrested?"

"No way!" said Charlie.

"It's true," said Abbie eagerly. "They're all in jail! They're wanted in Ohio for something."

Everyone laughed, and Dean said, "Now, that's quite a story."

I noticed Mark listening with an amused look. He looked good. His eyes were bright and clear, his face was tan, and he may have gained a little weight. "How's it going, Mark?" I asked. "So nice of you to come out this morning."

"I'm doing really well, Bud." Mark stood and we shook hands. "I'm working two jobs and paying the bills. I'm hoping I can land something better, but it's kind of hard with my background and record. I'll keep lookin' and praying, and hopefully, something good will happen. I'm just glad I can get over here on Saturdays to see Mom."

* * *

I asked Clayton and Kathleen if they wanted a cup of coffee. Clayton declined, but Kathleen said she did and followed me to the coffee station. I was pouring a cup of coffee and Kathleen was eyeballing the pastries when I saw Brett approaching. His face was beet red, and he was scanning the dining room like a lion on the hunt.

"Where is he?" he barked. Before we could respond, he seemed to fly across the room and stood within inches of Clayton. The tension was palpable, and everyone in the dining room watched in stunned silence. Kathleen and I walked over.

"I know it was you!" screamed Brett.

"What are you talking about?" Clayton said.

"Don't give me that bullshit, you lying son of a bitch."

Dean and Tony stood. "Wait a minute!" said Dean. "Don't be talking to him that way!"

"Mind your own business," snapped Brett. "This doesn't concern you."

I said, "Come on, Brett. This isn't the time."

He glanced at me. "Shut up." Then he looked back at Clayton. "You did it, didn't you? I saw the four of you in that bus."

"What bus?"

Brett put his hands on Clayton's chest and pushed, causing Clayton to take a step backward. "The fucking bus you drove, you lyin' bastard."

"Now, that's enough!" yelled Dean.

"You need to leave right now," said Tony.

Apparently sensing that Dean and Tony were about to grab him from behind, Brett put his hands in the air as if to surrender. "You're right. I apologize. I overreacted." He dropped his arms to his sides, turned away from Clayton, and said to Tony and Dean, "Excuse me, I'm going back to my office."

When they stepped back to let him pass, Brett spun around and lunged at Clayton, pushing him hard in the chest.

Clayton staggered backward and fell.

Chapter Seventy-Nine

Dean sprang on Brett from behind and wrapped his arms around him, pinning Brett's arms to his sides.

Tony yelled, "Somebody call 911!"

Brett squirmed and twisted like a trapped wild animal while yelling, "Let go of me!" He kicked hard at Dean's shins with his heels and tried to break free from his hold by elbowing him in the ribs. He leaned his head forward and threw it back, striking Dean in the nose.

"You son of a bitch," said Dean. A trickle of blood rolled out of his right nostril. Without letting go, he whipped Brett to his left. Just then, a rolled-up sandwich bag flew out of Brett's breast pocket and onto the floor. Brett kicked the bag while struggling with Dean, breaking it open and spilling pills all over the floor.

Tony, who looked like he'd had enough, grabbed Brett firmly by the collar with his left hand. Then he cocked his right arm to deliver a punch to Brett's face. "Knock it off, or you will lose those pretty white teeth," he said. "Understand?"

Brett immediately stopped resisting. Dean said, "I'm going to loosen my grip, and you're gonna sit in this chair and remain there until the cops arrive. Are we clear?" Brett nodded. "Any more bullshit, and my brother and I are going to stomp you into the floor. You got it?" Brett nodded again.

Dean pivoted toward the chair and said, "I'm letting you go now. You're going to sit, right?" Brett nodded.

Dean released Brett, then Tony put his hand on Brett's shoulder and pushed him down until he sat. Brett was breathing hard from the struggle and still had a defiant look in his eyes—until he saw the pills on the floor.

He started to stand, but Tony and Dean pushed him back down. He looked around with a desperate expression, then put his hands to his face and began crying.

Dean and Tony stood next to him like sentries as Dean blotted his bleeding nose with a napkin.

Kathleen and I were on our knees next to Clayton, who was writhing in pain and moaning, "Oh, my hip." Kathleen was crying and holding his hand.

I was trying to stay calm and assess his injuries. "Clayton, listen to me. You probably fractured your hip. I'm going to call an ambulance."

"No!" he responded.

When Clayton's moaning and groaning continued, I said, "That's it. I'm calling an ambulance!"

I pulled out my cell phone and was about to dial when Clayton moved and pressed his knee against my knee. I glanced at him, and I thought he winked. Kathleen didn't seem to notice. She was tenderly rubbing his arm, her eyes red from crying.

Clayton's writhing and carrying on convinced me I was mistaken; there was no wink. Again he nudged me with his knee. This time, our eyes met, and there was no doubt about it—he definitely winked. Once again, I was being sucked into one of his goofy stunts, and I had no choice but to run with it.

"Are you going to call an ambulance?" said Kathleen impatiently.

"No, man. I don't want no ambulance!" moaned Clayton.

There was urgency and worry in Kathleen's eyes.

"Ah . . . let's wait until the police get here," I said. "I'll text his astrologist." I ignored Kathleen's puzzled look and tapped on my phone: "*He's faking. Play along!*"

Seconds after I sent the message to Kathleen, I heard the phone in her pocket buzz. She looked at me, appearing to be thinking about what had just occurred.

Then she stood, casually checked her phone, looked at me, and smiled.

Chapter Eighty

Mark was on his knees and looking at the pills scattered on the floor without touching them, like a detective examining a crime scene. He used his finger to point them out and identify them.

"There's oxycodone, that one's hydrocodone, there's Xanax, I think that's Percocet, and those are definitely Valium." He looked at Brett in disgust and said, "I bet he's ripping off the people who live here."

"I knew it!" said Abbie. She looked at Brett with disdain. "You dirty, rotten son of a bitch."

Two police officers jogged into the dining room and approached us. One of the officers stood by Brett and asked Dean and Tony what happened while the other asked Kathleen and me to stand back as he knelt and talked to Clayton. He asked about calling an ambulance, and Clayton said he'd like to try and stand first.

The officer said, "Well, just stay put until we get some help." He said something on the microphone pinned to his chest, and in a few minutes, two more officers arrived.

The officer who was with Clayton stood, briefly

conferred with the three other officers, then ordered everyone out of the dining room other than the people who were in the immediate area where Clayton was attacked. When most of the people were gone, the officer again knelt down next to Clayton and resumed his conversation with him about his level of pain and ability to stand.

The second officer got on his knees and began examining and photographing the pills on the floor while the other two began interviewing the witnesses.

The officer who had been examining the pills eventually stood and talked quietly to the two who had been interviewing the witnesses. After a short discussion, the officer with the camera got back on his knees and continued to photograph the pills while the other two approached Brett and told him to stand. Brett stood, and the officers told him to place his hands behind his back.

"Why?" Brett said angrily.

"Sir, you're being arrested for possession with intent to deliver controlled substances and abuse of a vulnerable adult. Now, put your hands behind your back."

Brett complied, and the officers handcuffed and escorted him out of the building.

After the officer finished taking photographs, he put on latex gloves and carefully picked up the pills and the sandwich bag they had been in, then put them in a clear plastic evidence bag. He wrote something on the bag with a Sharpie, then walked over and stood by Clayton and the officer who was attending to him.

The officer who was kneeling next to Clayton said, "Are you sure you want to try to stand?"

"I'm sure."

"I think we should call an ambulance," said the officer with the evidence bag. "If you have a fracture, standing up could make it worse. It's better to be cautious about a hip injury."

"Thanks, guys," said Clayton as he moved his legs. "I'm not feeling any pain when I move my legs, and I'm sure I would if my hip was fractured." He grimaced when he moved. "My problem is that my butt is really sore, and I think it may have a crack in it." The officer on his knees fought hard to keep from laughing. "You'll find out when you get to be my age that you want to avoid the hospital at all costs. They'll want to admit me, run a bunch of tests, then try to stick me with a bill for a few grand. That's the way they work it."

"Okay, we'll note in our report that you refused medical treatment," said one of the officers.

"That's fine. Don't worry about me. I have a very high pain threshold."

"Yeah! He cut his leg off with a pocketknife," blurted Abbie as she flashed a smile at Kathleen and me when the officers weren't looking.

The officers looked at each other. "You're the guy that did that?" asked the officer kneeling next to Clayton. "I heard about you from a buddy who's a cop in Bloomfield Hills."

The officer with the evidence bag smiled and said, "You're kind of a legend there."

Clayton smiled. "Wow! That's crazy. When I get up, maybe someone can take our picture, and you can send it to your buddy."

Kathleen buried her face in her hand and quietly said to me, "He just never quits."

"That would be awesome," said the officer with the evidence bag.

Clayton slowly moved to a sitting position and looked at

the officers. "So far, so good." The officers helped him stand, then pivoted him and slowly lowered him into a chair. "Now, that was a piece of cake," said Clayton. "Hey, I really kicked his ass, didn't I?"

The officers laughed. One of them said, "You sure did."

"Officers, I have to tell you something really important."

Expecting that Clayton was about to tell a whopper, Kathleen said under her breath, "Oh boy, here we go."

"What's that, Mr. Davis?" one of the officers said.

Clayton pointed to Abbie. "That woman right there in the panda bear sweatsuit—she's the real hero in all this. She suspected all summer that the guy you arrested was skimming pills from the residents. I didn't believe it, but she was right all along. You should talk to her. Not only is she a walking fashion statement, but she's very smart and incredibly observant."

Abbie smiled at Clayton's compliment, and Mark looked at her proudly.

"Thank you. We'll definitely talk to her." The officers asked Abbie to stay in the dining room for a few minutes and explained they had some things they had to wrap up. They went to every person who remained in the dining room and confirmed their names and contact information. When that was done, they told everyone they were free to leave.

Charlie told his sons he was proud of them, and I thanked them for intervening and restraining Brett.

"We love being around you guys," said Dean.

"Why?" asked Kathleen.

Tony laughed. "'Cause there's always action. A fight today. The cops at Bud's house during Woodstock. The Beverly Hillbillies thing. You never know what you're going to get. It's fun."

"And unpredictable," said Dean.

I laughed. "I never looked at it that way, but you may have a point. See you next Saturday?"

"You bet," said Dean. "Looking forward to it."

Kathleen and I filled two mugs with coffee and delivered them to the officers at the table with Abbie, Mark, and Clayton. The officers thanked us, and Clayton resumed telling them what happened from the moment he saw Brett at the coffee machine until Brett pushed him down. When Clayton finished, he slowly stood and said, "I think I'll be moseying down to my crib."

"Are you sure you're okay to walk that distance, Mr. Davis?" asked one of them.

"I think I'll be fine."

"Would you mind if we get that picture before you leave?"

"No problem."

Both officers gave me their smartphones. Clayton stood between them and draped his arms over their shoulders as if they were best friends. I snapped pictures on the phones while Kathleen smiled at the absurdity of it all.

After the photos, Kathleen and I left the dining room and went outside for a walk. Mark and Abbie remained at the table, and Abbie told me later she talked to the officers for over an hour about the missing pills and why she suspected medications were being stolen from residents at the three Serenity facilities.

The officers listened intently and took copious notes.

Chapter Eighty-One

As I walked to the dining room for a midmorning coffee the following day, I saw two police officers at the nurses' station talking to Brenda. A box was on the counter next to them. Brenda was smiling, and the conversation seemed amicable. The officers picked up the box, thanked her, and headed toward the entrance.

I asked Brenda what was going on. She told me the officers had arrived early in the morning with a search warrant for records from Brett's office and the nurses' station. She mentioned that Nurse Jackie didn't show up for work and that the cops were wondering where she was staying.

Brenda whispered, "I heard one of the cops say Brett was 'singing like a bird.'"

I told her we were concerned that state authorities would order the building to be closed and that we'd all be scrambling to find new places to live. Brenda assured me that wasn't going to happen. She said a night-shift nurse spoke to a part owner from California, and he assured her the business would continue operating.

I was surprised by Brenda's comment about a California

owner. I'd always understood that Brett and his two prep school buddies owned the three Serenity facilities. Brenda said she'd also heard that the owner was trying to arrange a meeting with the employees and residents.

That evening, I joined my friends, other residents, and a few Serenity employees around the TV in the great room to watch the beginning of the six o'clock news. The facility was buzzing with talk about Brett and what had happened in the dining room, and we were curious to see if the incident was being followed by the media. We didn't have to wait long to find out.

"Good evening, Detroit, I'm Ross Bluestone. Welcome to the TV 6 evening news. At least four people are in custody this evening, and others are being sought, in connection with a rapidly expanding investigation involving the theft of prescription medication from elderly residents of Serenity Assisted Living facilities in Farmington Hills, Grand Rapids, and Traverse City. Let's go live to TV 6 reporter Heidi Longstreet, who is at the Farmington Hills facility and has been following this story throughout the day. Heidi, what can you tell us?"

Heidi stood on the sidewalk in front of the Serenity sign, where the Woodstock photo had been taken.

"What the hell? She must be out in front right now," said Clayton.

"Ross, the details are still coming in, but we understand the police were called here yesterday morning in response to a report that a resident had been assaulted by an employee of the facility. That employee was Brett Beaudry, a co-owner and manager of the facility, who was arraigned late yesterday afternoon on multiple charges, including conspiracy to deliver controlled substances, five counts of possession of controlled substances with intent to deliver, and abuse of a vulnerable adult."

"How did a call for an assault turn into a major drug bust?" Ross asked. "And what does that have to do with the Serenity facilities in Traverse City and Grand Rapids?"

"Ross, during the altercation with the resident, a bag of pills, allegedly stolen from the residents, fell out of Mr. Beaudry's blazer and onto the floor. While investigating the source of those pills, officers spoke to a seventy-four-year-old resident who provided credible information that pills were also being stolen from residents of the Serenity facilities in Grand Rapids and Traverse City. Authorities acted on that information, and search warrants were served on the Farmington Hills and Grand Rapids facilities this morning. We also understand that a nurse, bookkeeper, and co-owner of the Grand Rapids facility are in custody. Traverse City authorities have declined to comment on the case."

"Have you spoken to the witness who cracked this case?"

"Not yet, Ross, but I'm working on it and hope to have more news on this breaking story at eleven."

"Good work, Heidi."

Chapter Eighty-Two

Heidi Longstreet entered the building and was disappointed to find that no one was in Brett's office. As she stood trying to decide where to go, one of the residents walked by.

"Excuse me, sir," Heidi said.

Don Durman stopped. "What can I do for you?" He studied her face. "Hey, you're that person from . . ."

"Right. I'm Heidi Longstreet from TV 6. Do you know where I can find . . ." She pulled out a small notepad from her pocket and glanced at it. "Abbie Miron. I'd like to talk to her."

Pointing toward some people gathered around a big-screen TV in the great room, Durman replied, "She's right over there."

"Hi, everyone," said Heidi as she approached the group. "I'm Heidi Longstreet. I'm a reporter for TV 6, and I'm interested in talking to Abbie Miron." She pointed at a nicely dressed woman who gave her a welcoming smile. "Are you Abbie?"

"No. I'm Abbie." Heidi's eyes shifted to the short,

plump woman in a sweatsuit printed with tiny carrot-eating bunnies.

Heidi was taken aback but extended her hand, and Abbie shook it. "So nice to meet you, Abbie."

"Why do you wanna talk to me?" asked Abbie.

"I understand you may have provided the police with important information that led to the arrests of at least four people associated with the Serenity facilities."

Abbie shifted in her chair. "I just told them about some things I saw."

Her curt response gave Heidi the impression that Abbie might deny her request for an interview, which she needed badly after her comments a few minutes earlier on the six o'clock news. This wasn't the first time she'd encountered a seemingly reluctant interviewee, but she'd learned that flattery and bullshit can turn a camera-shy witness into an eager participant.

"Abbie, I'm so impressed by everything I've heard about you. One of the investigating officers told me you should teach a class in criminal investigations to rookie cops. Would you mind talking to me on camera?"

Abbie looked at the others at her table, who seemed to encourage her with smiles and nods. "I guess I could. Right now?"

"That'd be great. My cameraman is waiting out by the Serenity sign. I'll see you out there."

Proud of her persuasive abilities and excited about being the first reporter to interview a key witness in a big, ongoing criminal investigation, Heidi smiled and headed out of the dining room.

She was holding a microphone and talking to her cameraman when she saw Abbie step outside. She waved, and Abbie waved back.

When Abbie reached them, Heidi said, "All set?"

"Sure. I guess so."

"Okay, great. Abbie, I've got to pin this tiny microphone on your beautiful sweatshirt." Heidi looked at the cameraman and winked. As she pinned the microphone to Abbie's collar, she added, "Those little bunnies are so cute. I bet that outfit cost you a fortune."

"Not really. I got it on sale at Target."

"Target? Oh my goodness, I would have guessed Neiman Marcus." The cameraman faked coughing to conceal his laughter.

Abbie nervously ran her fingers through her hair to try to flatten it down as Heidi stepped back a few paces and sized her up. "Just before we start, you'll need to drop your arms to your sides and try not to move. Remember, this is not a live broadcast, so don't worry about that. We'll record the interview, and then we'll take what parts we need for the eleven o'clock news. So, if you want to repeat yourself or start over, it's not a big deal. Does that make sense?"

"Sure," said Abbie. "Anything else?"

"I always tell people to relax, ignore the camera, and just be themselves. So when I nod, you should state your name and address, and then I will ask you a question. Any more questions before we begin?"

"No."

Heidi watched the cameraman look through the viewfinder and make some adjustments in the settings until he said he was ready to roll. When he nodded, Heidi gave Abbie a thumbs-up sign.

Abbie was looking at her left arm and then swatted her arm with her other hand. "Damn mosquitoes. Can't believe they're still out."

"All right," said Heidi. "You have to look at me because

I will nod, and you will state your name and address. Sound good?"

"Okay."

Heidi nodded.

"My name is Abbie Miron, and I live here at Serenity Assisted Living in Farmington Hills, Michigan."

Heidi smiled approvingly. "How long have you been living here at Serenity Assisted Living?"

"I lose track of time. I think it's been around three years."

"You have been identified as a key witness in the arrest of several people associated with the Serenity facilities in Farmington Hills and Grand Rapids. What information did you provide to the police?"

"From day one, I knew that son of a bitch—"

"Abbie, sorry for interrupting. You know, we plan to show portions of this interview on TV, so you can't be using expletives."

"Expletives?"

"Yeah, you know—swear words."

"Okay. Want me to start over again?"

"Sure."

"What was the question again?" Abbie asked.

"I asked you what information you provided to the police."

"I knew from day one that . . . I knew that no-good chump—"

"Wait a second, Abbie—"

"You said no swear words. *Chump* isn't a swear word!"

Trying hard to be patient, Heidi replied, "I know *chump* isn't a swear word, but we don't want any name-calling on TV. We'd prefer just to stick to the facts."

"Well, the fact is that he's a son of a bitch and chump who stole medication from the residents."

"Right. Those are the allegations."

"Allegations, my ass! I saw the pills fall out of his pocket and onto the floor."

Heidi decided to try a different approach. "So, you've been a resident here for around three years. Did you see anything suspicious?"

"Definitely."

"What did you see?"

"I always thought he was up to something, but I just couldn't put my finger on it. He'd spent a lot of time with his head nurse, and Clayton said he was probably sleeping with her, but . . ."

"Wait, wait, wait . . . Mrs. Miron, ah, Abbie. I assume you're referring to Mr. Beaudry, and you can't be speculating that he was sleeping with the head nurse. Something like that could get us all in trouble."

"I wasn't speculating. Clayton was. I never thought she was sleeping with Brett. I mean, Mr. Beaudry."

"Okay, fine. Let's just stick to what you saw. Please don't refer to what other people said. Can we do that?"

"Sure."

"A few moments ago, you said you saw pills. What was that about?"

"I saw Brett, um, Mr. Beaudry, attack Clayton, and when Tony and Dean grabbed that no-good son of a—"

"Stop, please!" said Heidi. "Again, you can't be calling people names. There may be children watching."

"Well, children shouldn't be up for the eleven o'clock news."

"That's not the point, Abbie! We can't use those words on TV."

"I've heard worse on Netflix."

"I'm sure you have, but this is the news, not a Netflix movie. Look, I know you don't like Mr. Beaudry, but you have to keep those feelings to yourself. Please, can you just stick to the facts? What we'll do is, I'll ask you leading questions, like lawyers do in court."

"I know all about leading questions. I watch *Law and Order* all the time. Go ahead."

"You gave a statement to the police, which led to the arrest of several people associated with the Serenity facilities, correct?"

"Yup."

"You saw some things that happened here at Serenity Assisted Living in Farmington Hills that you reported to the police."

"Yup."

"And you saw that one of the owners, Brett Beaudry, had pills in his possession that you think he stole from the residents."

"Yup."

Frustrated by Abbie's one-word responses, Heidi abandoned her leading question inquiry. "Other than the pills Mr. Beaudry had in his possession, why do you think he was stealing pills from the residents?"

"Objection! Not a leading question!" Abbie laughed.

Heidi pleaded, "Come on, Abbie, why do you think Mr. Beaudry was stealing pills from the residents?"

"Mainly by counting pills, but other stuff too."

"What do you mean counting pills?"

"It's simple. I knew how many pills I took, and I asked how many I had left, and the numbers didn't add up. So I talked to my friend Jim—he died recently—and I said, 'Jim, this is a bunch of BS. I think they're ripping us off,' and he

321

found out the same thing happened to him and another friend too."

"So you guys kept track of how many pills you took, and when you asked how many were left, you found out there were shortages," Heidi said.

"Right! That's when we knew for sure they were putting it to us."

"You mentioned 'other stuff.' What did you see?"

"One day, I saw Brett arguing with Ricci, that guy from Grand Rapids, and that other guy, ah, Pennington, from Traverse City, and one of the men gave him a briefcase, and he looked in real quick. I could tell by his eyes that he was thinking, *Holy shit*." Heidi cringed after Abbie uttered the last two words but decided to let her continue. "And another time, I saw a guy come in the building with a dark-brown briefcase, which he gave to Mr. Beaudry. Then he left with a light-brown briefcase."

"So, you saw William Pennington of Traverse City and Louis Ricci of Grand Rapids in a meeting with Mr. Beaudry, and that's when there was arguing, and Mr. Beaudry looked in a briefcase."

"Uh-huh."

"Did you see what was in the briefcase?"

"How could I do that? I wasn't in the office," Abbie said.

"You just thought the whole situation was suspicious?"

"Yeah."

"Tell me about the briefcase exchange with the other man," Heidi said. "Do you know the identity of the man?"

"No."

"So, a man came into the building with a dark briefcase and left with a light-colored briefcase."

"Exactly," Abbie replied.

"Do you know what was in the briefcase?"

"How the hell would I know that?"

"What made you think that was suspicious?"

"What was your name again?"

"Heidi."

"Heidi, would you go to a meeting with a black purse and come out with a brown purse?"

"No."

"They pulled the old switcheroo. Oldest trick in the book. They thought they were being real clever, but they didn't fool me."

Completely exasperated and ready to stop the interview, Heidi remembered her boss's instructions to get a sound bite about the Crime Stoppers Award. "Abbie, did you know there is talk that you may be nominated for a Citizen Crime Stoppers Award?"

"What's that?"

"It's a prestigious award from the Farmington Hills mayor and chief of police to citizens who have the courage to step up and provide important investigative information to the police. Prior recipients have received gift cards and other benefits from area merchants."

"Cool."

"Anything more you want to say about the Crime Stoppers Award?"

"No. I haven't even got it yet."

"Okay, that's a wrap! Thank you, Abbie. It was a pleasure talking to you." Heidi took the microphone off Abbie's sweatshirt and shook her hand.

"Is that it?" asked Abbie.

"That's it. Thanks again."

"How'd I do?"

Heidi glanced at her cameraman, who rolled his eyes. "You did great."

As Abbie made her way up the sidewalk to the building, Heidi grumbled to the cameraman, "The biggest story of my career, and I can't get a decent interview with a key witness. That's got to be the worst friggin' interview I've ever done! What the hell am I going to do with that?"

"Editing. A whole lot of editing."

Chapter Eighty-Three

"Well, how'd it go?" asked Clayton as Abbie approached us in the great room. She was smiling broadly and moving faster than usual.

"They said I did great." Abbie pushed her walker aside and sat down.

"I'm sure you did," said Kathleen. "Good job."

"It was pretty easy. I just followed Heidi's advice and was myself."

Clayton smiled. "Filtered or unfiltered?"

"What do you mean? I didn't make a damn cigarette commercial."

Clayton looked at me and rolled his eyes. "What I'm asking is if you steered away from some of the colorful words in your vocabulary."

"Oh, that." Abbie thought for a moment. "A couple of times, but Heidi reminded me to keep it clean."

"Not a big deal. They'll edit that out. I'm sure you did fine."

We agreed to meet just before the eleven o'clock news to watch Abbie's interview.

* * *

Just before the start of the news, a bunch of us gathered in front of the TV in the great room. As Abbie approached us, Kathleen stood.

"Ladies and gentlemen, let's have a round of applause for the hero of Serenity Assisted Living," Kathleen said.

Everyone clapped and cheered, and Abbie let go of her walker and awkwardly curtsied. As she got closer, several of the residents gave her high fives. Kathleen pointed to the middle of the couch directly in front of the TV. "I saved a spot for you."

When Abbie sat, Kathleen walked behind the couch and placed a plastic crown adorned with rhinestones on Abbie's head. "I hereby christen you The Hero of Serenity." Kathleen noticed me looking at the crown and giggled. "Clayton had it in his costume bag."

Abbie beamed with pride as everyone applauded.

Someone said, "It's on. Turn up the volume!"

The newsman was seated and looking solemnly into the camera. I picked up the remote and increased the volume.

"Good evening. I'm PJ McClure. Our breaking news tonight is the arrest of the operators of the Serenity Assisted Living facilities in Farmington Hills, Traverse City, and Grand Rapids, along with several people associated with them, in what police have described as a complex criminal conspiracy involving the theft and distribution of prescription drugs taken from elderly residents of the three facilities.

"According to law enforcement authorities, the multicounty investigation began yesterday morning when the police were called to the Farmington Hills Serenity facility to investigate the alleged assault of a seventy-two-year-old resident—" Clayton raised his arms with his fists clenched, drawing cheers. "—by this man, Brett Beaudry, a part owner and operator of the facility."

Several people, including some of the employees, booed when Brett's mug shot appeared on the screen behind McClure.

"Beaudry allegedly possessed a significant quantity of narcotics he had taken from the residents. He was arraigned late this afternoon in the Forty-Seventh District Court in Farmington Hills on felony charges of conspiracy to deliver controlled substances, five counts of possession of controlled substances with intent to deliver, and third-degree abuse of a vulnerable adult.

"Late this afternoon, Louis Ricci, the operator of the Grand Rapids Serenity facility, his bookkeeper, and a registered nurse were arrested by Grand Rapids authorities and charged with conspiracy to deliver controlled substances. And we just learned that William Pennington, who's the operator of the Traverse City Serenity facility, and a registered nurse were arrested this evening at the Traverse City Airport as they attempted to board a plane."

Pictures of Ricci and Pennington appeared on the screen behind McClure. Abbie turned to Clayton. "Remember when they were in Brett's office?"

"Indeed I do."

"According to our sources," said McClure, "information supplied by a seventy-four-year-old resident of the Farmington Hills Serenity facility was essential to cracking the case. Heidi Longstreet tracked down and interviewed that person, whom some are calling a hero. Heidi, what did you find out?"

The camera swung toward Heidi, who was sitting at the newsroom desk adjacent to McClure. "PJ, earlier today, I met with Abbie Miron, a resident of the Serenity Assisted Living facility in Farmington Hills, whom police describe as a key witness in their investigation. Ms. Miron told me she suspected for several months that her medication was being stolen because there were shortages in the pills prescribed to her."

Everyone watching cheered when a clip from the interview appeared. Abbie's disheveled hair moved in the breeze, and the bright sunshine accentuated the carrot-eating rabbits on her sweatsuit. "I knew how many pills I took, and when I asked how many I had left, the numbers didn't add up. So I talked to my friend Jim—he died recently—and he found out the same thing happened to him and another friend too."

"Sounds like Ms. Miron is as sharp as a tack," said McClure.

"Definitely, PJ. Like an undercover detective, she cleverly monitored suspicious activities at the facility, and the information she provided to the police led to the recent arrests in Grand Rapids and Traverse City. Nothing escaped her prying eyes."

Another segment of the interview appeared on the screen. Abbie ran her hand through her hair and said, "They thought they were being real clever, but they didn't fool me."

"Is it true that Ms. Miron may be nominated for the Citizen Crime Stoppers Award?" asked McClure.

"That's right. The chief of police alluded to that today

during his press conference. Ms. Miron was very happy about that."

McClure smiled. "Excellent report, Heidi. There was an explosion this morning—" Someone turned off the TV.

"That's it?" said Clayton. "You had to have been talking to her for fifteen minutes. I can't believe that's all they put on."

Charlie clenched his fists and began chanting, "Abbie, Abbie, Abbie," and soon, everyone joined in, including Clayton. Abbie was beaming with pride as she was high-fived and hugged by residents and employees.

Chapter Eighty-Four

The next morning, we were notified of a meeting at eleven in the dining room to discuss "recent events at the three Serenity facilities." All residents were urged to attend.

Rumors and speculation circulated. Would Serenity be shut down? Would we be on our own to find new places to live? Would other Serenity employees be arrested?

An aide confirmed what Brenda had told me. A guy from California was going to address the residents and employees of all three facilities by live videoconference.

Well before the appointed hour, residents began gathering in the dining room. A cart bearing a big-screen TV had been set up in a corner, and my friends and I nervously waited for the meeting to start. With the three owners in jail, who was left to talk to us?

At precisely eleven, the TV flickered and came on. I watched my son, John, sitting at a desk and tapping his earpiece. He was sporting a closely cropped beard, and he looked tan and trim in his casual white shirt with the sleeves rolled up.

"Ooh la la, I could look at this guy all day," said Abbie. Clayton shushed her. Kathleen smiled and looked at me, but I was too stunned to respond.

"If you can hear me at the Farmington Hills facility, will you please raise your hands?" We raised our hands. "Thank you. How about Grand Rapids? Thank you. And Traverse City? Excellent. Thank you.

"Good morning, everyone. After all that has occurred, I'm sure you're all wondering who I am and what this meeting is about. My name is John Livingston. The three Serenity facilities in Michigan are owned by the Serenity Corporation, and I am the majority shareholder. I live in California, and I was shocked and appalled when I heard about the recent events there."

The eyes of my friends were on me, but I felt frozen, unable to react or move.

"Wow! Is that your kid, Bud?" asked Abbie.

I couldn't respond. I noticed that Kathleen and Abbie exchanged puzzled looks before I turned my attention back to the screen.

"I have known the operators of the three facilities for most of my life. We attended the same school, played on the same teams, and graduated together. But if they are guilty of the crimes they are accused of committing, I have no problem saying they should be punished to the full extent of the law. I have no tolerance for people who abuse positions of trust. It's that simple. You may rest assured we will fully cooperate with the police in their investigation of the alleged crimes. Regardless of the outcome of the criminal cases, the people involved will never again set foot in a Serenity facility.

"I can assure you the Serenity facilities will not close. I am working closely with attorneys in Michigan to make the necessary corporate changes so those accused of crimes are relieved of their positions and responsibilities. Recent events were a significant blow to the business, that's for sure. But that will not stop us from continuing to provide you with the outstanding services you are accustomed to. If we take care of you, there is nothing to worry about.

"In the near future, each facility will be visited by experienced consultants who will be assessing our management and personnel needs and assisting us in establishing stringent procedures for the handling, storage, and dispensing of prescription medication. Our country is in an opioid abuse crisis, and I am deeply troubled by the allegations that narcotics stolen from our residents may have ended up on the streets.

"I have always recognized that our employees are the reason for our success, and I am sincerely grateful for your loyalty, hard work, and dedication. Everyone will have to step up over the next few weeks as we deal with the loss of some employees, the criminal investigation, and the inevitable investigation by the licensing authorities. To show my appreciation in advance for your steadfast loyalty, I will be awarding bonuses of $700 to full-time employees and $350 to part-time employees. Those bonuses will be in your next paycheck.

"For those of you who may have been victimized by a few bad apples, I am very sorry. We will work hard to regain your trust, and we hope you will remember that the vast majority of people who work at the Serenity facilities are ethical, honest, and caring. Thank you."

John sat looking into the camera until the screen went blue.

"Okay," said Abbie. "Was that your kid or not?"

Embarrassed, I stood and left the dining room.

Chapter Eighty-Five

I sat on one of the benches along the sidewalk leading to the entrance, feeling a mixture of humiliation and anger, when, after a couple minutes, I heard, "Mind if I sit, Bud?" It was Kathleen, her sweet face full of concern.

"I didn't notice you come out. Of course. Have a seat."

My stomach was in knots, and I was in no mood to talk about John and what happened during the videoconference. We sat quietly until Kathleen started to leave. I asked where she was going, and she said she wanted to give me some alone time. I apologized and asked her to stay.

"Do you wanna tell me what's going on, Bud? I assume that was your son."

"Yes, that was John, my son."

I didn't know where to start, but I launched into a long-winded rambling about April and John, the heartache they'd caused me, and my disappointment in them. I told her about April's tactics to convince me to leave my home. Then I speculated that she'd bitched to John about having to check in on me, that he'd moved me to the top of the waiting list, and that Brett had played right along. I said I was mad at myself for not realizing something fishy had gone on when I hadn't needed to wait, even though Clayton said there was a long waiting list.

Kathleen smiled meekly. "I'm glad they pulled it off."

"Me too, but the sneaky way they went about it was wrong. John had to know I was watching. Isn't it sad he basically owns the place and nobody ever bothered to tell me? It was humiliating for me to sit there watching my son while Abbie peppered me with questions."

"I'm sorry it played out this way, Bud. I understand how you feel, but . . ."

A female resident came out of the building with a young man. Kathleen shrugged, and we watched and listened while the two talked. Eventually, the resident thanked the man for dropping by, and the man said, "Love you, Grandma." After they hugged, the resident went back inside, and the young man walked past us toward the parking lot.

"That was so sweet," said Kathleen.

"It was, but I think you started to say something when they came out. What were you going to say?"

Kathleen sighed. "I don't know April or John, and I don't doubt anything you're saying. But do you suppose there's another way of looking at this?"

"How so?"

"Maybe John and April saw that living alone in that house wasn't good for you. That you needed to be around other people."

Shaking my head, I said, "You don't know my kids, Kathleen. Your theory assumes they arranged for me to come here out of concern for my well-being. I doubt that was the reason."

"You told me a few moments ago that you're glad you're

here, so things worked out no matter what motivated John and April. Right?"

"I guess."

"Bud, you don't check your problems at the front door when you move into a place like this. It's how you deal with them that counts." She paused and appeared to be trying to keep her emotions in check. "Bud, I was a mess when I came here." She pulled a tissue out of her pocket and wiped the tears from her eyes. "I'm sorry. This is still difficult for me to talk about."

"Take your time."

"On the day my husband died, he said he didn't feel right. He said his chest felt weird and he was lightheaded. He was in decent shape and not one to complain. I was preoccupied with whatever I was doing and didn't ask any questions or offer to take him to the emergency room. A couple hours later, I found him lying on the floor in our bedroom. He was gone. It was a heart attack.

"I might've saved him if I had taken his complaints seriously. I couldn't shake that. I was overwhelmed with guilt, and my daughters and their families were devastated. The months that followed were rough. I was depressed and not taking care of myself. That's when I had the stroke. When I came here after rehab, I still hadn't dealt with my guilt and depression."

"How'd you move beyond those things?"

"It took a while, Bud, and I had some help. But I don't want to make this conversation about me. Today is your struggle."

Kathleen stared at the flower beds in front of us and seemed to be deep in thought. Then she reached over and held my hand.

"Bud, it doesn't matter if you're here because your kids

had their own agendas or they thought they were doing what was right for you. You're here, and you can either let the issues with your kids weigh you down or you can move ahead. In a way, you're in the same place I was when I got here. Things from the past are affecting the present."

"I get it. I know you're right. But you didn't answer my question. How'd you move beyond the things that were holding you back?"

"I heard about the going-out-strong stuff Sister Mary Katherine told Jim, but at the time, it didn't really resonate with me. Then I got to know Charlie, who had his own set of struggles—loneliness, worries about the business and his early retirement, guilt that he didn't take his wife to a better hospital, and concern that he'd been a burden to his family. I felt bad for him. So, one day, I challenged him to a game of cribbage, and to my surprise, he accepted. He seemed so happy to have company, and we agreed to make cribbage a regular event. Over time, we helped each other let go of those things and live for the present. That's when we both found peace and contentment. And that's when the things Sister Mary Katherine said made sense."

Out of words, I shook my head. Kathleen squeezed my hand. "Are you okay?"

I remembered that she once told me Sister Mary Katherine helped her through some rough stuff, but I didn't know her well enough then to ask what she meant. I didn't give it a second thought. Charlie confided in me that he felt like he was drifting because he was not working, but I never considered that he had been burdened with other concerns. Even after Jim, Abbie, and Clayton told me about the things that were weighing on their hearts, I was too caught up in my issues with John and April to recognize that we all came to Serenity with baggage, but Kathleen and the others figured out ways to put it on a shelf while I was still carrying it around.

"I feel pretty damn foolish," I said.

"Foolish? Why?"

"I've been a moron. I've been saying I want to go out strong, but I really didn't have a clue what that meant in spite of everyone's efforts to enlighten me. I kept thinking it was about having friends, staying active, and having fun while I am still able. I guess I'm just a slow learner, Kathleen. It took me all this time to realize that it's more of an attitude—a way of living."

"What do you mean by that, Bud?"

"It's about making the most of the time we have, which means moving on from the negative stuff and not being bogged down by the past or things we can't control. That's what you guys do, right? Good grief, I think I just stumbled upon the senior citizen's secret to a happier life!"

Kathleen squeezed my hand and smiled. "I think you've got it, Bud."

"Kathleen, can two people go out strong together?"

Our eyes met, and as I leaned toward her, a flower delivery van came flying up the driveway and parked in front of the building. The driver jumped out, opened the van's side door, and grabbed a bunch of red roses in a vase. He walked briskly toward the building, smiling as he passed us. He went inside, dropped off his delivery, returned to his van, and sped off.

I pointed at the departing delivery van. "Next time we have a serious conversation, we may want to pick a different location."

"Good call."

We looked at each other again, and I felt that this moment was equally important to Kathleen. As I leaned over to kiss her, I heard the door open and saw Abbie grinning and using her walker as a brace to keep the door from closing. Behind her was Clayton holding the vase of roses that had just been dropped off.

"Hey!" Abbie yelled. "Check out what Mark sent! Surprised the livin' shit out of me."

Kathleen stood and hurried over to hug Abbie and admire the flowers. I smiled and joined her.

Chapter Eighty-Six

By late September, the police investigation had been completed. Consultants had visited the facility and made their recommendations, and some changes and additions were made to the staff. A well-liked RN from the night shift now occupied Brett's office, and a popular day-shift nurse was promoted to the head nurse's position, replacing Jackie, who still had not been located.

Mark, Dean, and Tony became the "Saturday morning regulars," always arriving early. One Saturday morning, the two brothers offered Mark a full-time position with benefits at Motor City Bus Repair, which he tearfully accepted.

Saturday mornings became the most anticipated entertainment of the week. The regulars' spirited conversations with Abbie and Charlie caused much laughter at their table. Soon, other residents seeking amusement positioned themselves at nearby tables to eavesdrop on the conversations.

Kathleen and I got into a routine of taking long daily strolls for the stated purpose of enjoying the beautiful fall weather and colors. The strolls always resulted in long conversations about our lives. Sometimes, the conversations were light and amusing, such as the time we talked about our first dates and kisses. Other times, our conversations delved deep into emotional and personal issues. We became closer, and everyone seemed to accept that we were more than friends.

One afternoon, Kathleen introduced me to her daughter Martha, who was a spitting image of her mother. She was the same height and build, had similar dark-brown eyes, short dark hair, and a smile that was undeniably Kathleen's. I felt like a nervous teenager hoping for the approval of my date's parent, but Martha's friendly demeanor calmed my nerves.

We were sitting in Kathleen's apartment, and Martha suggested we have coffee. Kathleen thought that was a good idea, so she left her seat next to me, walked into the kitchenette, and began running water for the coffee maker. When she was out of earshot, Martha leaned forward in her chair across from me and said, "Bud, thanks for being so good to my mom. She took my dad's death really hard, and it makes me happy to see her smiling again."

I wondered if Martha noticed my sigh of relief. "You're welcome. Your mom is a wonderful person, and I'm grateful for her friendship."

Martha winked. "You know she really likes you, right?"

I whispered, "I'll let you in on a little secret."

Martha glanced suspiciously toward the kitchenette. Leaving her chair to kneel next to me, she said, "What?"

"I really like her too."

She smiled, patted me on the knee, and said, "Fantastic."

Chapter Eighty-Seven

"I love fall," said Kathleen.

We had just completed a long walk and were sitting on the same bench in the front of the building where we had talked after my son's videoconference. The location of the bench gave us a panoramic view of the grounds, which were particularly beautiful on a warm fall afternoon. The sky was clear and deep blue, and the red and orange leaves on the old oaks dotting the property fluttered in a gentle breeze. Here and there, leaves fell from the trees and floated to the ground.

"I do too. I just don't like what comes after it."

Seeming surprised, Kathleen responded, "What? You're kidding me! You're a Yooper! I figured you loved the cold weather and snow."

"I used to. I did a lot of skiing and snowmobiling when I was younger, but I can't handle the cold anymore."

She reached over and grasped my hand. "Well, I guess we'll just have to hunker down here and make the best of it."

With winter approaching, I'd been thinking about

escaping Serenity with Kathleen, but I was unsure how I'd broach the subject. I knew she'd have reservations about moving away from her daughters and their families. Her comment about hunkering down gave me an unexpected opening.

"Kathleen, I've been thinking . . . we don't have to stay here for the winter."

Looking puzzled, she asked, "We don't?"

"No."

"What do you have in mind?"

"Going to Spain for a bullfighting tournament and stamp collectors' convention."

She knew I was kidding and giggled. "Gosh, that sounds wonderful and so romantic."

"Actually, Kathleen, I think we should become snow-birds and go to Florida. I own a condo on the Gulf near Venice. April has used it from time to time, but I haven't been there for three years. I didn't see any point in going to Florida by myself."

Her mouth dropped open, and she stared at me. "Are you serious?"

"Very serious."

"Just pack up and leave like the kids who dropped everything and went to Woodstock?"

"Right." I smiled. "I remember you saying on the Fourth of July that you missed being a part of all that. This could be your personal Woodstock—a spontaneous and liberating adventure into the land of warm weather and sunshine."

She rolled her eyes. "Here we go again."

I couldn't tell if she was being playful or sarcastic. "What's that supposed to mean?"

She gave me a *duh* look. "You know exactly what I mean."

Something smacked me on the top of my head. "Ouch!" I said as an acorn rolled down my chest and onto the sidewalk. We looked up and saw a squirrel high up in an old oak tree jump from one branch to another.

Kathleen laughed. "I have friends in high places! Serves you right for corrupting me!"

Rubbing the top of my head, I said, "That wasn't funny!" Then her word choice hit me. "Corrupting? What's that supposed to mean?"

"You know exactly what I mean. Before I came here, I was never a risk-taker, and I rarely did something on impulse. You, Clayton, and Jim pushed me well beyond my comfort zone, and I've done some things that would have been unimaginable a year ago."

"Like what?"

The entrance door flew open, and two boys ran out. One of them yelled, "Race ya to the car!"

As they took off running and blew past us, a frazzled-looking woman came out behind them and yelled, "Slow down, boys!" She rolled her eyes and apologized as she walked by.

I laughed. "I thought we agreed this isn't a very good spot for a serious conversation. Now, where were we? Oh yeah, you said you were corrupted into doing things that were unimaginable. That's a very serious accusation. Like what?"

Kathleen seemed to ponder my question. "Geez, Bud, that's a toughie." She giggled. "Oh, wait. I remember! How about eating a marijuana brownie, putting a snake in a couch, and wearing a Cher wig and pig mask while you put a corn-laced Tootsie Roll in Brett's car." She smiled. "Want me to continue?"

"No. No. I get your point."

Kathleen smiled and patted me on the knee. "So, I think you know from those . . . escapades that I can be convinced to push my boundaries. But I need to process things and think on it awhile."

"That's fair. So, there's a chance?"

"I don't know, Bud. I just need a little time. I need to talk to my girls and . . . What about our apartments?"

"The apartments are easy. We just continue paying rent. I may be able to swing a reduced rate since we won't be eating meals or requiring services. Keep in mind, I'm connected to Serenity management."

"Yeah, you're connected all right. How would we get there?"

"Catch a flight from Detroit Metro and rent a car when we arrive in Tampa."

"How long would we be gone?"

"Well, I was thinking we could leave around early October and come back at the end of March or early April, when the snow is gone and the robins are back. But I'm flexible."

The wind gusted, briefly picking up the leaves on the ground and swirling them around like a tiny tornado. Kathleen seemed deep in thought as she watched the leaves settle to the ground. "I've never been away from my family that long."

"I thought about that. We could come home a couple of times, maybe Christmas and Thanksgiving. We could also arrange for your daughters and their families to come and see us."

"Oh, Bud, they could never manage that."

"I'd pay their airfare, Kathleen."

"I wouldn't want you to do that."

I squeezed her hand. "Kathleen, I'd do it in a heartbeat

because I know it would make you happy. There's plenty of room in the condo, and I would feel good helping out your family. I have the money, and I can't spend it when I'm gone. I remember when I was first married and Sharon and I were living from paycheck to paycheck. I'm sure your girls and their families would be thrilled to take a winter vacation."

"I'm sure they would."

"We both have more miles behind us than in front of us. Man, I want to cram as much fun, laughter, and adventure into the time we have. I hope that will be for many years, but you never know. We gotta go out strong, Kathleen."

She smiled. "Just throw caution to the wind?"

"Well, not entirely. But we're in good health, we can travel, and we can look out for each other. Why not go for it?"

Kathleen's eyes brightened. "Just get in that multicolored Volkswagen bus with peace symbols and go to California and become a flower child?"

I laughed. "Now you're getting it."

She was quiet for a moment, and the excitement seemed to vanish from her eyes. "But what if . . ."

"What if what?" My mind was racing, trying to anticipate what was coming. *What if I'm not as healthy as you think? What if my doctor says I can't travel? What if my daughters think it's a bad idea?*

"What if you decide you don't like me once we're there for a couple of months."

I sighed, feeling greatly relieved. "Not a chance, Kathleen. I've been around you long enough to know what kind of person you are. We're friends, and we've been through a lot." I smiled and patted her on her knee. "Besides, I wouldn't want to let Marian down."

345

She looked perplexed. "Clayton's mom?"

"Right. Remember the day we went to the nursing home to visit her? You said goodbye and waited for me in the hall?" Kathleen nodded. "Do you know what she told me after you left?"

"No, what?"

"She said you were a keeper and I shouldn't let you get away."

Kathleen smiled. "Oh, that was so sweet."

"You wanna know what I told her?"

"Yes, what?"

"I said, 'I think you're overmedicated and becoming delusional.'"

Kathleen laughed and seemed to be excited again. "Oh, Bud, you make me laugh, and I really like that about you." She was silent for a moment before asking the obvious question. "Okay, let's hear it. What did you say?"

"I said, 'I know, and I won't.'"

Kathleen smiled. "You're a good man, Bud. Just be patient and give me a little time to think this through. You know I want to be with you, right?"

"I do."

Chapter Eighty-Eight

One afternoon, I was scrolling through my unopened emails and found one that looked like a response to one of the emails I'd written after Woodstock. I read it and muttered, "Bingo!"

Eager to share my find with Kathleen, I printed the email, shut down my computer, and left for her apartment, where we always met before dinner. Her door was already open.

She smiled broadly as I entered her apartment.

"So, when are we going to Florida?" she asked.

I froze. "You're serious? You really wanna go?"

"Definitely! I talked to Martha and Elizabeth, and they practically ordered me to go."

"You're kidding! What'd they say?"

"They said to get the hell out of here and enjoy my life while I still can. So, let's do it!"

Bubbling with excitement, she did a cute little dance like a high school cheerleader, then sprung into my arms. She gave me a tight and sustained hug, followed by a kiss. It wasn't an open-mouthed, passionate kiss, but a gentle, soothing kiss that made me feel wanted, appreciated, and maybe . . . loved.

I placed my hands on the sides of her face, looked into her dark eyes for a moment, and said, "Kathleen, you have two very smart daughters."

"I know!" Still animated and giddy, she grabbed my arm. "Let's go tell the gang."

My other news was forgotten for the moment as we left the apartment and strolled arm in arm to the dining room.

We decided it would take us about ten days to get ready to leave. We looked at a calendar, counted out ten days, and booked a flight to Tampa. Our departure date fell on a Saturday, and we chose an afternoon flight so we'd have time in the morning to spend with our friends before we left.

The days passed quickly as we prepared for our trip. Kathleen spent a lot of time with her family, and Martha took her shopping several times. I compiled a long list of chores that needed to be completed at my house to prepare it for winter. Clayton and I spent a lot of time there, knocking off one chore at a time. In the evenings, Kathleen and I talked about exploring Florida, and we spent hours on the computer researching places to visit.

The Friday evening before our departure, we went to Martha's house in Farmington. Kathleen's entire family was gathered for a dinner and send-off party. She had the full support of her family, which was very important to her. It had been a long time since she'd smiled and laughed as she did that night, and as we headed out the door, I heard Martha whisper to her husband, "I think Mom is in love."

On the way home, Kathleen asked me if I'd told April and John about our plans. I said I hadn't.

She sighed. "Bud, you promised you'd let them know. Why'd you wait so long?"

"Kathleen, I don't expect my kids to react like yours. It'll be a contentious issue. I just know it. I plan to call April as soon as I get to my apartment. I'm just going to shoot an email to John."

I hadn't seen or heard from John since the videoconference a few weeks earlier, so I didn't feel obligated to call him. I sat at the kitchen table, turned on my computer, went to my email, clicked on New Message, and wrote:

Dear John,

I saw you on the videoconference when you spoke to the residents of the three Serenity facilities. You did a very nice job, and people here felt better afterward.

I was very surprised and impressed to hear you are a majority shareholder in the corporation that owns the three facilities, and now it makes sense that no other options were discussed when April was pressuring me to leave the house. I had to come to Serenity, and that was that. I used to think April was primarily responsible for uprooting me, but now I realize you were also involved. April's job was to execute the plan.

When I first arrived here, I was resentful that you two pressured me to leave the house, but now I know you did the right thing. I didn't realize how lonely I was until I arrived here, and I have made some great friendships with some very interesting people. I'm the happiest I've been in a very long time. I have heard residents say there is a long waiting list to get in here, but I never had to wait. I suspect you used your position and influence to get me in here quickly. I thank you for that.

Tomorrow, I am leaving for Florida with a good friend I met here. We will be staying there until April. In the mean-

time, we will continue paying our rent, and we will check in from time to time with the facility.

I am proud of your accomplishments and hope we can get together sometime.

Love, Dad

As I hit Send, I said, "There you go, John. Now you know where I'll be."

I hadn't seen or heard from April since she dropped by the house during Woodstock. I considered sending her a similar email but knew that wouldn't go over well. She was going to give me shit.

After a few minutes of pacing, I walked over to the kitchen table, picked up my cell phone, and placed the call. April picked up after four rings.

"Hi, Dad. I've been meaning to call you about Brett's arrest and all that drug stuff." *Sure you were.* "Are you okay?"

"I'm fine. There's nothing wrong. April, before I leave, I just wanted to thank you for your role in getting me in here. I know I wasn't very happy about it at the time, but things worked out. I made a lot of friends, and I'm happy."

"You're welcome, Dad. You said you're leaving. Where are you going?"

"I'm going to the condo in Florida for a while. I'll be back in April."

"Wait. You're leaving Serenity and going to Florida but still keeping your apartment at Serenity?"

"Right."

"Dad, I don't think that's a good idea."

"Why?"

"Who's going to look out for you? What if you fall again? Who's going to run your errands and do your grocery shopping? I don't think you're thinking this through, Dad."

350

"Look, I've made my plans. A friend is going with me."

"A female friend?"

"That's right. Her name is Kathleen. She's a lovely person. You'd like her."

"Dad, this is crazy. You can't possibly know this person well enough to go to Florida and live with her for a few months. Stay put, Dad."

"Maybe it's crazy, but we're going. I didn't call to get your permission. I just wanted you to know where I am in case something comes up and you need me. We're leaving tomorrow."

"Dad, you're acting like a teenage boy who's never been laid. You're infatuated with some woman, and now you want to run off and live with her for a while. That's ridiculous for a person your age."

"A person my age! Maybe you intended for me to sit around and play bingo until my number comes up, but that's not happening, April."

"Was that woman—"

"Her name is Kathleen."

"Whatever. Was she at the house during that freak show in August?"

"When you ran into the pizza delivery guy?"

"Here's what's going on, Dad. She saw the house and knows you have money, and now she's sucking up to you. It happens all the time. Smart, manipulative women smell money and offer company and other benefits so they can get a share." She was describing herself, and she didn't realize it. "I'm sure she—"

"Her name is Kathleen."

"Right. Kathleen probably doesn't give a shit about you, Dad. It's all about the money. Trust me."

"Up yours!" The words came out of nowhere, but I

didn't regret saying them. I took a deep breath and said, "I think we're done now, April. See you in the spring."

I turned off the phone and said, "That was fun." But instead of feeling agitated as I had so many times in the past in dealing with April, I felt good.

Chapter Eighty-Nine

I woke up when my cell phone rang. I picked it up and looked at the display to see who'd be calling me before seven on a Saturday morning. It was Kathleen.

"Good morning," I said.

"Good morning to you! I'm so excited, I've been up for two hours. I wanted to call you right away but decided to let you sleep in. That was really hard."

"What have you been doing for two hours?"

"I don't know. I went over my list three times to be sure I have everything and did some more research about things we can do when we are down there. How do you feel about swimming with dolphins?"

"That'd be fun."

"Good. I really want to do it. Hey, I've got some coffee on. Can I bring you a cup?"

"Sure, but give me half an hour to wake up and take a shower."

After I showered, I put on my boxer shorts and wiped the moisture off the bathroom mirror to reveal Gene Simmons's menacing stare from the poster on the bathroom door behind me. It seemed like years ago when I first arrived and Gene scared the bejesus out of me.

"I'm heading out today, Gene. Take care of the place for me, okay?"

I finished dressing and was stuffing miscellaneous items in my carry-on bag when I heard a knock at the door. Kathleen was right on time.

I hurried to the door and opened it.

"Good morning, Bud," said Clayton. He was in street clothes, which was a bit unusual. He wasn't an early-morning person. "I know you're leaving for Florida today, and I was wondering if I could tag along. I really need a change of scenery. The blue-hairs around here are driving me nuts. You said you have a three-bedroom condo, right?"

He seemed dead serious.

"Well . . . I . . ." Clayton laughed loudly and pushed me on the shoulder. "Damn it, Clayton. I still can't tell when you're serious or when you're bullshitting. Come on in."

He walked in, and I shut the door. My friend seemed preoccupied and didn't sit. He glanced at his watch.

"I won't be long. I just said goodbye to Kathleen, and I wanted to catch you before I go to Detroit. I'm meeting with a guy from *Rolling Stone* who is doing a story on Graham Nash. Graham suggested he interview me. Pretty cool, huh?"

"That's great, Clayton! You'll kick ass on the interview."

Stroking his mustache, Clayton gazed out the window, then looked back at me. "We've sure have had a lot of laughs over the last few months."

"Definitely. It's been fun."

He laughed. "That shit we pulled on the Beverly Hill-billies was classic, and the Brett payback—I keep thinking about you standing there in full cowboy, dropping your

354

drawers, and mooning the camera. I'll never forget that—the Serenity moon. What a lovely sight."

I smiled. "I don't know what got into me. I guess I got all caught up in the moment. That cowboy outfit of yours, combined with the Donald Trump mask, brought out my inner exhibitionist."

"I guess so." Clayton seemed lost in thought for a moment, then he struck a serious tone. "There were some bummer days too. Losing my mom, then Jim. That really sucked."

"For sure. We've been through a lot over the last few months."

He put his hands in his pants pockets and looked down, and I wondered if he was thinking about Jim and his mom. When he looked up, he said, "I'm really going to miss you, Bud."

Those words really hit me. A few months earlier, I could have croaked, and no one would have missed me.

"I'm going to miss you too. I keep thinking about my first ride in the Mothership, when I went on and on about how much my life sucked. You barely knew me then, but you listened. Thanks for that. Looking back, I think I needed to get all that shit off my chest in order to heal."

"Oh, I remember our conversation very well, and it wasn't all one-sided. After you confided in me, I spilled the beans about Candace and Marie." He thought for a moment, then added, "Until that day, I'd never told anyone about them, even Jim. It was just too painful. I don't know why it all came out that day. Maybe your trust in me gave me trust in you, or maybe we realized our ships were sinking and we needed to send out an SOS before it was too late. Whatever the reason, I felt better after we talked. I'm glad you were there for me."

I noticed Clayton glance at his watch again. "You're welcome to come and see us anytime. You know that, right?"

"I do. Maybe after the first of the year." He cleared his throat. "Bud, I've been thinking . . . You made me go to the Graham Nash concert, and that opened up some doors for me, and I just feel better about my career. I owe you, brother."

"You owe me nothin'. I was in a pretty dark place when I arrived here in June. Living alone in that house was sucking the life out of me. When I came here, you and Jim accepted and included me, and your asinine pranks made me laugh and feel alive again. I owe you."

"Whoa! Asinine?" said Clayton, acting offended. "That really cuts to the bone, Bud."

I smiled. "My apologies. Bad word choice. *Juvenile* is probably a better word."

"Right. *Juvenile* is much better. Let's get this shit over with, Bud."

We briefly shook hands, then hugged.

"Brothers forever, man," said Clayton.

Chapter Ninety

"Okay. Time-out," said Charlie as Kathleen and I approached the table.

Seated next to Charlie were his sons, Dean and Tony, and across from them were Abbie and her son Mark. They were all smiling and animated, and I assumed they'd been up to their usual Saturday morning bantering, providing entertainment for the regular resident eaves-droppers.

Charlie had a puzzled look and turned to Abbie. "Where are they going again?"

"Venice, Florida."

Kathleen and I sat at their table, and it didn't take long before the BS began to fly.

"So, Charlie. Mark has been working for Motor City Bus Repair for almost two weeks. How's that going?" I asked. I winked at Mark, who was squirming in his chair.

Charlie looked blankly at me, as if he was trying to remember. "Mark who?"

Abbie's jaw dropped, then she looked at me and back at Charlie. Charlie cracked a smile.

"You turkey. You're messing with me, aren't you?" I said.

Charlie smiled. "To answer your question, Mark is doing great. He's on time, he works hard, and he's well-liked. He was a good hire for us."

The conversation shifted to Abbie's penchant for wearing brightly colored and patterned clothing, then to the Lions' dismal start to the 2019 season. Describing himself as a diehard Green Bay Packers fan, Charlie delighted in needling Tony and Dean, who were Lions season ticket holders.

I had a feeling the conversation would inevitably turn to Kathleen and me, and I was right.

"Do you remember back in June when I told you I thought Kathleen liked you?" asked Charlie.

"I do," I said.

"Wait!" said Kathleen, who was blushing. "You told him what?"

"I told him I thought you liked him," Charlie said forcefully.

"You're a slut," Abbie said to Kathleen, drawing laughter from everyone at our table and the surrounding tables. Kathleen laughed too, but she persisted in questioning Charlie.

"I'm curious. Why did you say that? I barely knew Bud then."

"I don't know. Maybe it was the way you smiled at him. I could just tell."

Abbie interjected. "The very next day, she had Clayton take her to a tattoo parlor, where she got a 'Bud the Stud' tattoo. Show it to 'em, Kathleen."

Again, everyone laughed, and Kathleen's face turned a brighter shade of red. "I did not!" she said emphatically.

After Charlie and Abbie finished razzing Kathleen, the banter continued until I checked the time and told Kathleen we needed to get going.

She seemed momentarily stunned, and I assumed, with all the excitement about living in Florida, that she hadn't thought about leaving our friends. She looked at Abbie and Charlie and smiled. "We're going to miss you."

"We'll miss you too," said Charlie.

We all stood, and Kathleen began to cry. As she hugged Charlie, she said, "I'm going to miss our cribbage games."

He gently patted her on the back. "Me too. Let's have a few marathon sessions when you get back."

"Okay," she said, letting go of him and wiping away a tear that was running down her cheek.

Abbie said she and Mark were going to walk with us to our apartments, so they stood aside while Kathleen and I finished talking to Tony, Dean, and Charlie.

While Kathleen was hugging Charlie's boys, Charlie said quietly, "Bud, they say my memory thing can be progressive, so I don't know how I'll be when you get back. But I'm gonna hang onto my memories of the Serenity Gang as long as I can. I treasure them."

"Me too, my friend." We shook hands and hugged.

"I don't know why I'm so emotional. We're not going to be gone that long," said Kathleen as she wiped the tears from her eyes.

"Because we're family," said Abbie.

Kathleen looked at her meaningfully. "You're right. We are family."

Chapter Ninety-One

We talked about Mark's new apartment and the work he was doing at Motor City Bus Repair as we ambled out of the dining room and down the hall toward the apartments. When we arrived at my door, Abbie said, "Well, I guess this is it. I hope you'll keep in touch."

I hugged her and shook Mark's hand. I asked Abbie to keep us updated and let us know if she heard anything about Brett and the others. She assured me she'd be calling us. As we said our final goodbyes, I teased Mark about keeping an eye on his mom. He and Abbie laughed and headed down the hall with Kathleen. I told Kathleen I'd meet her in her apartment in ten minutes.

I went into my apartment, brushed my teeth, confirmed the refrigerator was empty, and did a quick walk-around to be sure I'd packed everything I needed. Confident I was ready to go, I sat at the kitchen table, turned on my laptop, and checked the Delta Airlines website to confirm the flight was on time and verify the rental car was secured. As I was opening my email, I heard a knock at my door.

"Come on in!"

The door opened, and Abbie slowly pushed her walker into the apartment. "I know you're trying to get out of here, but do you mind if we talk for a minute? I promise I won't be long."

"I don't mind at all. C'mon in."

Abbie pushed her walker into the living room, and I closed the door behind her. She had white powder at the corners of her mouth and on the front of her polka-dotted sweatshirt.

"Where's Mark?" I asked.

"He's in my apartment, watching TV. I bought him his favorite donuts."

"Powdered?"

"How did you . . ." Abbie quickly wiped her mouth with her hand and looked at the powder on her fingers. "Did I get it all?"

"There's still some on the front of your sweatshirt."

She quickly brushed the powder off her sweatshirt.

"What's up?" I asked.

She hesitated for a moment and said, "It was really hard for me to come back down here. I'm not very good at this sort of thing."

"What's on your mind, Abbie?"

"All my life, I've had trouble showing or sharing my feelings. I don't know why. It's just the way I am, I guess." She shifted her feet and leaned forward on her walker.

"Do you want to sit down?"

"No." Abbie stared at me and appeared to be struggling for words. "Bud, I loved my husband. He was a good man. We had a good life together, and I always felt we didn't have to tell each other how we felt. We just knew. Know what I mean? After he died, I wished I had told him more often that I loved him and how much I appreciated him. He deserved to hear me say it."

"I'm sure your husband knew how you felt."

Abbie ran her hand through her disheveled hair. "You get attached to people, like Sister Mary Katherine and Jim. And then, one day, they're gone. I keep thinking about things I wish I had said to them. We're not getting any younger, Bud. It could happen to any of us."

"You're right."

"I just don't want to risk it."

"Risk what?"

"Risk having something happen to one of us and lose the chance to tell you how I feel."

"Okay."

"Remember when you and the others were encouraging me to go to Mark's drug court graduation? You knew how scared I was, but you kept pushing me to go. I didn't like that."

"I'm really sorry, Abbie."

"Nothing to be sorry about, Bud. I didn't come here to bitch about that. It's just that . . ." She removed a tissue from the pocket of her sweatpants, then said, "Sorry," and blew her nose. "I wouldn't have gone to Mark's graduation if you hadn't gotten that Uber. God bless you for making it possible. That was one of the proudest days of my life."

"You're welcome."

We hugged, and I could feel her body quivering as she silently cried.

"You take care of my good friend, Kathleen. She's one in a million," said Abbie tearfully.

"I will. I promise."

Chapter Ninety-Two

A week after Bud and Kathleen left, Clayton received a call from Lance Glardon, the station manager of WREF, Detroit's premier classic rock station. Lance said he'd heard about the great interview Clayton gave to *Rolling Stone* and asked if he'd like to give a live interview on October 4—the expected release date of the October issue. Lance said it would have the Graham Nash story, and he'd heard it might have an article about Clayton.

Clayton eagerly accepted.

On the day of the interview, Clayton's cell phone buzzed just as he was getting ready to leave. He recognized the number and decided it was time to take the call.

"Hello."

"Is this Mr. Davis?"

"Yes, it is."

"This is Corrine from St. Anne's Nursing Home."

"Hi, Corrine."

"I've been trying to reach you for several weeks. I left you several voicemails. Did you get them?"

"I did. I'm sorry I didn't get back to you. I just wasn't ready to deal with it."

"Totally understandable. We loved your mom. As I mentioned in the voicemails, we have some of your mom's personal items in a safe, and we'd like you to come and pick them up."

"What personal items?"

"I have the inventory sheet right here. Let me see. There are two rings, a watch, a cell phone, bathrobe, slippers, comb and hairbrush, assorted clothing, a small purse and its contents, toiletries, and some personal papers."

Hairbrush. The word hit Clayton like a body blow. He slapped himself on the forehead. "You dumbshit."

"Excuse me?"

"Oh, I'm so sorry, Corrine. I was talking to myself. Something you said reminded me of a conversation I had with my Mom. I apologize."

"No problem. Do you think you can come and pick them up?"

"Sure. I'm leaving for Detroit in a few minutes. I'll stop by on my way back."

"That sounds great. Looking forward to seeing you."

Clayton hung up and checked himself in the mirror. His new shirt and jeans looked good. He rolled up the sleeves of his shirt and adjusted his belt. Then he pulled his hair back into a ponytail. Satisfied that he looked presentable, he grabbed his keys and left.

The live interview went very well. Clayton's knowledge of music and the music industry—coupled with his animated style, sense of humor, and obvious embellishment of stories of life on the road with famous musicians—had the two radio hosts and their support staff in stitches. At the end of the interview, Lance explained that while he was not in a position to make an offer, he wondered if Clayton would be interested in appearing every other week as a paid member of the morning show. Clayton said he would, and Lance promised to get back to him after he spoke to his boss.

They shook hands, and Lance gave Clayton a WREF Classic Rock sweatshirt. Clayton looked at it admiringly and thanked Lance. As he turned to leave, Lance said, "You probably noticed we didn't bring up your recent interview with *Rolling Stone* or the rumor that the October issue has a story about you. The damn October issue wasn't available, and we wanted to review it before we discussed it on the air. With all my luck, it will be out late this morning or early afternoon. Hopefully, you'll be coming back, and we can discuss it then."

Clayton made a mental note to swing by Barnes and Noble on his way home.

He drove directly to the nursing home and parked in his usual spot. He hesitated, remembering his mom and thinking about his life without her. Swallowing the big lump in his throat, he climbed out of the van and went inside.

"Good morning, Mr. Davis," said Corrine, who was standing in the nurses' station near his mom's former room. "You look really nice today."

"Thank you, Corrine. I'm going for the chick magnet look."

She laughed. "You got it! Hey, is it starting to heat up out there? It's supposed to be a stellar October day."

"It's beautiful, Corrine. Have you ever seen satellite images of Michigan in the fall?"

She shrugged. "I don't think so."

"You should check 'em out. The fall colors can be seen from space. It's nuts."

"Wow! I'll definitely do that."

"When I was in the space shuttle, I couldn't believe how cool things looked."

Corrine's eyes widened. "Oh my gosh! You were in the space shuttle? Really?"

"Sure was! They let you go right in at the Kennedy Space Center in Florida."

Corrine smiled and shook her head. "Oh my! I've missed your sense of humor. I'll get your mom's stuff out of the safe. I'll be right back."

When she left, Clayton peered into his mother's former room. A frail-looking man dressed in a red plaid bathrobe was slumped in a wheelchair parked in front of a blaring television. The stand where his food tray sat had been pushed aside, and the man appeared to be sleeping.

Clayton clasped his hands and said, "Oh Lord, please take me before I get old."

"Here you go, Mr. Davis," said Corrine as she handed him a plastic bag containing his mom's possessions. "I just need you to sign this receipt."

Clayton quickly looked in the bag, picked up a pen, and signed the receipt.

A few minutes later, he was in the Mothership, heading toward the strip mall near Reptile World.

Chapter Ninety-Three

C layton smiled as he drove past Reptile World and thought about the prank they'd pulled on the Ohio dipshits. He drove into a nearby parking lot, climbed out of the Mothership, and walked into the shop he'd spotted when he'd gone shopping with Kathleen. An hour later, he was back in the Mothership, looking at himself in the rearview mirror.

"Hope you're happy, Mom."

Clayton drove the short distance to Barnes and Noble, where he was delighted to find the October issue of *Rolling Stone*. He was surprised and disappointed that Graham Nash was not on the cover.

He sat in a chair and turned the first page, finding a note on the inside cover indicating that Graham Nash would be featured in the November issue. He continued thumbing through the paper until he found a story titled "Up Yours for Over Fifty Years." There was a picture of him with a lengthy article about "Up Yours" and his life as a behind-the-scenes musician for some of the most famous bands of the sixties.

Clayton was so excited, he had a hard time concentrating. He got up, paid for the magazine, and headed out the door to the Mothership. He'd read it more thoroughly when he got home.

Chapter Ninety-Four

"Wow! This is quite the place," said the Uber driver to his passenger as he drove his car down the driveway toward the Serenity building. "Check out the colors on those trees."

"They're gorgeous," was the reply.

They passed the parking lot, where the Mothership and a few cars were parked, and eventually stopped at the entrance. There was a man sitting in the sunshine on a bench in front of the building. He seemed engrossed in his reading material and barely looked up. The passenger exited the car and thanked the driver, then walked up the sidewalk and into the building.

She walked directly to the nurses' station, where Brenda sat.

"Excuse me. Could you tell me where I might find Clayton Davis?"

"Let me ring his room for you." Brenda picked up the phone and dialed Clayton's extension. After several rings, she hung up and said, "I'm sorry. He's not answering."

Seeing the disappointment on the woman's face, Brenda volunteered to locate Clayton. After checking the dining room, she said, "No luck. I'll see if his van is here." She walked to the front of the building, looked out the window, and spotted the van in the parking lot. As she turned to walk back, she did a double take. She returned to the nurses' station and told the woman she could find him sitting on the bench outside.

The woman slowly approached the doors, then stopped to observe the man she had traveled so far to meet. She had searched the internet and found some photos of him taken when he was in his mid-twenties, but she had no idea what he would look like in his early seventies. Now he was just beyond the entrance doors, sitting on a bench in the sunshine. He was a nice-looking, clean-shaven man with neatly trimmed salt-and-pepper hair. He wore an untucked, long-sleeve black dress shirt with the sleeves rolled up, jeans, and casual shoes. The reading glasses resting on the end of his nose, coupled with sharp features, made him look dignified and classy.

Clayton moved in his seat and flashed the cover of the material he was reading. She recognized the cover and smiled. He was reading *Rolling Stone*!

She took a deep breath and slowly walked out the front door.

"Excuse me. Are you Clayton Davis?"

Clayton looked up at her standing a few feet away from him. She smiled.

He folded his magazine and took off his reading glasses. "Yes, I am."

For weeks, she'd practiced what she would say at this moment. But the moment was here, and the practiced words were not.

"I'm Marie Whitman."

Clayton's eyebrows furrowed. "Marie Whit . . ." He stared at her in disbelief as realization dawned on him. "Marie?"

"Yes, your daughter, Marie."

Clayton put his hands to his face and said, "Oh my God!" When he pulled his hands away, he stood, studying her face. Marie could see the tears in his eyes. She was also fighting to keep her emotions under control. "Do you mind if I hug you?" he asked.

"I'd welcome it."

They hugged each other firmly, and when they stopped, Clayton stepped back and said tearfully, "Marie, there hasn't been a day when I didn't think about you. For all these years, I've been wondering what you looked like, if you were married, if you had children . . . I just can't believe you're here."

Marie smiled as the tears were welling up in her eyes. "I'm so glad I found you. I was so afraid you might not want to be found or that you wouldn't want anything to do with me or your grandsons. There's just so much to talk about. I can't wait to tell them you were reading *Rolling Stone* when we met."

"Grandsons?"

"Yes, grandsons. You have two grandsons, both in college. Andrew is twenty, and Matthew is twenty-three. They're musicians, and they've been researching you like crazy."

Clayton wiped the tears from his eyes and stared at his daughter, who was a spitting image of her mother. This was almost too much to take in. It seemed unreal.

"How . . . how did you find me?" he asked.

371

Marie smiled. "Oh, I had some help," she said mischievously.

"Help from whom?"

"I'm surprised he didn't tell you."

"Who?" said Clayton impatiently.

"Your teacher friend, Gene Simmons."

Acknowledgments

There are so many who have inspired, encouraged, and supported this effort, beginning with Candice, my lovely wife of thirty-four years, who tolerated my obsessing over this book for over six years. Your love, patience, and understanding are everything. And to my children, Abbie and Chad—thank you for believing in me. You're the best!

I owe thanks to the memory of my loving father, Bud, who died from the complications of Alzheimer's. And to the memories of Mike Koenig, John Ackerman, Dan Morley, Bill LeMire, and Brian Nicholas: good friends who died too young. To my brave cancer-surviving older brother and sister and my friends: Howard Dedow, Tom Davis, Cindi Davis, Kim Coggins, and David Sanders. All are constant reminders of the unpredictability of life and the importance of living life to the fullest.

My thanks to the graduates of the Delta County Drug and Sobriety Court, whose courage, resilience, and determination inspire me, and to the dedicated and caring men and women who work in nursing homes and assisted living facilities. God bless you all.

Many thanks to Caren Nicholas, Jim Parks, Martha Parks, Tom Butch, Ann Schwartz, Patty Antaya, Sara Cromartie, Betty LaPointe, Cara Brockway, Janet Rogers, Cindi Davis, David Sanders, and Tom Davis for taking the time to read the manuscript in its early stages. Your comments and input were invaluable. J.L. Hyde, one of

Upper Michigan's finest authors, inspired and guided me, and I am grateful for her input and suggestions. Also, special thanks to my editor, Carly Catt, for polishing the rough edges and strengthening the voice of this book, and to my talented niece, Heidi Goodman, who took the author profile photo.

Thanks to Jeff Bacon, Amy McGreaham, and Tim Dedow for being good-natured victims of a couple of the pranks described in the book.

And last but not least, to the rapidly vanishing musicians of the sixties and early seventies, who wrote and played some of the best music ever made.